The **M**arriage *of* **R**aphael **K**err

By the Same Author

Novels
Summer Sure to Die

The Hampshire Romances
Edmund Persuader
Tomazina's Folly

Stories
Tales of Arcadia

A Novella
Elissa Wyatt

The **Marriage**

of

Raphael Kerr

A Fable of Two Wives and Two Worlds

In *Five Acts* in *Five Volumes*

of Which This Is

Volume 5

by Stuart Shotwell

MERMAID PRESS OF MAINE

N.B.: In this volume, four passages originally written in Latin but quoted in the text in English have been marked with an asterisk to indicate that they are adapted from the so-called standard edition of the writer in question, which is itself a product of centuries of adaptations from the first translation into English. A fifth passage, marked with two asterisks, has been repeated verbatim from the standard edition. The intent behind this form of quotation has been to provide verisimilitude by representing the texts in a state closer to that in which they would have been encountered by the protagonist. Passages without such marking have been translated by the author.

This is volume 5 of 5.
Volume 1: 978-1-941864-07-4
Volume 2: 978-1-941864-08-1
Volume 3: 978-1-941864-09-8
Volume 4: 978-1-941864-18-0
Volume 5: 978-1-941864-10-4
Publication Data
Shotwell, Stuart (1953–).
The Marriage of Raphael Kerr/Stuart Shotwell
p. cm.
ISBN 978-1-941864-07-4 (volume 1 : alk. paper) — ISBN 978-1-941864-08-1 (volume 2 : alk. paper) — ISBN 978-1-941864-09-8-1 (volume 3 : alk. paper)—ISBN 978-1-941864-18-0 (volume 4 : alk. paper)—ISBN 978-1-941864-10-4 (volume 5 : alk. paper)— 1. England—History—19th century—Fiction. I. Shotwell, Stuart (1953–). II. Title.

Conceived, written, edited, designed, typeset, and produced by Stuart Shotwell.

This book is distributed directly from the publisher at www.stuartshotwell.com. Mermaid Press of Maine regrets that it is not able to acknowledge, consider, or return manuscripts submitted in any form.

Act 5

Serve Yet Seven Other Years

Serve with me yet seven other years.

—Genesis 29:27

Chapter 53

O life! what letts thee from a quicke decease?
O death! what drawes thee from a present praye?
My feast is done, my soule would be at ease,
My grace is saide; O death! come take awaye.

I live, but such a life as ever dyes;
I dye, but such a death as never endes;
My death to end my dying life denyes,
And life my living death no whitt amends.

Thus still I dye, yet still I do revive;
My living death by dying life is fedd;
Grace more then nature kepes my hart alive,
Whose idle hopes and vayne desires are deade.

Not where I breathe, but where I love, I live;
Not where I love, but where I am, I die;
The life I wish, must future glory give,
The deaths I feele in present daungers lye.

—Robert Southwell

And behold, a woman of Canaan came out of the
same coasts and cried unto Him, saying, "Have mercy on me, O Lord, thou son of David; my daughter is
grievously vexed with a devil."

—Matthew 15:22

Millions of spiritual creatures walk the earth
Unseen, both when we wake and when we sleep.

—Milton

Raphael's promises to the Wonderful had been difficult enough
when he uttered them, in that man's inspiring presence, and in

the bright reality of the other world. Here in the Dim World, it seemed his very flesh conspired against hope and pulled him down into confusion and abnegation of the power of the will.

He arose that first day of his return and went about his ways harrowed by conflicting thoughts and emotions: a deep sense of grief at losing Awen yet again, despair that he was sentenced for life to the prison of this world and to the loneliness her absence occasioned, irritation at Veronica as the indicated focus of the goodwill he ought to practice; all contrasted with his earnest longing to be better than he was, to win through to Awen again, to love Veronica for her own sake if that was possible.

He found, as the next week passed, and the next, and day followed still on day, that his loss of Awen was as the reopening of a wound—a wound now thrice inflicted; and it was as if his body gave up the rehealing of it. Three times was too much to bear: there was her first supposed death on Vigia, her second and true death from this world the previous spring, and then this loss of her at the prohibition of the One, and of the Wonderful, and of the guardian angel waiting by the gate. He was dulled and defeated, and everyone noticed it, and some even remarked upon it to him—those who dared, such as Mrs. Mc-Quillit and Mr. Strong.

Veronica piled hopelessness on his hopelessness; for from her loss of Manwaring she too despaired. She attended meals as if only to inflict her silence upon him. She watched him closely and steadily, perhaps trying to unnerve him; and she ate nothing, or very little, for day after day, until her excess flesh began to be consumed from within. A fine pair they made—silent, broken, lonely, and bitter, facing each other down the long table, each in a separate agony of loss, and neither helping the other through it.

One morning, about a month after Raphael's final dream, he felt strangely woozy as he climbed back up the hill from a walk to view the fields with Mr. Kettie. He sat the rest of the day in a chair in his study, with the cat Musa on his lap, sinking deeper and deeper into a physical malaise; he went to bed that night, thinking he would sleep it off and wake the next morning at least as lively as he had been of late; but the next dawn he was feverish.

The apothecary was summoned, declared the ailment trifling, advised rest and cooling food and drink, and went away. And still the decline continued.

For five days he slipped, by almost imperceptible degrees, down the short slope that leads from health to death. Each day the apothecary was called back, expressed more and more concern, took increasingly stronger measures; and finally brought a physician with him, who concurred in what was being done, but gave signs of even graver alarm over the condition of the patient.

By the seventh day there was no doubt that Raphael was dying.

The doctor asked for Veronica, who in all this time had taken no interest in Raphael's condition. The patient being now considered to be far gone, the doctor spoke to her in Raphael's very presence; and he said: "Mrs. Kerr, I am afraid that your husband is not long for this world. His ailment indeed seems trivial, or at least such as a man of his strength and years could readily shake off; but he has no will to do so. I have never seen the like of it; he seems almost to be willing himself to die."

Veronica said nothing, but her gaze went from the doctor to Raphael, where he lay pale and silent in bed, unmoving.

"If there is anything you can do," said the doctor, "now is the time to do it. If there is some word or difficulty between you that has caused this despair on his part, now is the time to mend it. Indeed, I pray that it is not already too late."

And he went away with a demeanor that suggested that he did not expect to be called back again.

Raphael, though in body he felt crushed and leaden, as though all the weight of the Dim World lay upon his frame, was yet lucid in mind. He was impressed by the doctor's acumen: for he was in fact willing himself to die. As a schoolchild seizes upon illness as an excuse to stay home, he had seized upon this trivial sickness to absent himself permanently from this world.

It would not be his fault, he told himself, if his body perished. His body and its illness were beyond his control; neither the One nor the Wonderful would be able to blame him for passing into the Bright World if his body had no longer been able to support him. He had been given a ticket home, and he would take it. All he could think of was Awen as he had last seen her, walking away *with himself* up the shore of the lake. Soon he would be back beside her, where he belonged, and then death could not come between them again, because they would both be on the same side of that Dutch door.

After the doctor left, Raphael lapsed into his memories of Awen and took no further notice of Veronica. Some time later, perhaps ten minutes, he happened to notice that she was still standing in the same place by the door of the room, watching him.

She wore an unfathomable expression. He assumed, indeed, that she was glad to see him die. She would lose possession of Fulkothing Hall, which was entailed away to a relative in the default of any male offspring of their own; but she would have Wapstrake Hall and enough money to live comfortably for the remainder of her life. He had provided very carefully for the care of Titus, and given a great deal to Lucy and Reuben Keith, and had established as well pensions for his long-time servants, so no one had any claim upon her. This chapter of her life was ending, and she could at last escape her marriage to a man she had always despised. He had no doubt that she was gloating at having outlived him; but he cared nothing for that.

When she saw his glance at her, she started slightly. Then, while he watched her through the haze of his sickness, she came to him and sat on the chair that the doctor had put beside the bed; and she looked on him with that same expression he could not read; and she watched him in return, but not narrowly, or gloatingly, as he expected.

And there she sat for an hour entire, little moving; and her eyes traveled over his face, as if she was remembering their life together; and sometimes he saw her, and sometimes he saw only his inner memories of Awen; and in either case, he cared nothing for Veronica, except to be glad that he was leaving her at last.

The daylight began to lessen, and the first shadows of evening began to gather in the corners of the room. It was then that Veronica turned to Mrs. McQuillit, who was sitting at a distance, and who had been tending at intervals to the patient in any way she could; and she said: "Leave us alone, Mrs. McQuillit."

Mrs. McQuillit bolted up from her chair in a mixture of astonishment and indignation. "The master needs care, ma'am," she protested.

"I know," said Veronica. "And I am not such as can give it to him. But I want ten minutes alone with my husband, and you shall not deny it to me. He will not die in ten minutes for lack of you."

All amazement, Mrs. McQuillit acquiesced. "Ten minutes, then, ma'am," she said; and she went out of the room, shutting the door behind her.

Veronica looked at Raphael, and he, feeling some faint stirrings of wonderment and curiosity, gazed dimly back at her. He expected she wanted time to wound him if she could, taunt him with her plans for future life without him—for rejoining Manwaring and fulfilling whatever other self-destructive yearnings she had. But her expression did not seem to be gloating.

The bed was a wide one; it was, in fact, their marriage bed, the one from which she had departed years ago. He was lying more or less in the middle of its width, and so it was too far for her to lean over from her chair and reach him. And now, much to his surprise, she rose from the chair and crawled onto the bed, swiftly, driven by impulse; and she lay beside him, and she clutched his nightshirt. It was as though she were trying to hold him back physically from the brink of death.

For a moment she lay there, half on the bed and half off it, with her face pressed to the bedspread; and then she raised her face and looked into his.

"*Raphael,*" she whispered urgently. It was the first time she had spoken to him since the business with Manwaring, and more than that, it was the first time she had used his given name for many a year. "Do not *go*, Raphael. *Do not leave me.*"

He stared at her, puzzled.

He was closer to her than he had been for years; so close that he thought he could see the outlines of her beauty beneath the concealing flesh. And the bitterness of her soul for once was not visible; her expression was not scornful or reviling or angry or shamed; it was only frightened and pleading.

"If you leave me," she said, "*I shall die.* I know I shall—I shall die without you. *Do not leave me.* I *must not* die—I am so frightened of dying, Raphael; you must stay and help me. If I die now—"

She did not complete the sentence, but her body shook with a bitter convulsion at the thought.

"You *must* stay," she said, with more than a little of her old selfish petulance. "It is your duty to stay with me and care for me, and you cannot abandon your duty."

And he thought to himself: *What am I doing? It is true! I cannot leave her—I promised the One that I would love her and care for her; and here I am, trying to give all my promises the slip! And if she did die, in the condition her soul is in, it is true—she would go straight to the Dark Lands and live in thrall of people like Manwaring for the rest of eternity.*

"Get Mrs. McQuillit," he said to her.

She raised herself on her arms and stared at him in surprise.

"Get Mrs. McQuillit," he repeated.

She climbed swiftly down from the bed and ran to the door, which she flung open. "Mrs. McQuillit!" she called.

The housekeeper, who had been waiting not far away, now bustled into the room in alarm and stared at Raphael.

"I shall want some broth," said Raphael in a determined, if still somewhat faint voice. "And bread; and a little beef. Bring them at once. And have some candles lit—plenty of candles. The dark is beginning to be oppressive.—And find the cat, and have her brought to me here. And send for Mr. Coldunham, if you would; I would like him to read to me from the Psalmbook."

"Yes, sir," said Mrs. McQuillit, both astonished and joyful.

When she had left on these errands, Raphael said to Veronica: "I shall not die this time."

If he had expected any expression of relief or happiness, he would have been disappointed by her response; but she reacted as he had supposed she would: now that the result she had wished for had been achieved, she lapsed back into silence and hostility, turning abruptly away from him and leaving the room.

Thank the One! he thought. *Through this unlikely messenger I have been recalled to my task! Who knows what would have happened if I had tried to take the easy way back to Awen?*

And this time he was the one who felt fear and horror.

ⓔ ⓔ ⓔ

Veronica did not return to visit him for the remainder of his convalescence. It was, however, of short duration, and soon enough he was eating meals in the breakfast room, although he was still quite weak. There he saw her again; and though she had resumed her silence against him, he made an effort to speak to her. His principle was that ancient one, that genuine feeling follows upon even a forced practice: he spoke kindly to her and, without insisting on any response, raised subjects that he hoped would engage her. His one rule was to utter no gossip: he spoke instead of art, music, literature; of love of God and love of neighbor. At first she listened, or seemed to listen, with a frank if unspoken contempt for what he said. She was like a recalcitrant student compelled into a lecture hall; but then it seemed she began to take interest in these mealtime discursions, however grudgingly; she seemed to be almost on edge on each occasion when they sat down to dine, until he resumed where he had left off, and then she gave herself over to the listening and at times almost forgot her food. The day came when she forgot her pique against him momentarily and asked a question about something he was saying; and once the rule of her silence had been broken, it was only a matter of time until it was set aside and forgotten, and she occasionally responded to him and challenged him on points he made. Though her responses were sometimes bitter and contemptuous, and though she still bridled at the mere idea of listening to him, she continued to be engaged and to engage with him.

As the weeks passed, she continued to lose the unhealthy weight that had literally disfigured her; she began to care for her person again, to groom and dress with more interest and willingness. With the loss of her excess body, it seemed she began to rise out of the ruins of self that Manwaring had caused in her. There comes the day for the alcoholic when, deprived long enough of drink, he sees the day dawn clearer, brighter, more worth having than the bleary timelessness of his disease; and likewise there was for Veronica a gradual recollection of the person she had been before Manwaring had dragged her down by inches. In fact, she had never been evil, as Manwaring had. Very few of those dark souls in the parallel world had clustered around Veronica and infected her thinking and speaking; the major number had been attached to the servant, and influenced the mistress only vicariously.

The transformation of her physical image was very gradual, almost imperceptible, but it was certain. She began to look and even to act like a Grancomb again; she began to remind Raphael of his Aunt Harriet. She stood and sat straighter; she carried herself with more ease and yet with more awareness; she began to acquire some healthy self-esteem and to shed that desperate substitute for it, empty pride. She began to play the piano again, and did so very seriously, earnestly attempting to reawaken the technical virtuosity she had once possessed.

More remarkably, she began to shy away from her old habits of bitter gossip. In this she was assisted by circumstance. From the Chaters she was, of course, permanently severed by her unspeakable history with them; but in any case they moved away not long after her brief affair with Mr. Chater. Mr. Taunton suddenly died, and Mrs. Taunton went to live with relatives in Kent. Of the circle of harpies, that left only Mrs. Mayliss; and she, if not led into neg- ative thinking, could follow the example of her husband and treat others with some respect. And Veronica seemed to relinquish her role of leader, now that she herself in turn was not being led by Manwaring. She was like someone who awakens after being mes- merized to find herself naked before an audience, mocked and sneered at; and she resented the effect her gossips had had upon her even as she came to resent Manwaring's influence.

Everyone felt the new lightness of the atmosphere in the house. Raphael would have said that Manwaring's evil aura had left it. And if all the servants felt Manwaring's presence and the presence of her evil companions pass from the house like a fe- ver-bearing miasma, Veronica must feel it too. Her fury ebbed to anger, her anger to resentment, her resentment to irritation; and this was finally overborne by a sense that life was not as dreary as she had known it to be for the decades Manwaring had been with her. When the Great Silence came to an end, during which she had loured at all around her, she seemed to relent in her hatred of the world, and to some extent, even in her hatred of herself.

She was still Veronica, however. She thought primarily of her- self in all things. She was constantly late to every function and appointment, and blamed all but herself for her own thought- lessness and rudeness. She tried constantly to put Raphael in a place lower than she was, though it was obvious to him that she did so only because she feared that her place in the universe was irretrievably lower than his. She treated the servants like a less- er species or order of being; she was positively cruel to those of whom she was envious—for example, mothers like Lucy—and the mere mention of the Quinns by a neighbor plunged her into a funk of jealous hatred that lasted for days.

As for Raphael—he struggled as well. To speak her fair re- quired his constant self-discipline. He sought everywhere in the world around him for models, and found them in unlikely plac- es: in Lucy, who saw even a bawling, colicky baby as affording a joyous opportunity to give more love and care; and in the couple who cared for Titus, who seemed with time to have come to love him almost like a son of their own, and almost seemed to treasure his odd ways. In some respects, loving Veronica, he saw, must be like loving Cath or Musa or any alien animal: she must be accepted on her own terms, and she could not be expected to love with a truly human form of love. But if she had been even a fraction as affectionate as those animals had been to him, she would have made his effort far easier.

It was as the Wonderful had said: Many are those who find themselves in partnership with a spouse who lacks imagination and loving kindness. Only a few do find a way to love those difficult spouses. They understand implicitly that not to love would draw them down into the Dark Lands, and they want nothing to do with that place. By choice they avoid it; they take the narrow way. Raphael was determined to find that narrow way and stick to it.

My kindness to Veronica, he told himself, *is my love of the One. The two are indistinguishable. I cannot be cold and cruel to her and have any presentable, creditable claim to love God.* And this understanding helped him greatly. It was not as if he were trying to fool the One with a pretense of affection for her—he knew perfectly well that that was impossible. He was only trying to find the certain wellspring of love within him that arose from the One and that would allow him to feel genuine love for her. *After all,* he told himself, *the One loves Veronica; who am I to despise her, to be irritated with her?*

And thus, gradually, he began to feel more love for this broken creature who was his spouse on earth. And with equal slowness, she began to respond to his sincerity; at first with frequent lapses back into suspicion, but in time with more certainty.

෨ ෨ ෨

He had not visited his brother since the incident with Manwaring, though during this period he asked for regular reports about

Titus's well-being. There was something about his brother's situation that was unbearable even to contemplate at this juncture of his life. But as his health returned after what he came to think of as his willful illness, he began to think of Titus more, and when he was recovered enough, he called for the carriage and drove to the cottage where his brother lived with his two caretakers.

Titus was about fifty years of age at this time. His condition had continued without alteration since the day Raphael and Roland Kerr had brought him home nearly twenty years before: though his madness had its seasons, he was still quite mad. Over the years his mental state had wrenched his features into conformity with it. Where once, on the journey home from Middlesex, his appearance might have deceived an onlooker, and he might still have been thought a gentleman, now he was patently insane: his face was deeply etched with his constant anguish, so that his features seemed exaggerated and almost like those of a caricature: his eyesockets were sunken, even while his eyeballs seem to protrude; his nose was bony and hooked, his nostrils flaring and bristling with coarse hair; his lips were thin and through them—because they were not sufficient to cover his yellow, malodorous teeth—his breath generally came in rough groans and pants. He had gone white, and his head had become curiously skull-like; he seemed, in fact, a living skeleton, held together by loose skin, for he was gaunt everywhere but over his belly, which had acquired a paunch of fat as hard as stone.

He still spoke of the Prince and Lord Canby and others of the Prince's circle of twenty years agone as though he had visited with them yesterday. His main attention, however, was focused on those he called "my people," and in no affectionate manner—in a tone, in fact, generally reserved by the oppressed for the goons of the regime that terrorizes them. He spent his days indoors, except when he could be coaxed outside to sit in the sunlight; and even then he would complain that "his people" did not like the sun, because they were difficult to see in its radiance. It was as if the beauty of the natural world distracted him from paying his demons the attention and homage they considered to be their due. His hours passed, day after day, mainly in one particular chair in a room reserved for his use. Here he would perch, literally on the edge of his seat, often writhing or rocking back and forth, rolling his head on his neck as if to keep all of his tormentors in view at once, twisting his hands together until he had chafed them raw, or tugging at his shirtfront until he plucked a hole in it. He murmured incessantly to these invisibles, defending himself against their accusations, as it seemed, or currying their favor by poorly feigned laughter at their jokes, or engaging in a babble in what he called "their language." Raphael had had occasion over the years to listen to this chatter, and the thing that impressed him most about it was that there was a meaning discernible in it. He could not by any means follow the drift completely, but it was not without rationality; and he often had thought to himself that if he could have heard the other side of the conversation—the cruel utterances of Titus's interlocutors—he could have made some kind of sense of it all.

His brother was, or so Raphael was by now completely convinced, utterly harmless. Indeed, he was too fearful to strike anyone, and dared do nothing that would alter the status quo. He was grateful for the safety of the cottage, for he believed that the Prince's men (whom he saw as distinct from his ordinary tormentors) were trying to find him and kill him. He even at times expressed the belief that they had already killed the Prince and had put one of their own in his place; and this belief was a source of considerable fear to him, as he thought that, being the only one who knew that the current Prince was literally a pretender, he was sure to be a target for the assassins of those who had murdered the authentic one. Any conversation with him must inevitably deal with these fictions, just as it must be interrupted by his pleas and excuses to his invisible companions. Caught as he was between these two obsessions, he was unable to discourse for more than a few minutes on any other topic.

This human wreck was watched over by Mr. and Mrs. Hexford—Bob and Nancy, sometimes Nan, as Raphael had come to call them; for they were of the servant class. The Hexfords had been chosen by his father, and Raphael had not at first liked them, for they had been clearly eager to take the position only for the financial security it would bring them, and he did not see much lovingkindness in them at the time. But now their affection for their odd adopted child was unquestionable. They loved him indeed more wisely than Raphael had ever expected: they did not foster any tendency in him that might lead to danger, but they indulged as many harmless pleasures as they could. Perhaps the worst that could be said about them was that they gave Titus too many sweets, which he greatly loved, and had inadvertently assisted in the ruin of his teeth, which Titus was loath to clean, and which no dentist would dare to examine and treat, in the fear of being bitten by the madman. Their most annoying defect of character was to observe toward Raphael a nauseating obsequiousness that caused him to be shorter with them than he might otherwise have been. They set no bound on the bowing and scraping that was due him, and fawned on and praised him until he must dislike either them for their silliness or himself for all the ways in which he fell short of being worthy of their adulation, or both. Their exaggerated servility had no particular purpose—they were not in fact trying to wheedle anything out of him; it only seemed to them to be the appropriate manner in which they should behave to their employer and benefactor. Its almost histrionic intensity formed a sharp contrast to the comfortable usefulness of servants in the Bright World.

The cottage in which this odd trio dwelt was a pleasant place, chosen (for some relief against endless gossip) out of the houses of the next parish, and situated on the brow of a low rise, facing south; Raphael had insisted that his brother's habitation should be well lit. Over the years the Hexfords, assisted by Raphael's generosity, had capitalized on its location and created gardens on both sides and adown the slope before it. From these beds they took fresh vegetables in all but the worst of the winter season, and fresh flowers as well, with which Nancy Hexford filled the house.

The couple was otherwise—that is, except for Titus—childless; but they had made a kind of son for themselves out of a madman, and beloved grandchildren out of their flowers. On this particular day it occurred to Raphael, as the carriage pulled up to the walk that led to the house, to wonder what symbol Awen would have seen in these loves that had blossomed in the Hexfords.

Though it was the beginning of December, the day was quite warm and fair, and when he arrived they were working in the garden, putting it to bed for the winter. They came to the gate, bowing and curtsying, respectively, Bob Hexford with hat in hand and head lowered on his neck as though he were putting it out to be struck off by an axe, and Nancy with eyes by turns demurely downcast and fluttering anxiously.

Bob said: "Greetings, greetings, Mr. Kerr, sir—we heard as you were better—we heard with great relief, sir, with great relief. The word as we had was that it was touch and go for a time there."

"I was called back from the brink, indeed, by my duty," said Raphael.

"Nay," said Bob, "you could not leave your brother alone, could you, sir?"

"Nor my wife; nor my sister and her family. So you see, there is much that binds me to this world; I shall not be leaving it soon."

"Indeed, sir, indeed," said Nancy Hexford. "And you, sir, of all the brothers in the world, know and observe your duty, sir. You are your brother's keeper, sir, though there's many a man would have nothing of it. Is that not so, sir?" It is a particularly annoying trait of such flatterers that they are constantly requiring their victims to assent to their praise, and thus forcing them to new ingenuities to evade it.

On this morning in particular Raphael was not willing to play their game with them; and he said simply, "My brother is inside?"

"Indeed he is, sir," said Nancy. "We tried to persuade him to come out, as the sun is so fair, and we know you like it when he can be talked into sitting howsoever long in it; but he would not come. We tried ever so hard, sir, you may be certain."

"He is quite safe by himself, Mr. Kerr, sir," added Bob. "He is quite safe, you know, sir; he would not harm himself—not like some other ones."

"I know that, Bob," said Raphael. "I have no objection to his sitting alone if he prefers it.—I shall go in and see him."

"Let me make you some tea, sir," said Nancy.

"No," said Raphael, a bit more firmly than he meant to. "Do please continue what you were doing—it is a pleasant occupation, and there is no need to alter your plans for the morning."

"Plans?" objected Bob. "What plans could we have but to make you comfortable on your visit to your brother, sir? Nan shall put on the kettle, and I shall stoke up the fire, and we shall have you a cup in no time, sir; and it will be heartening to you after your illness, sir."

"I forbid it," said Raphael determinedly. "Now, do go about your ways. I shall go in and see my brother."

Despite this undeniable negative, they followed him to the house, protesting that they would serve him in every possible way; and he had literally to close the door behind him before he could persuade them to leave off and return to their gardening.

The room he entered was both kitchen and dining room, for the house was indeed very humble, though immaculate and comfortable. The floor was of highly polished deal that gleamed dully in the light streaming through the bay window, and the walls were whitewashed plaster, bare and stark except where the homemaker had hung wreaths or clusters of flowers and herbs to dry. The residual heat of the fire that had cooked breakfast filled the room with an almost soporific warmth, a contrast to the more fresh morning without. Perhaps it was that the place reminded him of the house at Vigia—perhaps that was why; but Raphael had thought it a very salubrious place for a madman to dwell and to seek what peace he might win from his confusions.

But this pleasantness evaporated instantly as Raphael went on to the threshold of the room where his brother dwelt. A stench engulfed him, fouler than any mixture of excrement, urine, vomit, carrion, rotting fish, rotten egg; it was like a physical blow, and his eyes stung with it, his nasal passages and throat seemed to burn. For a moment he was incensed by the thought that Titus had fouled himself and been neglected; but no, as he looked into the room from the threshold, he saw that his brother was dressed in quite fresh, clean, and neat clothing. He was sitting in his usual chair in his usual dejected and anxious posture; nothing in his attitude indicated that any unusual circumstance beset him.

Raphael's second thought was that the chamber pot had not been emptied for a week, and as he walked forward into the room, pressing his handkerchief over his nose, he looked about for it—and saw it on the floor in the corner, as clean as such a vessel could be kept.

Titus belatedly noticed Raphael's entrance and looked up at him with that mingled hopelessness and distracted interest that the mad show to those whom they love; and Raphael, still looking about for the cause of the stench, said to him, "What is that smell, Titus? It is absolutely foul in here!"

"It always is," said Titus.

"What are you talking about, Brother? I have visited you many a time and it has never smelled like this here."

"That smell has been everywhere," said Titus, looking away and darting his eyes about, as though he were telling Raphael something he ought not to reveal.

"Everywhere? For how long?"

"Always."

"What do you mean, 'always'? I have never smelled it before."

"Since I was . . . since I began to be with . . . since *they* have been with me."

And now, as he looked down on his innocent brother, Raphael realized that this was not a physical smell. It was like the smell that had filled the room when Manwaring's evil companions had thronged about her. And lo, as he paused, and for the first time really *looked* at his brother and at the room where he sat, he realized that his brother was not alone here. It was almost as if he could see shadowy forms crowded around him, plucking at him with shadowy hands, leaning over to whisper in his ear, rocking with laughter, mocking him and slapping him. And as Raphael sensed them, it seemed he could catch bits of the words they spoke, fragments of the invective they hurled at his brother.

"These creatures," he said suddenly, "they are always with you?"

Titus raised his head and looked at him with surprise, though whether it was a surprise at being asked the question at all, or at someone's having at last noticed the presence of his tormentors, Raphael did not know. "Oh, yes," he said. "They are always with me. They have been with me since . . . since I began to . . . I do not know—since I was young. Twenty years and more."

"This cannot be right!" cried Raphael. "You did not invite these evil beings to beset you—did you? I cannot believe it! Why should *you* be tortured in this way? Do you love them, Titus?"

"How *could* I love them?" asked Titus, breaking into tears. "They never cease to torment me. From time to time I see someone different—a person who comes like light shining on me; but he does not stay long. The others, the dark ones, they crowd him out."

"Well," cried Raphael, "they shall torment you no more!"

And stepping forward so that he was directly before Titus, he clasped his hands together before him and held them over his brother's head. "Great and good One who rules all," he prayed, "grant this innocent soul relief!"

It was as if an electric charge had gone through the dark cloud of evil around Titus. Though before they had not seemed to sense Raphael in their turn, now they did so; he could feel their horror and hatred; and after pausing thus, as if to assess the seriousness of his challenge to them, they abruptly fled in all directions. The stench that had clogged the air dispersed simultaneously with their departure.

And as instantly it seemed that other beings were present. They, too, could not be seen, except as a faint radiance of light; it was all around the two brothers, but seemed to have no specific point of origin. These beings brought with them another smell, a fragrance indescribable, lightning-fresh, a scent of warm earth and flowerhead, of fruit and clean skin, of remembered childhood.

Titus groaned and then broke into wild sobbing. Raphael knelt beside him and put his arms around him, and Titus clung to him, blubbering in grateful shock. "What did you *do?*" he asked between his sobs.

"I only prayed," said Raphael.

It was late in the day before Raphael could persuade Titus to let him leave. His brother was sure that the evil beings would return to plague him; and as a defense against that eventuality, Raphael taught him to pray. It was like teaching a child; for though Titus had been instructed in religion, like all British churchgoers, from the time he was a boy, he seemed to have regarded all religious acts as meaningless rituals enjoined upon him in order to induce a conformity to the beliefs of the general populace. He had never imagined that the dry, dead forms dinned into his ears so often might contain, hidden in them, the wellspring of hope against his eternal despair, or the sun of light that would irradiate and illuminate his endless darkness. "And this, too, you must remember," Raphael told him. "I will always be here, never far from you. If they plague you again, you can send to me by Bob or Nan, and I shall come and drive them away again. You are weak now, I suspect, and they may well attack you again—I do not deny it is possible; but a prayer will send them away as effectively again as it did before."

"But why did you never send them away before this?" asked Titus.

"I never sensed them before."

"But why do you now?"

"That is a long story, Brother, which I do not know if I am permitted to tell. Suffice it to say that now I know of the other world, the real world, of which this first, dim world is only a part. The real world, which I call the Bright World, is all around us. Other people, untrammeled as you and I are by the dimness and heaviness of this world, are constantly walking beside us in space and time. It seems that if we think, feel, and do evil, the evil in that larger world are attracted to us; if we think, feel, and do good, the good throng joyfully around us. Or perhaps we could say that *we put ourselves* in the company of the evil or good of that world depending on what we think, feel, do."

"But am I so evil?" asked Titus. "Have I deserved this torment?"

"No," said Raphael emphatically. "There is something wrong here—something I do not understand, and may never understand. I believe that the One has so ordered the universe that we here in the Dim World cannot *consciously* sense the other world, and those in the Bright World cannot sense us here. But there are exceptions to this order, for reasons unknown. I am an exception, though a feeble one at best. And you are an exception, though to your own great anguish. The barrier in your mind that should prevent your perception of the other world is broken. Perhaps you once cherished bad intentions—I do believe that in your younger years you did—and the evil ones were drawn to that. Ordinarily you would never have known they were there, known who was tormenting you; but because that barrier was broken in your mind, you could not help it. Perhaps what we call sanity is only the soundness of that one barrier, and the instant it is cracked, *we are cracked*; and through that crack the evil forces of the other world wedge their way, breaking open the gap, making it wider from year to year, and holding us in a cycle of despair and misery that prevents our ever closing the gap again. Whether the crack is caused by an organic defect or a spiritual or mental one, I do not know."

If he had proposed this theory to anyone else in his acquaintance, he would have been thought as mad as Titus; but Titus, perhaps because he was mad, understood it perfectly.

They went outside and sat in the sun for a time, and that was clearly pleasant for Titus; but Raphael could see that there was still something very wrong with his brother. His brain did not work properly. All normal and healthy train of association was absent; his mind leapt from one topic to the next, from one fear to the next, without any order or pause. It was as if the many compartments of his mind were all ruptured, and instead of a house of many rooms, each shut off by wall and door that could only be entered in an orderly way, his brain was a ruined building through which thoughts ran unimpeded and helter-skelter. But for some minutes on that day, as they sat overlooking the garden and the two happy workers in it, Titus did have some peace; and Raphael hoped that as time passed, he would have more.

And thus was the case: in coming years, Titus did have longer and longer intervals of peace, though not of anything approaching lucidity. The frame of his brain was broken and would not be repaired on this side of death. Sometimes the dark forces attacked him again; sometimes he successfully held them at bay and summoned back the forces of light; but more often he had to send desperately for Raphael, who was always able to send the molesting crew back to the Dark Lands.

If this form of healing was incomplete, it still was a kind of miracle. From that day the mental health of Raphael's brother was very obviously improved, and the Hexfords saw it was so immediately. They questioned Raphael as closely as they dared, and later Titus; and though the latter freely told them everything that Raphael had said to him, the Hexfords could make little sense of it, and could only repeat to others that Raphael had effected some kind of healing with prayer.

People in the little parish where the Hexfords lived quickly appreciated the change. They came by the cottage and saw—previously a rarity—the madman sitting quietly and contentedly in the sun; for now Titus began to like to be outside in all weathers and seasons, and it became a matter of some difficulty to coax him back into the house. Paradoxically, the out-of-doors turned him inward to the light, as the world indoors had kept him focused on the externals of his self. Out of doors, he was in connection with the clearer, brighter forces of limitless love; inside he was at risk of falling into the dark abyss of his own limited person.

Rumor went abroad from the parish, and even its twisted, broken vessel retained some truth; and it led on to a further incident worth recounting.

One day about a month after Raphael had banished the dark beings from Titus's life, Mr. Strong came to him in his study and announced that "a tradesman-looking sort of fellow" had called and begged to see him. "His wife and child are with him too, sir," said Mr. Strong. "And there is something quite odd about the daughter. Shall I send them away?"

Raphael, puzzled, said: "No, I shall see them; show them into the little parlor and I shall be along in a minute."

It took him several minutes, in fact, to finish up what he was doing; and when he arrived at the door of the parlor, he found the family waiting for him, under the intimidating watch of Mr. Strong. It was like the day he had visited Titus: the moment he stepped into the room, an evil smell rolled over him. It was not, however, as vile and suffocating as the one that had surrounded his brother: it was more sour and vomitlike than excremental. One glance at Mr. Strong told him that the butler could not sense this stench.

The man of the family was an intelligent-looking fellow of about forty-five. He had the appearance of a schoolteacher who had failed at his calling, for whatever reason, and had been forced into the trades. Raphael expected he might be a haberdasher or draper or stationer. His wife was a good ten years younger; and though pretty in a faded way, she was pale and drawn, as if either exhausted by their journey here or worn out by continuous anxiety. Both husband and wife had an air of seedy poverty, and he guessed that their enterprise, whatever it was, just barely provided them with a living.

Such couples were common enough in the England of any era; what interested him more was the daughter they had brought with them. She was standing slightly behind her father, peering from his protection at Raphael: a girl about twelve years of age, dressed in her finest clothes, which yet seemed second-hand, outdated, as if they had once belonged to her mother. She was ill, mentally ill; he could see it at once when he looked at her; and it took no special power to do so, as indeed Mr. Strong had been able to see it. She looked—not *stupid*—but *stupified,* as if something dreadful had happened to her and she was still in shock because of it. Her eyes were hollows, quite dark, and she was preternaturally thin.

Later Raphael was to remember this child in particular because it was on meeting her that he first saw a personal aura made visible in this world. In the Bright World he had sometime caught glimpses of brightnesses around individuals, and though he could sense auras there in many different ways, he had not *seen* them as he could see this child's aura. It was gray, like a grainy, dark smoke, but it was not so much a physical thing as a hueless-ness that seemed veritably to suck color out of the world around it. From time to time shapes were visible in this gray cloud, as if of people coming and going.

"You may leave us now, Mr. Strong," he told the butler. "But do please ask Mrs. McQuillit to bring us some tea, will you? These people must be quite famished after their travel this morning."

When Mr. Strong had gone, Raphael gestured to the chairs. "Do sit down," he said.

"It would hardly be proper, sir," said the man, "to sit in the presence of such as you, being such as we are."

"I insist," said Raphael.

The wife looked at her husband, hoping his pride would not prevent her from sitting down; and the man, seeing that almost hopeless gaze, said to Raphael, "Well, sir, if you insist, then I shall most gratefully see my wife seated, as she is quite tired."

She settled into a chair as if she could not have stood for another ten seconds together; and upon Raphael's sitting down, and coaxing the fellow a little more, the man conceded enough to his host's authority to sit down himself, though he remained literally on the edge of his seat throughout the interview. His daughter put herself immediately behind his chair, standing; and Raphael, on some instinct, did not address her directly to encourage her to take her own seat.

"Now," he said, "what is your name, my good fellow?"

"Drayer, sir; Michael Drayer. And this is Mrs. Drayer; and my daughter, Louette."

"Very good, Mr. Drayer; and what brings you to me today?"

Mr. Drayer looked at once fearful and disappointed. "Can you not guess, sir?"

"Perhaps I can," said Raphael thoughtfully. "But it would be best to hear you say it."

"It is Louette, sir. She is . . . she is going mad. Nay, sir, I shall admit it: she is mad, quite mad, we are afraid."

With this confession, the gates of his speech were broken, and he blurted out the tale. Mrs. Drayer was soon weeping at the telling.

"My daughter," Mr. Drayer began, "has had fits since she was a baby. To other people who do not know her, they are frightening, but they are nothing—nothing, sir, for any intelligent person to be afraid of. She falls down, she foams at the mouth a little—her eyes roll back, she is stiff, she arches her back. But those are just occasional fits. In all other ways she has always been the sweetest child, sir. You cannot conceive; you cannot conceive how sweet.

"When she was a very little girl she started pretending she had a playfellow—quite imaginary—we thought nothing of it at first. She would talk with . . . this playfellow, in her imagination; and at first she would stop when we told her to. But then she would not; she spoke to . . . the person she imagined was there, spoke all the time. And as she got older, we realized that her conversations were not just with one person, but with many. She began not to listen to us at all, as if she did not even hear us at times; she spoke of brightness, and beautiful people, and looked into plain space as if she could see some other world; she described the houses they lived in, the gardens where they walked—it was all so real to her—I cannot tell you how strange it was, sir, as if she were truly seeing what she told us of.

"It was bad enough that people thought her odd; but then she began to say strange things about religion, and to laugh in amazement when we took her to church, as if the rector did not know his own business. It became impossible to take her anywhere, and my custom began to suffer, and we had to keep her out of the shop altogether. Not that she ever hurt anyone, sir! She could not hurt a fly or a flea. It was just that she was strange, and people fear what is strange.

"At last we took her to a surgeon in Norwich, and he told us we must send her away if we wished to save her mind. We were loath to do it, sir, loath; but for her sake we did it. She was at St. Mary's School in Yorkshire—we did not like it, not at all; it seemed a grim place to us, but we believed it was all for the best.

"Well, it was not for the best. When the holidays came, I went to bring her home; and I found her in a cell—a cell it was, no schoolroom—and all changed. At least before she had been happy, even if she was daft. Now she was frightened, miserable. Now all the imaginary beings around her seemed to be cruel and to taunt her."

Mr. Drayer paused and his eyes made a pathetic appeal to Raphael. "Can you imagine, sir, what that is like?" he asked. "To think what they must have done to her, to turn all her pleasant fancy into a painful one?"

"It is indeed a frightening thing to contemplate," said Raphael, who could guess that the girl had suffered endless beatings, lectures, and imprisonment in a cruel and ignorant attempt to discipline her out of her odd ways.

"Now, sir," continued Mr. Drayer, "I shall not take up any more of your time with our troubles than is absolutely needful— so I shall not go into how we brought her home and tried our best to mend her back at least to what she had been. We have failed, that is the sum of it.

"And here is the thing: We have heard that you have done something wonderful with . . . someone related to you, sir, if you will pardon my referring to it. We are hoping you can . . . try the same with Louette. We are not asking you to cure her; but if you can make her happy again, sir—" And with this plea he himself began to weep.

Raphael was unsure what he ought to do, to say nothing of his uncertainty of what he was able to do. The girl had placed herself behind her father in such a way as to most effectively conceal herself from the stranger, and he now rose and tried to look upon her. She continually shifted her position, however, so that he could not see her without obstruction, until her father said, "Nay, my dear, you must hold still. The gentleman will not hurt you." Then she stayed put long enough for Raphael to obtain another good look at her.

She had the face of someone far older than her years. She must have seen and heard things, with her ability to see into the Dark Lands, that children—and indeed no one—ought ever to see or hear: foul speech, fouler deeds, unspeakable brutalities and spoken blasphemies unperformable. What had happened to her in the school, too, could only be thought of with a shudder of helpless and thus dismissive horror. It came to him that there was a little of Veronica's hurt peering back at him from those too-experienced eyes, though none of Veronica's shame and anger.

On an impulse, perhaps thinking to be less frightening to the girl if he did not loom over her as an adult, he knelt on the floor. Mr. and Mrs. Drayer, who had risen from their chairs with him, now knelt as well, perhaps thinking that they ought not to remain standing when he knelt, and assuming that he meant to pray. But he did not do so, or at least not at first. Instead he spoke to the girl.

"I know what you see," he said.

She seemed startled; and though she had been looking determinedly away from him, now she turned to face him.

"You can leave the Dark Lands, you know," he said. "You can go back to the Bright Lands, where you used to live."

Now her eyes truly grew wide, and she looked at him almost yearningly, and took a half-step toward him.

"You must think yourself there," he said. "You must will yourself there. Think of the friends you had in that place and ask to be in their company."

She looked dubious.

"It is true," he said. "We can be in any company we want—or at least, in company as good as we can endure. We have only to truly want to be among the best, and there we are."

She still seemed unsure.

"Come," he said. "I will show you. Come here and kneel down, and we will pray together, all of us."

She came forward, uncertainly at first, but she did as he suggested, kneeling about three feet before him.

"Now, fold your hands together," he said.

She did as he told her, though awkwardly, as if she had not prayed for many years.

"Now," he said, "I want you to pray. And when you talk to God, do not use that name; say, 'the One.' Can you do that?"

She nodded a little stiffly.

"Now, pray to be in the Lands of Light."

The girl looked frightened and confused. The swarm of personages around her, which Raphael could sense only very dimly, seemed to be growing agitated as her tormentors felt her turning away from them, and they seemed to be trying to shout down her attempt to focus on prayer.

"Pray to the One for light," said Raphael gently. He looked at Mr. and Mrs. Drayer too, and said, "You pray as well; pray that your daughter may walk in the Lands of Light again."

They were both frightened at the strangeness of all this, he could see, and looked as if they thought he too must be mad, and perhaps they even wanted to give up the visit and leave at once, but they did not dare be so rude.

"Oh, *One,*" said the girl suddenly, in a thin, lisping, childish voice, "let me walk in the Lands of Light again."

Instantly the stench was gone from the room. The gray cloud around the girl vanished, replaced—at least to Raphael's vision—by an aura almost golden, faintly glowing. The girl looked around herself in wonder; then she looked joyfully at Raphael—jumped to her feet, spun about on her heel as if gazing in all directions on that other world (which he perfectly believed to be the case), and clapped her hands together in girlish pleasure.

At that moment the door of the room opened and Mr. Strong and Mrs. McQuillit entered. They were surprised to find the master and his two adult guests kneeling, and they hesitated and almost retreated; but Raphael rose to his feet and said, "By all means, bring in the tea—we are in need of sustenance here."

And thereafter for an hour he sat with the Drayers as though they were of his own class, much to the wonder of his servants, and drank tea with them. Louette was able to join them—to be mentally in this world—and had a little tea and ate a few cakes happily, though she said nothing. From time to time she looked shyly at Raphael, smiling as one does who shares a secret; and he smiled back, gently, glad of what relief she had found.

It was obvious that she was still too much in that other world to cope with this one for long. He suspected that some organic damage had taken place in her brain, either concomitant with or consequent to her epilepsy, that had, in essence, weakened the membrane between the worlds. At first she had lived among the good there, but her difficult experience at the school had some-how relocated her among the cruel. He had redirected her to a better part of the Bright World, but he could not repair the bar-riers in her mind that were supposed to prevent her from seeing that world or even knowing of its existence.

When Mrs. Drayer cautiously asked him if Louette would ever be like other girls, Raphael shook his head. "She will al-ways be different," he said. "She will never be fully present in this world. I know nothing that can be done about that, I am sorry to say. We must be content with seeing her happy where she is."

The Drayers were, fortunately, able to feel grateful for this improvement. Raphael put them into his own carriage for their journey home, after making them promise to send word to him about Louette's condition at least once a fortnight for the next few months, and to bring her back if she relapsed into her former suffering.

Then he himself went for a walk, pondering the universe, wondering why it was made the way it was, and thinking on the strange part he had now to play in it.

He saw, he believed, that the lessons of these two strange cases—Titus's, and the girl Louette's—applied to his own life. He could now understand how his irritation with Veronica had drawn him downwards over the years. In retrospect he even wondered if at times during his marriage to her—when he had grown particularly angry with her for some petty attempt to hurt him— he had not seen dim, dark forms being attracted to his anger and beginning to assemble around him. If that were so, then in future he thought that if he could only be prompt to pray and repel his irritation, those shadowy shapes would vanish, and beings more light would take their place. It must be possible to attract the attention of those in the other world who were good and whose effect on him would be more positive. He must deliberately set out to win the company of those brighter beings, by fostering within him a love and affection toward all.

Veronica, too, was affected by melancholic or angry beings drawn to her by her consistently negative mental state. There seemed to be an intangible connection between this world and that, through the membrane of the mind: those beings in the other world who thrived on one's mental attitudes were drawn to one, or rather to a point on the other side of the membrane immediately contiguous to one's location here. They did not, in the Bright World, have any sense of "going to" any "place" where mortals were, for their world was without space, as it was without time. They were "with" mortals in this world only in spirit. Their sudden departure—as when, in the case of Titus, Raphael had actually seen them dispersing in all directions—was only an appearance; they were in fact only disconnecting from their engagement with an aura that had formerly attracted them because it was like their own—spiritually departing from a spiritual locus. The beings that had afflicted Louette were not evil so much as they were full of despair; their presence had kept her isolated in melancholy because she was not healthy enough to block them out and choose a new and happier frame of mind.

Such were his speculations. He tested them by observing Veronica through fresh eyes; and over the next few weeks, he grew able to see her aura and sense the beings that flickered through its gray cloud. He prayed for her frequently, but curiously this brought no mitigation of her psychic pain. It was clear then that she was in love with her suffering; and if she was to be cured of that unhealthy love, it must be by degrees, by a thousand thousand acts of kindness that drew her out of the company of the gray into the company of the light.

Yet, though he saw her situation with new clarity, he still had no expectation of her healing. He had spent too many years of his life in those hopes to adopt them again now.

He himself was afflicted by melancholy from time to time. These dark periods followed hard upon his brightest moments, when it seemed he could feel the presence of Awen just on the other side of the membrane, when her aura was present to him in all its richness and emotion, its fragrance and sexual heat. When he lost that sense—as he inevitably did from time to time, in dealing with the business of living in this heavier, duller world—it was as if his life went blank for a period. He lost his connection with the One, or so it seemed; he drifted, purposeless, for an hour or an afternoon, yearning for his sojourn here to be over. And if his despair descended on him in the evening, before he lay down to rest, he sometimes found himself, in his dreams, pacing along the wall that barred him from the Bright World, or even peering longingly through the gate of horn, until the stern figure of the guardian angel, glimpsed through the mists, sent him reeling back into consciousness of the Dim World, to awaken in a sweat of terror, horrified that he had even contemplated disobedience.

Another strange new awareness grew on him at this time. He had always read the Bible as a historical document, a narrative of the Jewish religion and of the Christian church that had grown from it. But one day, having opened the book to one of the driest passages of Leviticus, it occurred to him to read not the narrative but the symbols, as if the book had been written in the Bright World and were presenting not a literal meaning but a stream of images in the mental and poetic language of that place. And instantly the hard, gray, even cruel world of the ancient Israelites, in which people were stoned to death by their own community, took on a golden luster, and its violence dimmed and dissolved; and he saw that its strange word paintings had to do not literally with intolerance and excess, but, in the strange paradox of symbolism, with love and with bettering our faults.

At first he clung to this understanding as a man clings to the brink of a precipice. But his new apprehension of meaning in the Bible did not slip away from him; he was able to confirm his grip on it, to raise himself until he stood on that level, though he could indeed barely grasp the depth and power of the symbols he was reading. It seemed to him that there are two languages, the first being that language in which the mind of the One expresses itself, unfathomably and infinitely rich; the second being human discourse, limited by space and time and the pettiness of human knowledge and feeling. The Bible seemed to be a lamination of the two.

He plunged his mind into those deeper symbols as a boy throws a stick into a torrent and then chases it along the banks, watching it vanish in the rapids and then bob to the surface again, as it follows the contours of the land and the mighty pull of gravity, responding to the summons of the sea, the great sea of symbol that was the mind of the One. Sometimes, indeed, he felt that his mind disappeared under the surface of the symbols of the story, only to reemerge after mental adventures he could not have rendered into speech.

And having seen this sudden blossoming of beauty and love in that ancient and crabbed book, it was not long before he was seeing the same blossoming in the Dim World itself. He had glimpsed the beauty of the Bright World leaking through the membrane between this life and that one; now he saw that this world around him was a vast symbol of that other world, that the symbols here spoke to the symbols there in endless conversation, just as Titus and Louette and Veronica and he himself and indeed all people here drew to themselves, in endless conversation of spirit, the people of that other world.

Sometimes it was all he could do to remain aware of the world around him in its literal sense. He sat in the Paradise, or on the top of the hill slope at Fulkothing, and the beauty and symbol of the Dim World was so infused with the meaning and beauty of the Bright World that he was overwhelmed, and for intervals lost the ability to follow the ordinary sense of this world, to recall the purposes of the actions and speech of those here.

It occurred to him that our materiality here is only the consequence of a symbolism we require. We are no less *substantial* in the other world, but we no longer require to eat, sleep, urinate, defecate, to be bound by gravity and age and sickness, all in representation of our limited lives. He suspected, indeed, that the denizens of the Dark Lands were still attached to those bodily functions and limitations, still required them as part of the symbols they made of their lives. And he thought it might just be possible to let go of such needs even here, in this world, if one were spiritually advanced enough; but this altitude was beyond his reach.

Perhaps he was in those moments of reverie perfectly insane. At the very least he was in some visionary state. He gave up the tenuous game we call reality (which by the standards of the Bright World means unreality) and let his mind flow with the stream of beauty and meaning coursing out of the Bright World, coursing (ultimately) out of the One at the center of all things.

Then he knew wonders he had never known before, a knowledge beyond speech, beyond the powers of his mind to recollect, an angelic knowledge. It was too powerful, indeed, for his mortal brain and body to hold and retain. For example, there were times, when he thought of Awen, that the intensity of his love for her smote him like a mighty inrush of spirit, as if a hurricane had breathed all its energies into his meager body, inflating him to the bursting like a stopped and frail reed. In those moments he became so physically aroused that it seemed he must die, literally be rent apart, and he was deafened by the surge of his blood and the hammering of his heart, dizzy in brain, alternately gasping and sinking in breath, both sweating in a rage of heat and burning with cold, his limbs flaccid, and yet his phallus so engorged it nearly bled, and indeed ached for hours afterward.

Only in the Bright World could one safely know the secrets of the Bright World, he realized. That was one reason the One had put that barrier between the worlds. The insanity of Titus and Louette were warnings to him. But the beauty and love of that place drew him irresistibly; and he felt that the One did not censure him for these glimpses he took of that higher reality, but instead had granted him these moments to encourage him and steady him on his way.

Chapter 54

I knew a man in Christ above fourteen years ago (whether in the body, I cannot tell; or whether out of the body, I cannot tell: God knoweth) such an one caught up to the third heaven. And I knew such a man (whether in the body, or out of the body, I cannot tell; God knoweth). How that he was caught up into paradise and heard unspeakable words, which it is not lawful for a man to utter.

—2 Corinthians 12:2–4

After Raphael had been banished from the Bright World, and after he had recovered from his illness, the words of the Wonderful began to haunt him: *There I was known as the Swede* and *Those who seek shall find.* He sent to his bookseller, Mr. Lissome of Lissome and Brickit, and inquired as to the availability of any books in Swedish about the afterlife, as well as any texts from which he might learn that tongue.

He and Mr. Lissome had been in regular communication by mail for some twenty-five years, though they had never met. Mr. Lissome was one of those odd figures, previously mentioned, who are common in the book trade: though not a reader himself—indeed, at times Raphael wondered if he had ever made his way through an entire volume of anything from cover to cover—he loved books; that is, he loved dealing in them. The buying and selling of august literature put him, in his own eyes, in the class of those who could write it and read it with appreciation. It was as near as he would get to that fraternity of letters of which he longed to be a part. He was, in fact, courteously tolerated by writers and readers, by librarians and scholars, almost as if he had been one of their number; but he remained always on a slightly lower level. His popularity may in fact have been the greater for that inequality, because everyone likes to feel superior to others, and a person like Lissome, whom you treat as an equal, while you secretly harbor an assurance of superiority to him, is a very valuable fellow to know, inasmuch as he reassures you of your humility at the same time he feeds your vanity. Raphael, however, had a genuine liking for the man: his letters, though curt and dry, were direct, and occasionally concluded with a fillip of humor, thrown in almost as an afterthought, like salt to season the rest.

Raphael received Mr. Lissome's reply to his inquiry within a few days. He opened it while at the breakfast table, though he did not ordinarily read mail if Veronica was at the table with him during breakfast: Veronica almost never corresponded with anyone, except in the case of the polite notes that were passed back and forth within the neighborhood, and he had always thought it rude to occupy himself with the business of reading letters when she could not join him in it. But this morning she had some invitations she was glancing over, and between her preoccupation and his eagerness to learn what Lissome might have found, he made the event an exception. This is what he read:

> Geo. Lissome
> Lissome & Brickit
> No. — Albemarle Street
> London
>
> Mr. Raphael Kerr
> Fulkothing Hall
> Nedwich
> Norfolk
>
> Dear Sir:
>
> Yours of the 23rd: Nothing on the afterlife in Swedish theology known to me short of various tracts of the Lutherans. This what you would be wanting? Texts concerning the Swed: tongue also few and far betw:, but shall send what I can find.
>
> It occurs to ask If you meant Swedenborg? An enthusiastical fellow—do not recommend him—but know you are interested in religious curiosities. Wrote in Latin, not Swedish.
>
> Your servant,
> GEO. LISSOME

The effect of this letter on Raphael was startling to Veronica and the servants in the room. When he read the contents, he gave a muffled exclamation and rose from his seat. Veronica stared coldly at him, with that look that said she was offended by anything and everything he did; and though he did not care for her opinion, he remembered his manners and sat down again, to make at least a pretense of finishing his meal.

Veronica said, "And what can your bookseller have to tell you that is so exciting to you this morning, Mr. Kerr?" She meant him to know that she had seen the letter lying on the table before he had come in, and discovered whom it was from.

"A bookseller, my dear," he said, in a kind and eager tone, as if he really thought she might be interested, "can have the most exciting news in the world for one, if one is seeking a particular book."

She seemed to be weighing whether it would hurt him more if she showed no interest and terminated the conversation, or if she found out what book so intrigued him and then mocked it. In her indecision about how most effectively to wound him, she resorted to a third option and said: "And were you jumping up from the table to run off to London and secure this tedious book you so suddenly cannot live without?"

"No; for Mr. Lissome's letter informs me on a point of which he himself is unaware: I have realized that the very book I asked him to seek out is in my own library, unread."

"Oh," she said, in a sarcastic tone, "do you mean to say you have not read everything in your library, sir? I am shocked to learn that."

Raphael smiled gently, completely proof to her irritations. "Oh, I have many books I have not read, and I trust I always shall. They are my bulwark against boredom and my stored sunfire against the days of rain to come. They are my acknowledgment that the wonders of the world are infinite in comparison to one's ability to know them, though their magnitude shrinks to nothingness when set against one's desire to do so."

"Always the posturing scholar!" she said bitterly.

"Oh, yes," he said genuinely. "I am a failure in countless ways; but you will not impeach my eagerness to learn."

"Then why do you not go seek out this book, Mr. Kerr? I shall not miss your company."

"It would be rude," he said. "I apologize for starting up like that; I forgot myself for a moment."

"And I tell you I do not care if it is rude. Indeed, it cannot be rude, if your companion at table takes no offense at it; and as I care not one way or the other whether you are present or absent, I can take no offense."

He only smiled at her, his good spirits unquenchable, and continued his breakfast.

When the meal was finished, however, and she went back upstairs to her sitting room, he went directly to his study, barely able to refrain from running. There the golden morning sun was spilling into the room; the cat was in her favorite chair by the fire, and stretched and yawned when he came in, and then went away to hunt; and the books in their cases beckoned him like a lover on a balcony. He knew, or thought he knew, the very case in which the book should be; but books intended for later reading are sometimes temporarily included with others of that ilk, and at other times are assigned to their permanent dwelling, and between the two go missing. So it was with this book. He went through several cases not once but twice; but eventually, in double-checking everything they contained, he came again upon a volume he had before passed over too rapidly—it was bound in a pale vellum, and he had been picturing the book he sought as being in unsewn signatures.

The vellum was unmarked, unstamped, and so, thinking that he would only confirm his assumption that it was some other forgotten book, he opened to the title page; and to his surprise he found it was the very one he wanted, for his eyes fell on these words:

DELITIAE SAPIENTIAE

DE

AMORE CONJUGIALI;

———

POST QUAS SEQUUNTUR
VOLUPTATES INSANIAE
DE
AMORE SCORTATORIO.

AB

EMANUELE SWEDENBORG
SUECO

Which might, though it defied intelligible literal translation, be rendered in English as:

TREATING
THE DELIGHTS THAT ARISE FROM BEING WISE
ON THE SUBJECT OF
MARRIED LOVE

———

AND AFTER THOSE, ALSO TREATING
THE RECKLESS GRATIFICATIONS
OF
PROMISCUOUS LOVE

BY
EMANUEL SWEDENBORG
A SWEDE

The work had been published in Amsterdam in 1768, and Raphael had acquired it from Lissome himself in 1805—he had written the date of accession on the title page, as was his practice—though the bookseller had evidently now forgotten the transaction; it had arrived in a large box for purchase on approval, and though Raphael had kept it as a curiosity, he had, like Lissome, regarded it as a work of third-rate interest, the self-indulgent fantasies of an amateur theologian—indeed, of a crackpot.

He began at once to read it, and for three hours he stood without moving an inch except to turn the pages. He was, from the first sentence, in no doubt that the Wonderful and Swedenborg were the same man.

The book spoke very definitively and authoritatively about theology and marriage and the relationship between the sexes—too authoritatively, it seemed to Raphael. It seemed to be a digression from the course of a larger theological construction—Raphael was aware that Swedenborg had written many other books on theological themes; and that theology, as it appeared in this book at least, seemed to Raphael to be a mere human's best guesses at doctrine, based on experiences the Wonderful had had while wandering in the Bright World. It was this human interpretive element—regretted, as Raphael had heard, by the Wonderful himself—that tangled the presentation no end, though the theology in itself was strangely beautiful as well as highly sensible and practical. A further complication was the odd Latin in which it was written, the composition of a man who, though thoroughly familiar with the best classical models, seemed deliberately to reject them in order to write in a simpler, looser style.

But what a joy to read those words, printed on a page in this Dim World, of another man who had traveled through the Bright World years ago—if Raphael had ever doubted his own experience, here was proof and more than proof enough for the very last skeptical fiber in his brain. It took him those three hours to read the first sixty-five pages of that strange Latin, packed as it was in small type in a large single column on the quarto pages; but when he had reached that far he closed the book on his index finger and went, almost reeling, to the chair by the fire and sank into it; and held the book against his chest and was swept away by a whirlwind of eager thought.

What Swedenborg had seen in the Bright World was in many cases very different from what Raphael had seen, and he described it not as Raphael would have. But—the finding that shocked Raphael most of all the things he read there—some of Swedenborg's experiences had been very closely parallel to his own. He too had gone on a journey to visit the Golden People; he had climbed the same mountain, and would have gone astray in the same labyrinth of paths on its slopes if he had not been led by a guide, who showed him the olive trees and the vines growing on them, and brought him at length to the cedars on the upper heights, and finally to the plain at the peak. The very conversation that Swedenborg had had with those people was similar to the words Raphael had exchanged with them. He had visited the Silver People as well, and seen the rainbow artwork of the Image Makers; he had been to the lawyerly city of the Bronze People, and seen the foul polygamy of the Iron Folk; but he was not, like Raphael, spared the sight of the People of Clay—he had been there, and he described it in detail. Perhaps that was the reason he had turned Raphael aside from the wide way, so that he might be spared that disgusting portion of his journey.

But these minor differences aside, the similarity of their experiences was so close that Raphael could only wonder at the meaning of it. It seemed that when one first went to the Bright World, one saw what one needed to see in order to learn what one needed to learn; and indeed this first guess was to be borne out by his further reading, which included countless representational encounters with the inhabitants of the other world, clearly arising out of Swedenborg's own fervent interest in the questions of theology. As a wanderer there, he had attended elaborate debates on such obscure questions as the nature of the soul, doubtless among communities that delighted in such things—certainly he never went to the city of the Image Makers, where Raphael's own interests had drawn him.

For another hour he sat in astonished reverie on these matters. Then he leapt up and dashed off this message for Lissome:

> Sir—
>
> Disregard my previous about Swedish theology. Do buy me with the utmost haste anything you can procure of the works of this Swedenborg. Use the utmost dispatch—send it to me posthaste—you know me—I shall pay your charges.
>
> RAPHAEL KERR

He called for a man to take the letter to the inn at once and there hire a messenger to carry it on by the most urgent means to London. He then ordered his meals brought to him in his study until further notice, and laid in a supply of candles against the coming of the night.

These preparations made, he sat down to the book again. He would read on until he could read no more, and resume as soon as his strength to do so returned.

He found that Swedenborg had attempted to describe the nature of marriage in the Bright World. More than that, he had attempted to write a kind of manual of spiritual marriage love. In some respects he was quite successful; in others not so. He himself seemed not to have married while on earth, and his scope was in consequence somewhat limited; but he did report what he saw, or what he learned from the didactic experiences the One had granted to him.

He distinguished between true marriages, in which the partners were united spiritually, and simulated marriages, in which both or at least one of the partners was incapable of the spiritual life. Of the true marriage he had little to teach Raphael—indeed, Raphael could have taught him much, or at least he could have taught much to that Swedenborg who had composed the book during his mortal life. The most condensed gist of the book was that the One promised those who wished for true marriage the opportunity to achieve it in the Bright World, if they did not find it in the Dim World; and as Swedenborg had observed, both in his conversation with Raphael as the Wonderful and in his book, few people ever found the true marriage here. But Raphael had already discovered as much.

Of the simulated marriages, by contrast, Swedenborg had many things to say that were of use to Raphael. One such passage was as follows:

> The cause of these simulated marriages is that a person who has a deep spirit acts on the basis of good judgment and what is right. That is, such a person does not consider a simulated marriage to be at odds with his or her inner life, but as requiring to be aligned with it. He or she acts in full earnestness, looking toward the possibility that his or her spouse's behavior

will undergo amendment; and if this does not follow, then the hope is for an accommodation, so that there will be order in the house, or so that the two spouses may assist each other, or so that they may care for their children, or so that they may have peace and tranquility. A sense of what is right directs such a person to pursue these goals, and he or she brings them about through the use of good judgment. A spiritual person lives with a nonspiritual person in this manner because a spiritual person treats others spiritually, whether those others are spiritual or not.

When he read this, he felt the Wonderful was speaking directly to him. He was particularly impressed at the phrasing of the words "he or she acts in full earnestness," *ille serio agit,* which literally read "that person acts earnestly," for the word "earnestly" was *serio,* the very word in his own family motto—"Late but in earnest."

On reflection it seemed to him that he had, to some extent, always attempted to follow this principle. He had tried to return calm and kind words to Veronica's attacks on him, only occasionally slipping into caustic rejoinders at her expense. He had avoided humiliating her in private and in public; he had not encouraged the servants' complaints against her; he had not interfered in her occupations and pleasures, though they were far different from his own; and certainly he had never reproached her, as some husbands in that era well might have, for the lack of children in their marriage. But he had never accepted her for what she was; he had always resented the fact that she was not what of course she could never have been, the equal of Awen.

This corroboration in Swedenborg bolstered his work of bringing his outer show of kindness toward Veronica in line with his inner beliefs, in strengthening it with spiritual conviction. She was *not* his true wife; she was only his partner in a simulated marriage. If he fully accepted that, he could have compassion on her as someone who found the situation in which they had been placed as unpleasant and unfortunate as did he. He could love her as a fellow creature—a child of God, as the saying goes; he could look upon her needless anger against him with equanimity, tranquility, serenity, as the One must look calmly on all the petty spite of the created. After all, Raphael had been granted a longer view and a greater knowledge of life and death. When he himself went on to live in the Bright World, his *memory* of Veronica would die away, but the *character* he had built in acting lovingly toward her would remain. He could, while still in this Dim World, advance himself a few steps further toward the inner realms of the Bright World, by cultivating a love for her that was consonant with the love that the One had for all.

It was a matter of choice, after all. He could love his cellmate or loathe and skirmish with her. And when he considered the great, radiant light and heat that streamed into all the universe from the One, there was no doubt in his mind and heart as to which he preferred to do.

⟲ ⟲ ⟲

Before he had finished a careful reading of the work on marriage— which took several days—a box arrived from Lissome and Brick- it. Nay, it was not a box, but a trunk: George Lissome had taken him at his word, and found and sent many, though not all, of Swedenborg's published works. The bookseller noted that two small works on the worship and love of God were missing, along with an exposition of the Book of the Apocalypse. Several massive Latin volumes were from a period before "Baron Swendenborg" (Mr. Lissome was now consistently misspelling the author's name) had "claimed his revelation"; these were on various topics in natural philosophy—on what would today be called atomic structure, on cosmogenesis, and particularly on anatomy, of which it appeared Swedenborg had been a dedicated student. Some of the books Lis- some sent were not in the original tongue: the first editions being still the only editions in almost all cases, the Latin versions were becoming quite rare. In particular, Mr. Lissome reported, the eight original volumes of the *Arcana Coelestia,* "The Celestial Arcana," were impossible to find these days, although he understood that the universities had copies; but the work had been translated into English, and a copy of that rendering was included. "To my mind, the translation is as good as any Latin," wrote Lissome in one of his dry flourishes, "for it is at least as incomprehensible."

The great prize was an original copy of *De Coelo et Ejus Mirabilibus, et de Inferno ex Auditis et Visis,* "On Heaven and Its Wonders, and on Hell: From Things Seen and Heard." This book Raphael immediately seized upon for his next reading, for he guessed correctly that it was the most condensed of Swedenborg's travelogues. After that he read the *Arcana Coelestia,* in which Swedenborg had presented a rich and beautiful and highly imaginative reading of the inner meaning of the first two books of the Bible, accompanied by accounts of "the Wonders in the World of Spirits and the Heaven of Angels." These books alone gave him great cause for reflection; and in these days he was deeply occupied with analyzing Swedenborg's reports, comparing them to his own, determining which part of them to accept and which to reject, and copying out passages into a special notebook he kept for this purpose, making his own translations, or altering the translator's prose as he saw fit, if all he had to work from was the English rendering.

He had long since seen how Swedenborg referred to the Bright World as heaven and the Dark Lands as hell; he referred to the dwellers in the Lands of Light as angels, and the dwellers in the Dark Lands as genii or demons; and instead of the One, he referred to the Lord. To Raphael those were serious misnomers—the world in which Awen lived had nothing to do with any place called heaven in all of the Dim World's literature or theology, so far as Raphael could see. He could not recall that any one who lived there, aside from the Wonderful himself, had referred to heaven and hell in his hearing, or had enumerated the heavens as only three, as Swedenborg seemed to do. He did not remember having heard the words *angel* or *genii* or *demon* used once in the Bright World, and he was equally convinced that he had never heard the term *the Lord* used for the One. But it was character-istic of Swedenborg that he had interpreted what he had seen in terms of what he knew already—indeed, as Raphael discovered, Swedenborg was himself aware of this defect in his reporting. Be-sides, Raphael was sure that Swedenborg would have considered any similar reports Raphael himself wrote and published to be equally limited and biased. As observers, they were each equally blinded by their preconceptions and by their own particular pas-sions. For Raphael, the greatest interest of the Bright World lay in his there being able to reunite with Awen in a symbol of the One; for Swedenborg, it lay in the unpredictable interplay between its truths and the religious beliefs of the Dim World.

There were both beautiful and ugly things in Swedenborg's writings. He seemed not to understand the faith of Mohammad at all, and to grossly mischaracterize it; and he had dreadful things to say of Jews and Roman Catholics, though at least he never advocat-ed physical violence against them. In the midst of these dark prej-udices were moments of loving lucidity, like crystals of perceptive-ness suspended in the dried excrement of ignorance. He said that "the neighbor" we are enjoined to love consisted of all the individu-al members of the human race. He said that no matter what religion people were born into, they could live in the Lands of Light. He even went so far as to insist that the One loved *variety* of religion:

> The Lord has provided that everyone shall have a place in heaven who acknowledges God and refrains from doing evil because it is against God. Heaven cannot be made up of people who are all of one religion; it must be made of people of many religions. Therefore all who make these two universal principles part of their lives have a place in heaven.*

In any case, Swedenborg's prejudices were not the focus of his voluminous works; ultimately, his purpose was to denounce what he saw as the empty faith of the ordinary Christian, faith without the *bona fide* intention to do good works and love God and one's neighbor. He would have preferred to do away with doctrine altogether in favor of these basic Christian principles:

> In the Christian world it is doctrinal matters that distinguish churches; and from them people call themselves Roman Catholics, Lutherans, and Calvinists, or the Reformed and the Evangelical, and by other names. It is from what is doctrinal alone that they are so called; which would never be if they would ensure that love for the Lord and charity toward their neighbor was the principle of their faith. Doctrinal matters would then be only varieties of opinion concerning the mysteries of faith, which true Christians would leave to everyone to hold in accordance with his or her conscience, and would say in their hearts that a person is truly a Christian when he or she lives as a Christian, that is, as the Lord teaches. Thus from all the differing churches there would be made one church; and all the dissensions that come forth from doctrine alone would vanish; yea, all hatreds of one against another would be dissipated in a moment, and the Lord's kingdom would come upon the earth.*

To Raphael these passages were far sounder teaching than the attacks on particular religious groups or beliefs. To him—and to the Wonderful himself now, as Raphael knew—the One was what mattered, not the artificial constructs of theologians that supposedly explained the One. What did a quarrel between churches, Old or New, Protestant or Catholic, Lutheran or Anglican, have to do with the One and the world to come? These differences were only a distraction from the very simple injunction that one must love the One and love one's neighbor as oneself. The human relationship with the Divine was thus both utterly simple and infinitely, intimately deep.

Like Awen, Swedenborg saw all of the Dim World and the Bright World as representational. He wrote:

> Things internal are drawn forth when with the eyes of our body we contemplate the starry sky, and thence think of the

Lord's kingdom. Whenever we see anything with our eyes, and see the things that we look upon as if we saw them not, but from them see or think of the things that are of heaven, then our interior sight, or that of our spirit or soul, is "drawn forth abroad." The eye itself is properly nothing but the sight of our spirit drawn forth abroad, and this especially to the end that we may see internal things from external; that is, that we may, from the objects in the world, reflect continually upon those which are in the other life; for this is the life for the sake of which we live in the world. "Heaven" in the Word, in the internal sense, does not signify the skies that appear to the eyes; but the Lord's kingdom, universally and particularly. When we are looking at internal things from external and see the night skies, we do not think at all of the starry skies, but of the angelic heaven; and when we see the sun, we do not think of the sun, but of the Lord, who is the sun of heaven. So too when we see the moon, and the stars also; and when we see the immensity of the heavens, we do not think of their immensity, but of the immeasurable and infinite power of the Lord. It is the same when we see all other things, for there is nothing that is not representative.*

He found corroborations of his experience in the Bright World, and of what the Wonderful had explained to him there, throughout Swedenborg's works; he had only to readjust the language to understand it. For example, Swedenborg confirmed the views of the Image Makers countless times in sayings such as the following:

> Everything has its marriage or its coupling, without which it could not possibly continue in existence.

> For each of us, the excellence of our lives varies according to our marriage love.

Another of Raphael's favorite corroborations was this:

> They who are in mutual love in heaven are continually advancing to the springtime of their youth, and to a more

and more gladsome and happy spring the more thousands of years they live, and this with continual increase to eternity, according to the advance and degree of mutual love, charity, and faith. Those of the female sex who have died in old age, enfeebled with years, and who have lived in faith in the Lord, in charity toward the neighbor, and in happy conjugial love with their husbands, after a succession of years come more and more into the bloom of youth and early womanhood, and into a beauty that surpasses all idea of beauty such as is ever perceptible to the natural sight; for it is goodness and charity forming and presenting their own likeness, and causing the delight and beauty of charity to shine forth from every least feature of the countenance, so that they are the very forms of charity: some have beheld them and been amazed.**

In one of Swedenborg's posthumously published books he found this remarkable description of the very kind of sexual love he had had with Awen in the Bright World:

I would like to say a few things about the marriages of angels in heaven. The angels tell me that they have unfailing potency. After the act they never feel weary and never the least depressed, but instead experience a keen sense of being alive and of exhilaration of spirits. Married couples spend the night in a close embrace; it is then as if they had been created as one entity. Consummation is constantly available, and it never fails provided they have the desire for it, since without it their love would be like a spring with a blocked channel. Consummation opens that channel and brings about continuity and connection so that they become as one flesh; the vital power of the husband merges with the vital power of the wife and forms an intimate bond. They say that the bliss of their consummations cannot be described in the words of any language in the natural world, nor even be *thought* in any but spiritual concepts, and even the latter do not exhaust the depths of those experiences.

Though he took issue with many of Swedenborg's conclusions, and kicked back against the pricks of what Swedenborg had called his "true Christian religion," there were many explanations that Swedenborg made that he realized would have been beyond his own powers to discover based on his much more limited experience in the other world. Swedenborg had traveled widely there—he was an explorer, even what later ages would call an ethnographer, of the Bright World, and he was not the least afraid to journey through the Dark Lands, which he referred to, in a plural term expressive of their sinister extent, as "the Hells." Raphael was too uxorious, in the most positive sense of that word, to concern himself for long with any place that did not hold his wife; Swedenborg, a lonely and utterly bold spirit, had searched insatiably through as much of the Other Realm as he was permitted to see. At times his report read like the adventures of a Baron Munchausen, not a Baron Swedenborg. He even claimed to have seen spirits from other planets; and although he apparently had confused those far worlds with Venus and Mars and other planets in the Sun's system, Raphael did not doubt that there was some kernel of truth in his account. He had seen *something;* perhaps he was too free in interpreting exactly what it was and in understanding his experiences as gospel truth and divine revelation, but he had been *there,* in the very world where Raphael had been. There could be no question of that.

Furthermore, it was very likely that Swedenborg was not telling as much as he knew, but only what he thought his readers could understand. There were many clues that suggested this, hints of greater wonders, of societies and even heavens beyond those he enumerated. Perhaps he had only been able to penetrate to the outermost of three heavens and had suppressed discussion of the rest as something too holy even to mention. Perhaps the One had formed and limited what Swedenborg could see: on many occasions, in fact, the experiences he related had the appearance of *research,* and the reports were those that were to be expected from one who had gone to the Bright World with a definite theological agenda—for example, to find out what happened to people there whose belief in God did not lead them to do good to others, or was only assumed in an effort to fit into earthly society, or was any one of the infinitely many other variations on human foolishness. And as Raphael had seen, the One seemed to grant certain experiences specifically to induct newcomers there into the wondrous realities of that higher world. This would explain why so many of Swedenborg's experiences seemed encounters with straw men: those interlocutors had been assembled for the very purpose of rendering a lesson.

In Swedenborg's accounts, then, Raphael penetrated to a truth he himself had till then only dimly grasped. As Jesus had said, the kingdom of heaven is within. That place Swedenborg had visited *was within him,* and thus his own subjective experience of it had molded what it was. Likewise Raphael's encounter with the Bright World had led him not outward to some other place, but inward into the idiosyncrasies of his own self. For Swedenborg, the Bright World had been a kind of debating hall of theological topics; for Raphael, it had been the affirmation of the love he bore Awen and his passion for everything that was a passion to her—lovemaking, poetry, music, deep benevolence to all. So not only was the Bright World within the Dim World, it was within the very self of the individual, just as it was within the very self of the One.

Raphael's notebook detailing his fascination with Swedenborg soon grew to several volumes. There was one curious account in Swedenborg's works, however, to which he returned again and again. It appeared at the end of Swedenborg's lengthy, even epic, exegesis of Genesis and Exodus, which seemed to have been intended to go on throughout the entire Bible, but dwindled to a halt after the last chapter of Exodus—closing not in a hermeneutic passage, but in one of Swedenborg's travelogues of a visit to another planet. In recounting what the inhabitants told him of customs there, Swedenborg said:

> With regard to their life, they said that they go about quite naked, and that nakedness is no shame to them. . . . As regards

betrothals and marriages among the inhabitants on that earth, . . . a daughter of marriageable age is . . . conducted to a certain wedding house, whither also have been brought a number of other young women who are marriageable; and they are there placed behind a partition that is raised as high as the middle part of their bodies, so that they are seen undressed merely in respect to the breast and face; and then the young men come thither to choose one for a wife; and when a young man sees one who is like himself, and to whom his mind draws him, he takes her by the hand; and if she then follows he leads her into a house that has been made ready, and she becomes his wife. For in that earth people see from the faces of others whether they agree in their minds, because there the face of every person is the index of the mind, being quite free from pretence and deception. . . . They said further that a husband has only one wife, and never more, because that would be contrary to divine order.*

To Raphael this drew powerfully on the long bell-rope of memory. It was not only a symbol of how man and woman come together in everyday life, it was a reminder of how he and Awen had come together in Vigia and at Fulkothing, and of course it put him in mind of the Hall of Recognition near the Temple of True Marriage. Furthermore, it was a curious and dreamy symbol appropriate to the end of this great and rich book. *You who read this,* it seemed to say, *you may take from my book the truth you recognize and wish to wed to your soul. Those other truths that do not fit you, leave them behind; for it is right for each soul to be wedded to one truth and one truth alone among the many radiating forth from the One.*

Chapter 55

Some Swedenborgians in our streets are found,
Those wandering walkers on enchanted ground

Who in one world can other worlds survey,
And speak with spirits though confined in clay.
Of Bible-mysteries they the keys possess,
Assured themselves, where wiser men but guess:
'Tis theirs to see around, about, above,—
How spirits mingle thoughts, and angels move.
Those whom our grosser views from us exclude,
To them appear—a heavenly multitude;
While the dark sayings, seal'd to men like us,
Their priests interpret, and their flocks discuss.

But while these gifted men, a favor'd fold,
New powers exhibit and new worlds behold,
Is there not danger lest their minds confound
The pure above them with the gross around?
May not these Phaetons, who thus contrive
'Twixt heaven above and earth beneath to drive,
When from their chariots they descend,
The worlds they visit in their fancies blend?
Alas! too sure on both they bring disgrace,
Their earth is crazy, and their heav'n is base.

—Crabbe

Having discovered this strange link to the Bright World in Swedenborg, Raphael's thoughts turned naturally to the question of the man's followers. At this time in England they were somewhat notorious, if at the same widely understood to be harmless—just one of the many Christian-tinged, or Christian-drenched, mystic sects outside the established church, from Quakers to Moravians to Behmenists. To Raphael it seemed they must constitute a kind of city of companion believers—what Swedenborg would have called a heavenly society; and he looked about to find them. There were several dozen such congregations (actually called societies); apparently they were strongest in number specifically in London and Manchester, and generally in Lancashire and Yorkshire at this time. He sought out the group in Norwich.

He was wary, as always, of revealing anything of Awen or of his own experiences in the Bright World; he merely attended a gathering of the Swedenborgians without explanation of his interest. As is the case with any newcomer to a small religious group, after the meeting he was beset with friendly inquiries as to his identity and his interest; but these he satisfied with a vague comment on his curiosity about religions in general. In fact, it seemed he was known to several of the people in the meeting already as a gentleman scholar in religious matters who lived in the neighboring country; and though he was warmly welcomed, no great hopes were excited as to converting him and making him a member.

Which was as he wished; for he went away from his encounter with them much perplexed. Here were good people, intently concerned with discovering and believing the truth; and yet to them the life to come was only a dim dream. Some had read Swedenborg's accounts of the Bright World, but most had not—had only learned of them at secondhand; and even those who had read them had retained only a confused notion of them. They spoke of beautiful mansions, of streets covered with pearls and gold, and other such scenes of tawdry opulence, which Swedenborg had unfortunately proffered as images testifying to the desirability of life there. The stock themes and topics of heaven and hell were much on their minds; some spoke longingly of having wings someday, and a few even spouted the very misunderstandings of life in the next world against which Swedenborg had wittily inveighed, such as the belief that there one endlessly sang hosannas or wasted eternity in perpetual feasting.

Furthermore, in their company, Raphael again encountered the difficulty he had had with Swedenborg's own writings. These Swedenborgians were focused to the point of obsession on their revelator's corrections of the doctrines of what he and they called "the Old Church." In Raphael's view, the existence of the Bright World was a lance of light so intense and solid as to shatter utterly all of the teachings of religion but the most basic, sweeping away forever the superstructures of specificity; and yet these Swedenborgians spoke endlessly of the improvements wrought by their doctrines in discarding the three separate personhoods of the Trinity, the concept of Atonement, and other such historical accidents of religious understanding. He felt like shaking them and saying, "But this is all of no matter, no matter whatsoever! The great fact of which you must remain cognizant is that we live *forever,* and that we must prepare ourselves for that eternal life."

Furthermore, the more literate and knowledgeable among the society were full of the convert's zeal concerning certain aspects of Swedenborg's theology that had grown out of his own attempts to understand the workings of the physical universe, not out of a genuine revelation. It was in fact difficult to distinguish, in his writings, between the knowledge the Wonderful had acquired in his travels in the Bright World and the preconceptions and theories he had brought with him when he came. Some arcane philosophical notions offered as truths revealed to Swedenborg had, to Raphael's mind, the smack of purely human and even purely desperate construction. When he had conversed with several of the Swedenborgians after worship, the knowledgeable among them had spoken with authority and minced theological niceties into seemingly infinite fineness, while the less knowledgeable stood by nodding their heads, certain that something wise was being said. But all this had nothing to do with the Bright World as Raphael knew it. That place, that fact of eternal life, could not be contained in, reduced to, or summed by mere dogma.

In short, he felt as might a man possessed of sight who visits a particular village in a country of the blind, hoping there to find others who possess the faculty of vision; only to find that the rumor that they possess sight themselves is quite unfounded, though these villagers, unlike others in their nation, do at least believe that sight exists as a human sense.

In consequence, he was now more alone in his knowledge than ever.

After his return from his visit to the Swedenborgians, he wondered about what he had been told of his future as an inventor of religions in the city of the Image Makers. He did indeed long to write something of the truth of that world while still here, to give people some structure of belief that would support them in the difficulties of common life. Clearly some people craved the particular structure that the Wonderful had erected, but others would want something else. He gave much thought to this, but for a long while his thinking was inchoate, like that of a composer hearing themes in his head at random hours of the day, uncertain how to combine them into a symphony. His state reminded him of the way he had been in those early days on Vigia when he had craved Awen bodily, but scarcely knew how much he loved her: his desire had roiled in and tumbled through his brain and heart, his arms had yearned to hold her and his loins to enter her, while all the time his true love for her was building in him, all unknown to him, massing like a great storm cloud, ready to break forth in bolts of electric astonishment.

Then, gradually, it came to him that if he were to compose a religion, it would be of the most serene and essential type. It would teach two facts primarily: love and life. Its primary doctrine would hold that without a knowledge that life *is*—that is, that it has always existed, always continues, and never dies—one cannot fully and successfully love. And, conversely, one cannot fully and successfully live without fully loving the One and the created universe—the "one-verse" of the One, so called because it contains all within it in a oneness. In this he diverged from Swedenborg, who had made love and wisdom the two great principles of his system; for though Raphael agreed that wisdom was in some views the complement of love, most often he saw it as the means love took to its end. And one could not be wise without loving, that was certain, though one could love without being perfectly wise.

His own life gave examples of these laws. Every day he grew more loving and serene, as his acceptance of the eternity of life soaked deeper into his thoughts and understanding. How could he charge Veronica with spoiling his life, as he had once done, when he had an eternity of life yet to live, which would indeed be lived in merciful oblivion of her? What was Prosper to him now, what was Quinn, and all the outrages they had committed? They had not broken his love for Awen, for they could not. The more he forgave them, the lesser was their effect on him; ironically, the greater his triumph over them in forgiveness, the lesser his triumph became, as it diminished to insignificance what they had done to him.

He saw the vast pettiness of human affairs, too, with a calm, paternal humor, looking on the trials and tears of the dairy maid and her spilt milk as much of a level with the fulminations of members of Parliament over the supposedly vital business of the nation. The human world was a vast machine of government and economic systems, running out of control, crushing the weak and the poor, sometimes destroying even those who boasted they steered it; but that machine ought not to be broken and dismantled, it ought to be set to run straight and do good, fueled by the principles of love. These were enormous simplifications; but the twin truths of love and life were also simple, and far more powerful than the human complexifications in which they became obscured and were lost.

Secondary to those twin principles, offspring of them, was usefulness. This was a Swedenborgian doctrine of which he approved most heartily. Love insisted that one spend one's life being useful. Thus he himself strove to bring a loving, honorable, functioning peace into his own estate and his own parish; he saw this as his great use, and he sought to widen it with time.

Ultimately he decided that the composing of his religion in writing must wait until he moved on to the Bright World and the city of the Image Makers, when he would work by day in the tower overlooking the city, and know that Awen worked there too, never far from him. He did, however, write out a credo, which he worked to refine over a long period. It never fully satisfied him, but spending some time in the contemplation and writing of it was a pastime toward which he looked with pleasure and anticipation. The chief article of it ran as follows:

The universe is the creation of the One; it arises from the unification of two principles, love and life. Neither love nor life can be created or destroyed; they are radiated by the One into us; we depend upon them, being unable to love or live without borrowing love and life from the One. We may see testimony of the constant radiation and absorption of these principles in the urge to join and complexify, which is shared by all living beings.

Love and life are each in themselves infinitely complex, though each is also a simplex. Woman is commonly the symbol of love, man of life; and yet each sex also represents aspects of the opposite principle. Woman is the uniting principle, man the complexifying; and yet without love, complexification would not be possible. Woman joins; man builds. And yet so closely united are these principles that there are women who build and men who join, whether the building is a home or a bridge or a poem or a symphony, and whether the joining is a marriage or a community. Thus a man who works wood into complex new shapes is called a joiner; thus a woman who bears new life is said to be building a family.

The greatest truth of our existence is thus twofold: that we are always loved and that we never die.

Even when we are abandoned, left alone on a deserted island in a sea of humanity, hated and reviled by our own kind, the One loves us without hesitation. Even when our bodies are crushed and shattered by accident or war, or succumb to age or disease, we live in the One infallibly and infinitely.

When we live here, we believe we can see the full shape of everything we shall ever know; we believe death from this world is our limit. But beyond this appearance of everything that is our life in this dim earth, there is a bright existence, in which the One gives us the full scope of our ability to love and live. If we go on to that bright world without having learned to love, then we do not and cannot love; we choose more of the same, more of what we have known—unending rage and resentment. "If I have told you earthly things, and ye believe not, how shall ye believe, if I tell you of heavenly things?" Without love we live a living death. But if we have made even a beginning of love, that beginning is nurtured and complexified as our life continues in eternity.

What is more: in fact the next life is not next, it is now. The Bright World surrounds us; we live within it, embraced and bathed in its love and life; our companions in that world walk about among us, connect with us in thought and feeling, all unknown to us, unseen by us. If we choose to live in its darker parts, then so we do; if we choose to live in its brighter realms, then within them we dwell, even while we appear to live only here. But the wisdom of the One has so ordained the order of things that we seldom glimpse the larger life from the petty one that we seem to inhabit, so that we live here free of any coercion that knowledge of that world might impose upon us.

Indeed, there is no proof of these truths. Some in this world have claimed that they went to that deeper, brighter world; but their evidence is only the testimony of single minds, which may be deluded; and even our own mind may be deluded if we ourselves have sensory evidence of that larger reality. We can only know these truths by transcending ordinary intellectual knowledge; but that transcendent certainty is utterly complete and infinitely more satisfying than the petty half-certainties of logic and philosophic proof.

After he had written this, he reflected that he had almost inadvertently articulated why he found the Swedenborgians he had met to be problematic: They did not believe transcendently in the greater reality of the Bright World; they did not believe in it because they *perceived* it to be true through some deep, inward capacity of the soul; they only believed in it superficially, because they accepted the accounts, the testimony Swedenborg had given of it. And this was no better than believing in Moloch because one has been taught to believe in Moloch. Swedenborg himself had waxed polemical against basing one's beliefs on mere intellectual knowledge, mere facts culled from learning. His own works were full of countless contradictions and patent self-delusions and illusions engendered in his mind by people of the Dark Lands. He himself had decried reliance upon miraculous revelation, citing the words of the one he called the Lord: "Because thou hast seen me, Thomas, thou hast believed; blessed are they who see not, and believe"; and he had insisted that miracles tended to compel belief, which was against divine order, against the divine design. And yet in the same breath he offered his own miraculous experiences as evidence of what he said. He believed he had spoken with people who lived in worlds too near the Sun to be habitable; he believed he had spoken with Newton after death and Newton had recanted his belief in the vacuum of space. Clearly his literal accounts could not be accepted at face value; and yet he had seen *something*, known *something* of the Bright World, just as Raphael had; and when what he said of it rang true with the preknowledge of the soul, it had to be believed in that transcendent manner that surpasses the need of physical proofs.

⊚ ⊚ ⊚

During his brief visit to the Swedenborgian society at Norwich, Raphael had several times heard praise for one of the great lights of this "New Church," as it was called. It was a name with which he was already familiar, for the man had translated many of the works of Swedenborg from Latin into English, and Raphael had read his translations when he could not obtain the original Latin. This John Clowes was a clergyman in the Church of England in Manchester—his unorthodox opinions being tolerated by the church authorities, it was said, because of his undeniable piety. Raphael obtained some of his sermons, read them, and found them of more depth and sincerity than he had encountered in his own parish, certainly; and eventually he resolved to go visit this cleric to see for himself what the man was, before he gave up utterly on the companionship of Swedenborgians.

In the early spring of 1817, he told Veronica that he was going to visit a famous divine in Manchester. That killed any interest she might have had in accompanying him. He did not bring Jackman with him; he merely packed a small bag, had a horse saddled, and set out alone. He stopped at whatever inns he happened to find, and when the horse grew weary of carrying him, he spared it by walking beside it.

He arrived at Manchester late in the day, stayed overnight, and at a decent visiting hour the next morning he went out, leaving his horse at the inn, and walked to the rectory where Mr. Clowes lived. He was told by a servant there, a very elderly woman, that the rector was away at a picnic, a celebration in his honor. The picnic grounds were only a short distance into the country, however, and the servant urged him to make his way there and join her master. Having come so far, he was susceptible to this encouragement—which was unaccountably cordial, as it seemed to him; and he walked on, as the day grew to noon and to considerably more warmth than the early morning had promised.

He had long since begun to wonder whether he had lost his way when, in passing down a lane bordered by tall hedges, he heard a choir of children begin to sing somewhere on the far side of the hedge on his right; their voices carried to him with an uncanny clarity. Obviously he had found the gathering; and in another minute he came upon a gate in the hedge and turned in there.

The open space beyond was a fallow field, several acres in extent, gently sloping upward to the far side. At first glimpse he thought it amazingly thronged, perhaps by as many as a thousand individuals; but then, after halting and blinking his eyes, he saw that he was greatly mistaken: there were only about a hundred people present. For a moment he puzzled over this curious initial misapprehension; but then he realized that he had, in that first glimpse, seen an additional gathering that was not visible to those in the Dim World: a considerable convocation of good people in the Bright World who were drawn to the spot because of the presence of John Clowes.

In fact, as he looked across the little hollow, he could easily determine which person was that gentleman: a radiance was visible around him, or at least to Raphael's partly enlightened vision. He was an elderly man and physically frail in appearance; but he was listening to the children's choir with an expression of delight, delight that transcended physical infirmity, a joy and delight that might almost be said not to have any place here on earth, but to belong to the Bright World, where joy has its true context in the acknowledged love and understanding of the One. He was sitting in a chair that had been brought especially for him, surrounded by a group of his closest well-wishers, among whom Raphael saw no few of his fellow clergy.

When the singing was over, he called the children to him and spoke to them for several minutes. His voice reached Raphael only as a muffled prayer; and then the children ran away with shrieks of pleasure to some picnic sports—races and the like. Raphael guessed that Mr. Clowes must have promised them some reward after their games, and it struck him that this was symbolic of the preacher's role.

For a time he stood where he was, just inside the entrance to the field, and watched Mr. Clowes without attempting to approach him. The man was busy with his friends in any case; but after this interval, he seemed to start as if he had sensed something unusual about him. He looked around the field in surprise, and his gaze fell on Raphael. He evinced considerable interest, so much so that his companions also turned and looked where he was looking; and after staring at Raphael in wonder for as much as a minute, he beckoned to him, as an elderly person does who cannot easily go to the one with whom he would speak. Raphael approached him, winding his way through the gathering, which was now for the most part preoccupied with the holiday contests underway in the lower part of the field.

On closer view, Mr. Clowes was not prepossessing: he had lost all his teeth and his musculature was quite wasted. But his gaze was, by turns, piercing and mild, as if he saw through vanity readily in one moment, and forgave it the next.

"I do not know you, sir," he said to Raphael. He spoke not in a hostile tone, but a welcoming one. His toothlessness seemed not to affect his voice, which was very clear, though soft.

"Indeed you do not. I have made a journey to see you; I am come from Norfolk."

"To see me? Then I pity you; for there is not much to see."

"The man who translated the *Arcana Coelestia* is worth beholding," said Raphael.

"Ah, but you did not come merely to *look* at a scholar; you came to speak to me."

"I did."

Mr. Clowes looked around at the friends that stood near him. "Perhaps you will leave me for a time to speak with this interesting gentleman," he said. They acquiesced graciously, though they evinced no little curiosity about Raphael. One man, who had the clothing and the air of an impoverished curate, brought a chair for Raphael before he left, and placed it invitingly near Mr. Clowes, with a kindly smile.

"Thank you, Mr. Clarage," said Mr. Clowes. To Raphael he said, "Now, do, sir, have a seat beside me and let us talk."

Raphael sat down, and he and Mr. Clowes looked at one another with frank interest.

"And what is your name, if I may inquire?" asked Mr. Clowes.

"Raphael Kerr, sir. I am from Fulkothing Hall, near Nedwich, in the county of Norfolk."

"How did you find me so readily on this picnic?"

"Your housekeeper, sir, directed me here, or such I believe she was."

"Truly? She is usually quite protective of my person and privacy; but she gave you direction to this place?"

"Yes, sir."

"She must have sensed, Mr. Kerr, as do I, that you are an extraordinary individual."

"I am as ordinary as anyone, certainly," said Raphael, "although perhaps I may say that I am fortunate in having been particularly humbled; as perhaps have you." He was keenly curious as to whether Mr. Clowes had ever been to the Bright World, or had ever been favored with any sight of it from this, and he hoped that Mr. Clowes would drop a hint that he had; but the man seemed not to notice this opening.

"Ah, we are all of course equal in the eyes of God," said Mr. Clowes. "But to the eyes of man differences appear. I am certain that you are a receiver of the truths revealed by Emanuel Swedenborg; and though most of those present are also receivers, in one respect or another—even if some of them hardly know they are—I sense in you a *depth* of reception that is unusually great."

Raphael thought this mistake quite humorous, and smiled.

"And the great company you have here," he said quietly. "Do you call them all followers of Swedenborg?"

Mr. Clowes looked around the little hollow at the picnickers. "As I say," he said, "most of them are so, in one respect or another."

At that moment Raphael knew that Mr. Clowes could not see into the Bright World. He was, like the other Swedenborgians Raphael had met, a believer only through indirect revelation, not through personal experience. And yet the goodness of the man was beyond the merely extraordinary: he was a veritable Swedenborgian saint, and the cluster of company he had on the other side of the barrier of worlds was proof.

So quick and sharp was Mr. Clowes's perception that he observed at once that Raphael was disappointed in him, though he could not guess why.

"You expected to find something more in coming to me?" he said then. "But you find only a man—much worn by years, much broken in health; and as full of pettiness and vanity as others are."

"On the contrary, I find a man truly great in his goodness," said Raphael.

There was a minute of silence between them, if silence it could be called, broken as it was by the laughter and shouts of the gathering below. Mr. Clowes seemed to be puzzling over Raphael.

"What is it I sense about you?" asked Mr. Clowes then. "It is not just that you are a receiver of the doctrines."

Raphael had it in mind to say, as Swedenborg did, *I have seen, I have heard*; but he felt suddenly some inner inhibition, some prohibition against revealing what he knew to this man, like the one that Socrates mentioned, which always forbade but never commanded him. He understood in that moment what Awen had felt when she had wanted to tell him what she knew about the Bright World, but was unable to do so. It was as if the Guardian of the Gate had given him warning. Instead, then, he said what he could.

"I am not, in fact, a 'receiver,' as you put it," said Raphael. "I happen to believe in the . . . in the order of things that Swedenborg described for other reasons than his revelation."

"For *other* reasons!" exclaimed Mr. Clowes in wonder. "What other reasons could there be?"

Raphael did not answer the question directly; he only said, "I found in Swedenborg's works a great corroboration of the truths I knew already."

Mr. Clowes was still puzzled. "If you knew those truths before they were revealed by the Lord's appointed revelator, then you were blessed indeed, sir," he said, but in a doubting tone. He would have rejected the mere possibility of any such thing, except that he had Raphael before him, and he found him increasingly mysterious. "Of course," said Mr. Clowes, "some of these truths were known; because Divine Truth has its way of penetrating even through the smoke and haze of human delusion and irreligion, even through the lies of false religion. Swedenborg observes this many times: the simple folk know much of the truth of Divine Order that the supposedly wise, blinded by their book learning, cannot believe. That our souls have substance, for example, and that we live on in the next life as human individuals. So of such things you may well have known; but of the full order of things as Swedenborg describes it—I dare say, Mr. Kerr, no one could have known of that. It would have been contrary to the ordainment of God for anyone to know those things before he sent his teacher to tell of them."

Again, Raphael did not wish to address this point directly; he turned the conversation slightly instead. "Swedenborg was only a human being," he said, "reporting what he saw and heard. He did not perfectly interpret or understand what he experienced."

"But he was guided in his understanding by the Lord himself," insisted Mr. Clowes.

"Not so. As he himself would have told you, if he had been guided, it would have been a violation of the freedom God gives to humankind, to believe or not to believe."

"But he *tells* us he was guided."

"He was certainly guided by those to whom he spoke," said Raphael quietly, "as those who listen to you are guided by you. But he was not guided by the One in such as way as to be infallible."

Mr. Clowes marveled at him. "You believe he saw what he saw—that he traveled in the spiritual world—and yet you insist that he did not understand it? You admit the miracle of his experience of heaven, but deny that he was led to know what that miracle meant?"

"Precisely," said Raphael.

Mr. Clowes was silent another long moment; and finally he hit upon the strange truth about Raphael.

"You say you knew of these truths before you read the doctrines. Do you have any . . . *personal knowledge* of them? Any *experience?*"

"Anyone may," said Raphael evasively.

"Nay," said Mr. Clowes, falling back on his cherished admiration of Swedenborg. "That is not so. Only the chosen revelator has access to these arcana."

"Only one man can see the truth? I think not. I think we are all gifted with the power to see the truth, only we do not use it."

"Nay, it is not so. The power is particular, limited, granted only by God in special cases; and it has only been granted to one and one alone in our own times; and that was the Lord's revelator, Emanuel Swedenborg."

"With the utmost respect, Mr. Clowes—I disagree. We all possess it. Consider, sir: What is it that raises the power of love between man and woman to transcendent greatness from mere petty alliance of interests? What is it that allows the statesman to see beyond the hunger for base revenge against the enemies of the state, to a better day of prosperity and peace between nations? What is it that allows us to guess at the richness and abundance of the Divine order of the world? All these things are owing to one power, and one power alone, granted to each and all of us, but seldom used: the power of the imagination."

"Imagination? I would rather say the goodness of the Lord."

"The goodness of the One cannot be made use of if it is not perceived; and it is the power of the imagination that makes that perception possible."

"That seems to me a sophistic quibble. Does imagination allow anyone to see what Swedenborg saw?"

"Indeed it does."

Mr. Clowes scoffed. "Are you saying that Swedenborg *imagined* what he saw of the spiritual world, of heaven and hell?"

"I do. But I mean that in the best sense, or in an eminent sense."

"The best sense! What good sense can there be in what you say? I am disappointed in you, Mr. Kerr. You say you admit the truth of Swedenborg's revelations one minute, and then the next you impute them to mere imagination, you imply they were the mere mental playthings of an idle hour. You make no sense."

"I do not demean the vision of Swedenborg when I say it was the work of his imagination," protested Raphael, who, in his disappointment at finding Clowes only a follower, now waxed eloquent. "You do not understand me, that is all, my dear sir. You seem to err in understanding what the imagination is. What most people of this world think of as the imagination is only a dim and untrue shadow of the power that is our utmost sensory capability. To them the imagination seems the mere froth of a vacant mind. But Swedenborg—and others who have gone where he went and seen some little of what he saw—utilized the power of the imagination, that same power commonly derided as puny and unreliable, to open the very gates of heaven. If you scorn what I say, it is as a man scorns to believe that mathematics may describe the courses of the heavenly spheres because he knows only that two and two is four; or that a great painter may paint a likeness of living perfection, because he himself knows only the representations made by a child in chalk on a slate. God has given us all a glimpse of what the imagination can do, in those daydreams you so rightly describe as the products of an idle hour; but it is our own failing if we do not utilize that gift to its fullest. Indeed, most men and women cast it aside as a useless toy and never know that life is what we make of it, what we think of it, what we imagine it to be. The One gave us that power, and it is contemptible in us to contemn it."

"Nay, the power of the imagination is based on *proprium*," said Clowes. This was a term often used by Swedenborg to express the notion of human self-reliance or self-sufficiency, as opposed to acknowledgement of the animating Divine that flows constantly into humankind.

"Nay, rather: the power of the imagination is an inflowing gift of the One," retorted Raphael.

This answer checked Clowes for some reason; and looking at Raphael wonderingly again, he said, "Then you have raised imagination to a higher level than most people do; you have found and utilized a form of the imagination that most people do not."

Raphael did not answer; the two men only looked at one another, again silent, for another space of time; until Clowes, leaning forward, and speaking suddenly and urgently, said in his low but clear voice: "Tell me what you have seen."

"It is not permitted," said Raphael.

"Ah," said Clowes. He actually seemed satisfied, even pleased by this answer; he sat back in his chair and beamed at Raphael. "But if it were permitted," he said, "you would have much to tell."

"Much indeed," said Raphael.

And then, to Raphael's surprise, Clowes wept. He did not cease smiling, but several tears stole out of his eyes and ran down his face.

"The Lord has sent you to me," he said.

"What is it that the One does not do?" asked Raphael.

"Yes; but for me—this is a particular gift."

"Why is that? Surely you need no confirmation of mine."

"No; no, I do not. But I rejoice in every affirmation of the other world."

"Then perhaps I may tell you this: I have good reason to believe that there stand around us at this very moment, in that other world, a great concourse of good people who were drawn to this place by your own great love for God and humanity and your own great love and wisdom."

Clowes smiled, both happily and wryly. "If I am wise, Mr. Kerr, it is the wisdom of the holy fool."

"The best wisdom, sir."

They were again silent for a time; then Raphael spoke.

"But I should not disturb you in your pleasant company," he said.

"Ah, Mr. Kerr, you will not go away, will you? You will stay, and we will talk. I know you cannot talk of . . . of things you have seen. But we may talk on other matters, matters we know in common to be true. It will be most refreshing to me. You have no idea what it is like for me, always to be . . . a shepherd. There are times I yearn to be one of the sheep; and indeed, I look forward to that hour in heaven when I become one, and have a better teacher than I am. If you will stay . . ."

"I have perhaps already stayed too long," said Raphael, "and I have perhaps already said too much."

"But are you not lonely in your knowledge, your experience?"

"Sometimes I think so; but then I recall the partner of my soul, who stands always on the other side of the barrier, and I am lonely no more."

"Ah," said Mr. Clowes.

After a minute of silence, Raphael rose; when Mr. Clowes attempted to do the same, Raphael prevented him by placing a hand on his shoulder. The man was too frail to resist that command;

his shoulder, indeed, seemed a mere twig of bone inside his coat, without strength. Likewise his hand when Raphael shook it.

"I wish you a most useful life," said Raphael.

Mr. Clowes smiled happily. "And the same to you, my strange friend.—I feel almost as if an angel had visited me here today on this celebratory day."

"One among many, then," said Raphael, smiling.

He turned away and went down the slope past the celebrants. At the gate of the field he paused to look back toward Mr. Clowes again, and to salute him with a wave of his hat and a bow. Several of Mr. Clowes's followers had returned to his side and were trying to speak with him, but the rector was paying no attention to them; he kept his eyes exclusively on Raphael, and he waved back in farewell.

Raphael made his way back into the city to his inn and was bound away homeward by midafternoon. Despite his disappointment with Mr. Clowes—for which, he knew, the rector himself was not to blame—the visit to that saintly man was greatly inspiring to him. Here was a person who had taken Swedenborg's testimony on faith, not on the evidence of any experience of his own, and had grown into an innocent and holy being. Ought not Raphael himself be able to do as well, who had the evidence of his own spiritual senses and the promise of Awen's love—symbol as it was of the love of the One?

With the knowledge of Mr. Clowes and the works of Swedenborg he thus fortified himself; but there was soon to come into his possession a renewed testimony to the Bright World far more congenial even than these.

Chapter 56

Who hath ascended up into heaven, or descended?

—Proverbs 30:4

Quis ex coelo ad nos venit et narravit quod sit?

Who has come to us from heaven and told us what it is?

—Swedenborg

And another book was opened, which is the book of life.

—Revelation 20:12

Who telleth a tale of unspeaking death?
Who lifteth the veil of what is to come?

—Shelley

"The great disadvantage to living on such a great hill," said Veronica, "is that there is only one way for any and all to approach the house, no matter of what class they may happen to be."

She was taking tea with Raphael—an odd innovation of hers, as she had for many years taken tea in her own sitting room without his company. It was an afternoon in the summer after his return from Manchester. Indeed, since his return from the north she had been strangely clinging, though she had not altered her behavior otherwise in a manner that would have made him eager to be with her. Her present remark was typical of the unpleasantness to which he was subjected in these disparate tête-à-têtes, and he sought in vain for a long moment before he found a neutral reply.

"And who is approaching?" he asked.

"I do not know; she looks like a beggar. Rather haggard, actually; she walks as if she is quite exhausted."

He rose at once and went to stand beside her. The thought crossed his mind that it might be Manwaring, but Veronica would certainly have recognized her. The woman did strike him as familiar, but he could not place her on the basis of the visual information he could glean at this distance. She seemed to be in her thirties, and was rather tall and strongly built; and despite Veronica's aspersions on her clothing, it was neat enough and in good repair, though plain and simple, suggesting that she was of the servant class. The one incongruous element of her attire was a veil she wore; for servants rarely wore veils, even when traveling.

"Probably someone looking for employment," he said. It was an obvious conjecture, but he felt the need to say something.

"Then Mrs. McQuillit will know enough to send her away," said Veronica. "We are not in need of any more help at the present time."

Raphael thought that Mrs. McQuillit would very likely do exactly what Veronica had predicted; but he relied upon that bluff but good-hearted Scotswoman to give the applicant a meal or at least the end of a loaf before she dismissed her. The day would be getting dark soon, and their visitor would have a long walk to any lodgings. He left the window and went back to his chair, but Veronica remained standing there, watching the woman as she came to the door.

"There is something familiar about her," she said then.

"Yes," he replied. "I thought so too, though I could not have said what it was or who she is."

"She ought to have gone round to the other entrance," said Veronica darkly.

"Perhaps she has not come for work after all," said Raphael. As usual, he felt the need to defend the innocent against Veronica's spite.

"Then why does she come?"

He shrugged. "Perhaps she brings news of some sort," he said.

They both listened as the knocker on the door resounded dully in the front hall. Then they dimly heard a conversation; a conversation that went on for much longer than Raphael would have expected, and grew gradually into something like an altercation. It ceased abruptly, and Veronica looked down into the drive.

"She is not leaving," she said, in a haughty, puzzled tone.

Mrs. McQuillit entered the room. She seemed angry; she gave Veronica one dark look, as if she wished not only that she were not there, but that she had been transported to the antipodes, and then she addressed herself to Raphael.

"If you please, sir," she said, "there is a most importunate person here who wishes to see you. I have left her in the front hall under the watch of Mr. Strong. I shall send her away—I am sorry to disturb you, but she said she would not go until she spoke to you herself; and if I know from your own lips that you do not wish to see her, that will make my job that much easier."

"And who is she?" asked Raphael.

Mrs. McQuillit darted another look at Veronica again, and then answered his question with a certain stubbornness, as if she did not care what the mistress might think. "A servant, sir," she said. "A woman who was a servant at Rush Hill in the time of the previous tenants."

"It is that Fallows woman!" cried Veronica with instant heat.

"It is," said Mrs. McQuillit. "It is Bessie Fallows, sir."

"Send her away!" cried Veronica. "We have no wish to see the likes of her in this house."

Mrs. McQuillit was evidently of the same mind, but she hesitated, meaning to make sure that Raphael approved.

Raphael was powerfully taken with the desire to go to the hall at once. Here was someone who had known Awen closely; he would gladly do much for her if he could make the opportunity. But he saw that Veronica was inflamed at the mere recollection of Awen.

"How strange," he said in a calm voice. "Does she say in particular what it is she wants?"

"No, sir; only that she wants to talk to you."

His mind was instantly made up, but he did not want to show it; he paused, as if deliberating. He rose slowly.

"Very well," he said. "Let curiosity rule the day; I shall see her."

"Oh, no, Mr. Kerr!" cried Veronica. "You cannot be serious! You will see the servant of that wretched woman?"

"Why not?"

"Why not! This is the Fallows who accused you—in public—of a deed I shall not name. If you do not recall what she did, I do, and so do all of our neighbors."

"Yes," said Raphael, "I recall it perfectly. She accused me of something I did not do."

And at this cool reproach, Veronica was deeply ashamed; for she herself had most certainly done what Raphael had only been accused of.

As she stood frozen temporarily in shame and uncertainty, he left the room. He knew that anger would immediately succeed her shame, and then she would be willing to make any sort of scene.

When he entered the front hall he found Mr. Strong watching over Bessie Fallows much as he might have guarded a burglar apprehended *in flagrante delicto*. At his coming she raised the veil from her countenance; her gaze was a mixture of apprehensiveness and boldness. He could see at once, though she strove not to show it, that she was weak with hunger.

"Well," he said. "You wish to speak with me, Miss Fallows?"

"In private, sir," she said.

His heart leapt up in him. She had something to tell him about Awen.

For the sake of appearances, he paused a moment before answering, as if with some reluctance, "Very well; come into my study."

Mrs. McQuillit, who had followed him back to the hall, was further surprised and alarmed. "But you will not put yourself into this person's company alone, sir?" she asked.

"Why not, Mrs. McQuillit? Is she dangerous?"

"There is no telling what she might accuse you of, sir. You ought to have a witness."

He looked at Bessie Fallows. "I do not think Miss Fallows is so great a threat to us as that," he said. "Indeed, I shall go further; I think Miss Fallows is in need of some refreshment. Make up a meal for her, which she may have when our business is concluded.

Let her take it in the little sitting room, alone." The little sitting room was generally reserved for visiting servants if there were too many in the house to comfortably seat at dinner in the kitchen. He meant to isolate her from the other servants, both to spare her their cruel remarks and to prevent her saying anything to them that might further injure Awen's reputation.

Mrs. McQuillit was disgusted, but she would not disobey him; and so he led Bessie to his study, with as restrained a stride as he could manage, and closed the door behind her.

The first thing she saw was Musa the cat as she slept in the chair by the fire; and at the sight, Bessie's famished reserve seemed to break, and with a happy little cry she rushed to the chair and knelt before it, patting and stroking the animal. Musa responded with an unusual show of pleasure; she got to her feet, purring loudly, and not only allowed Bessie to stroke her, but pressed hard against her hand.

In another moment, however, Bessie remembered her place and stood up guiltily. "Begging your pardon, sir," she said. "But I could not help myself when I saw *her* cat."

"*Her* cat?" cried Raphael.

"Yes—did you not know? This is Mrs. Quinn's cat."

"Are you sure?"

"Sure as I can be. Why, we had her with us for six years, in one place or another; and Mrs. Quinn and I fussed over her as if she had been a baby."

"She came here after . . . after Mr. Quinn vacated Rush Hill."

"Then that would make sense. Mr. Quinn would have nothing to do with her; very likely he went off without making any provision for her. And I do not doubt she came here because . . ."

But she did not finish the reason she was going to give; the thought that Raphael loved her mistress seemed to put her in mind of her business.

When she was suddenly silent, Raphael—still marveling over the matter of the cat—asked her, "What did your mistress call her, then?"

"Why—Musa, sir; that was the name she gave it. She said it was a Latin name for the kind of goddess that inspires people to write poetry and suchlike. But of course you will know all about that."

"Musa! That is what *I* have named her," said Raphael.

Bessie did not quite understand. "Do you mean you knew nothing of the cat's name?" she asked. "You never heard it of my mistress?"

"I am certain I never heard a word of it from her, or anything at all about the cat, or even of its existence."

They stared at each other in mutual surprise for a long moment; and then Bessie said, "Well, if it is so, sir, it is not the strangest thing in all of this."

"No," said Raphael.

Bessie hesitated a moment more, but then at last blurted out her business. "Oh, Mr. Kerr, sir," she said, "I have fallen on very hard times since I lost my good mistress."

"I am sorry to hear that," said Raphael.

"I want you to know, sir, that . . . I did not like to accuse you as I did."

"You cannot be blamed for trying to tell the truth as you saw it, Bessie."

"No," she said, with something a little like defiance. "That was only right; and this much that I know: that my mistress—my good mistress, she that was and is no more—she loved you, and only you, of any man on earth."

He warmed within with a kind of pride at this; but aloud he said cautiously, "Be that as it may, it is a great leap from there to the assumption that she and I did anything wrong."

"I have come to see that I may have been mistaken in that," she admitted. He saw that she could not decide whether he and Awen had committed the act of adultery or not; she was perfectly poised between believing it and disbelieving it. "It grieved me to drag your name in the mud, as she loved you so; and even more it grieved me to drag *her* name in the mud, as she was so very,

very good to me—more good than I 'preciated at the time; but I thought . . . I thought . . . "

"What did you think?"

"I thought it would not hurt *her*, as she was dead; and most of all, I thought that *he* should not go free and clear of it, when we all know that he shot her a-purpose. He shot my mistress as planful and deliberate as any murderer who ever swung for it. And I knew that if no one knew about you and her, they would have no reason to think—no reason to *know*—that he meant it all along. He loaded his gun, he went out and lay in that spot in the woods, he knew it was her the moment he drew bead on her. He was that jealous of her, that it meant more to him to see her dead than to spare his own immortal soul. But it was too late for his soul! And I suppose he knew that. He had his fancy-woman in Norwich, who had been following us from place to place; and children by her—the mistress knew of it, and all the servants, even if none of the gentlefolk here ever did."

"Maybe it was a mercy to her, to die," said Raphael. "How do we know? At least it took her out of his company. Now your mistress is in a better place; she cares nothing for any of these events. Indeed, she does not remember them at all; she has better things to think about. And she is happy, happier than she ever was on this earth."

"May it be so, sir!" said Bessie, with an odd look at him.

"What is it?" he asked now, suddenly catching at that hint of further knowledge.

She hesitated again; and then she said, "It is only that . . . I am not sure where *she* is; but I know I am left behind, here on this earth, and I am . . . sore troubled, sir. I have no reference; I can get no work. I have been living off what I have put by these past fifteen year, and that is all gone. I am—as you yourself have noticed, sir—famished so as I can hardly stand."

"Sit down," he told her. "I shall order your dinner set at once. Eat that first, and when you are feeling stronger, then you can tell me what you have to say."

"No, sir, if you please—I shall push on to the end of it." And now she came back across the room toward him, thrusting her hand, as she came, into a bag of once-handsome cloth that hung at her shoulder, a kind of scrip. From this she drew a bound quarto book, not too thick, somewhat dirty and faded. As she stopped before him, she held out the book, as if teasing him with it, and her eyes took on a hard, greedy, desperate gleam.

And strange though the circumstances were, he guessed at once what the book was: a volume of Awen's writings.

He went to seize it, in a dream of joy and amazement; but Bessie drew it back.

"Begging your pardon, sir," she said. "I see you guess what this book is; but it is *mine* now."

"Oh, Bessie!" he said, in a wonder of disappointment. "You cannot be thinking to *sell* me her writing? You cannot be driven down so low, can you? Do you not know that my gratitude for this gift will repay you more than any bargain you could strike?"

Bessie was ashamed by this; but she looked sullen and said, "I cannot *eat* gratitude, can I, sir?"

"Silly creature!" he said, with a loving laugh, "Do you not know how dear you are to me—because she knew you? And because you loved her?—Very well, tell me: How much do you want for this book?"

She was even more ashamed, but she persevered in her desperation. "I must sell it dear, sir," she said. "It is all I have to make my way in the world with. I must have five guineas for it."

He produced the money at once from his pocket and held it out to her. She took it eagerly, almost incredulously, and at the same time she relinquished the book to him. He opened it at random, saw one spread of pages inscribed in Awen's neat and flowing hand, and then, overcome with joy at the rescue of this treasure, clapped it shut and held it to his brow for a moment. He seemed almost to feel her aura welling out of it into his brain. At that juncture he did not grasp exactly what the book contained;

he knew only that it was some part of the many writings Awen had set down over the years.

Meanwhile Bessie, overcome in her own way, had gone to a little distance to make sure of her money; and having done that, she put it up in her purse and turned back to him, a little fearful that Raphael might do something unpleasant now that he had what he wanted.

Of course he did nothing of the kind; he made her sit down, and sat down facing her, still holding the book, and said, "Now you must tell me how you came to have this."

"I dare not," she said.

"Ah, I know you must have stolen it. But I know that Quinn would have burned it, so I shall never reproach you for that. Besides, it is mine now—I have received stolen goods, and that makes me your accomplice, for all intents and purposes. Only tell me how you came to have it."

She continued reluctant for a few more minutes, but with more coaxing, she finally came out with it. "It is simple enough," she said. "The night after she was murdered, I lay awake till dawn thinking of how she had come to die, and of what I must do about it. That Mr. Thewitt of Lord Kintillian's had told me I would be asked to speak at the inquest, and I knew Mr. Quinn would not let me set foot in the house again once I had said what I had to say at Oakage; so I had to get all my things out of the house. Mr. Quinn was not there at the time, and I could come and go in the mistress's rooms as I pleased. So before dawn the next day I took . . . the book, and I put it among my own things, and I carried it out with them, and hid them all in the wood, to get back again after the inquest."

There was something not quite right about her account; the hesitation in the middle of it was telling, but he was not quite sure of what. He determined not to show his doubts and to continue to speak mildly to her.

"And it was only now, now that you have been quite reduced, that you have come to me to sell me this book? You should have come sooner. You will see; I shall help you, Bessie. I would hire you here myself, except that the lady of the house would make your life miserable. But I shall inquire of my sister, Mrs. Keith, if she needs a good servant—for I know you must be one, if you lived so long in *her* service."

"Ah, sir," said Bessie in a troubled tone, "I have not been so very good in my life. I did not realize how very bad I was until I began to live with my mistress. And even then, at first I thought she was just a kind of fool, soft-hearted. But as time went by, I saw that she was no fool, and that she had been through grievous hard times, much harder than I myself had endured; and yet still she found a way to love everyone, including me."

And to her great credit with Raphael, she now began to weep at the recollection.

"There is no question you loved her," said Raphael, "and that is all I need to know. Only go on, for her sake, trying to be a better person every day. That is what I do; and though I have far to climb, that thought lifts me upward and onward bit by bit."

"It is worse than that," said Bessie. "When he hired me—Mr. Quinn, I mean—he told me I must watch my mistress, and if I learned anything he ought to know, he would pay me for it. And I agreed—I agreed!"

"I expect you did," said Raphael. "Why would you not? You were only a young girl starting out in the world. How could you refuse?"

"Indeed, sir."

"And did you ever give him information?"

She looked at him, offended at the question; but not for her own sake, as it appeared. "What information could I have carried to him?" she asked. "What did Mrs. Quinn ever do that was in the least wrong? She was an angel—or at least until she met *you*. And for what she did then, an angel would forgive her."

"So you *do* believe we did wrong then," he said.

"I do not know, sir; that is all."

"Well, I am sure you will never take my word for it," he said, "but if you think on her character, you should know that she did nothing then—nothing that might need to be forgiven by any angel. The One itself would smile upon her conduct and actions."

Bessie apparently did not want to be forced to decide this matter one way or the other; she turned the topic by saying, "She herself used to call God 'the One,' just like that."

"She was the teacher who taught me to do so," he said. "But come, Bessie, I shall not pester you about any error you believe she and I committed. There is only one thing I do not want you ever to do again in my hearing, and that is to call her by the dreadful name of the man who murdered her."

"Indeed, it tears at my heart every time I do it," said Bessie.

"Then call her Awen," said Raphael.

"But she is above me," said the maid, in a protest made the more pathetic by a fresh upwelling of tears.

"She is above me as well, but she does not take offense when I call her by her name."

Bessie was suddenly silent. She seemed almost frightened.

"What is it?" he asked her.

"You speak of her as if she were . . . still living," said Bessie.

"She is," said Raphael. "Only not here where we can readily see her."

"If that is true, sir!" she exclaimed.

"If that is true, then . . . what?"

She shook her head as if she could not utter the thought that was at work inside her. He did not press her; and as it was, he did not understand her meaning until later. He reverted instead to the plan he was forming for her.

"Now, Bessie," he said, "if I send you to work for my sister, will you promise me to be a good servant?"

"Would you really do that for me, sir?"

"I would. But we must have your best behavior—no bearing tales for anything, and no filching notebooks."

She seemed struck again by something in what he had said, but she nodded and said, "I shall be good, sir. And as you say, I shall think on her, and grow better every day."

"And you will go to church on Sundays? It will be the better for you if you do."

"If you get me a place, sir, I shall go to both services on Sundays for the rest of my days."

"Hold to that. And when I am visiting my sister sometime, perhaps you and I shall talk further of what use one can make of the things they say in church."

"Yes, sir."

"Now go have your dinner. It is getting late; you shall stay here tonight. I shall write a letter to Mrs. Keith, and first thing tomorrow I shall have someone drive you over to Madgelet Lodge."

This time the fresh weeping was in gratitude, not in shame. Raphael saw the woman taken care of and then sat down to write the following letter.

Fulkothing Hall, Nedwich

Mrs. Reuben Keith
Madgelet Lodge
Ayresrill, Norfolk

Dear Lucy,

The bearer of this letter is the Bessie Fallows of whom I told you in my account of the inquest after Awen's death. She was Awen's maidservant for fifteen years; but you must be warned that though she has been much improved by that acquaintance, she has not by any measure been made angelic.

Ever since she spoke against Mr. Quinn at the inquest, she has not been able to find work. I think we ought to help her for the sake of the affection we bear to Awen, and I would hire her here myself, but that her life would be miserable, as the housekeeper, and for all I know the other servants, and certainly Veronica, dislike her for having borne witness against me.

Indeed, if you are willing to take her on, you must do so in full awareness that people will say we are trying to hush her up. But it seems to me a better principle to help where help is needed than to bow to fear of rumor. I know not if even in your good household she may be redeemed completely; but there is only one way to find out. If you are willing, and have work for her (as it seems to me you must), do engage her. I shall recompense you for her wages. If not, then send her back to me and I shall take fresh thought on what she is to do.

With all affection, your brother

RAPHAEL

That night Bessie stayed in a spare room in the servant's quarters—much to the distress and dislike of Mrs. McQuillit. Veronica, fortunately, knew nothing about it; and when she asked him at dinner to reveal Bessie's business, he told her only that the maid was hard pressed and in need of work.

The next morning he sent the gig to Madgelet Lodge, with Bessie in it; and when it returned he received this note from Lucy:

Dear Brother,

Your wish is my command; and where any friend of Awen is concerned, as in this case, your wish it shall be my pleasure to perform. Besides, we are much in need of another pair of hands, and we accept Bessie not just as a friend in need, but as a blessed offering of our brother to assist us.

With all our love, your sister

LUCY

The matter was not to be so simply settled, as it turned out; but both he and Lucy had the satisfaction of having tried this expedient first.

Chapter 57

Idem est apud Dominum, et inde in caelo angelico, quod venturum, aut quod praesens; quod venturum est praesens, seu quod fiet hoc factum.

Whether it is to come, or is so now, is all one to God; and since it is so to him, it is so to the angels in heaven. For them, the future is already present; and what *shall be,* even this has *already come to be.*

—Swedenborg

Establishing Bessie in her new position seemed a petty business indeed compared to the other matter that absorbed his powers of attention on that day: he began to read in the notebook. As in the interval when he had discovered Swedenborg's testimony of the Bright World, he shut himself up in his room; but on this occasion his preoccupation was not simply intellectual, but emotional. He was utterly overwhelmed by every word Awen had written; he wept from word to word, line to line, page to page, until his head was thick with weeping; and when it seemed he must have bled away every tear his body could produce—then he wept more. Time fell away from him, as it falls away from an animal that has been living on the keen edge of starvation for weeks and then suddenly finds food to sate itself; and if he was not stuffing his soul with her words, he was lying on the floor or on his bed in a daze, digesting their inexhaustible richness, savor, sweetness.

Time was indeed bent and twisted back and inwoven upon itself in that notebook in ways he could not begin to unwarp and unwoof and untangle. The first entry was dated some sixteen years before her death; and yet the events recorded in it had occurred only a few months ago, in Raphael's experience. For the notebook held the account of her time in the Bright World, from the day of her arrival there, through the time that she waited for him to join her, until the very day of his coming.

She had left a blank recto at the beginning of the book; but the second recto she had titled Journal, and on the third she had written this dedication:

> To You whom my friends have taught me now to call
> The One:
> May this celebrate and symbol You.

The journal began thus:

All these years have I searched for my love through dream after dream, always in vain. My sleep at night has been a wandering, and I have awakened more exhausted than I have lain down.

But now I know that in all my years before this, in day even more than night, I was asleep! And now I have awakened. But still I fear that my new waking dream is but one more place to search for my beloved to no success; and indeed, so it still may be, for all the promises and assurances of my heart; for even there my new friends are cautious about my hopes.

On this day a fortnight past, I first entered that world. As I sit here writing, I feel, though the very sun of *this* world warms my back, as if I am at the bottom of a well filled with fog so thick I scarce can breathe; and so I do denominate that *other* world the Real World; for in that place, there is no mist between the mind and the senses, between perception and the soul.

I first entered the Real World, then, on the night of August 4, 1800, when for all that anyone in this Unreal World could know, I lay in my bed asleep, and for all they would guess, I lay dreaming.

I was at first walking in a dark and dreary place—the far outskirts, as I know now, of the Unreal World, the shadowy margins of the mind—along a wall of great height, ancient, and of enormous stones, as if it had been worked and builded by the Cyclopes of old; and I was urgent to find a door in it. There was a path along the perimeter of the wall, though the soil there was all flint; and I could see that many had passed along there before me, passed and repassed, futilely seeking what I was seeking; perhaps also like them, I was barefoot and the flints of the path hurt my feet at every step. But it seemed to me even then that the door, if I could find it, would lead me *back into life;* and it was then, in my dream, that I first realized that *this world,* the Unreal World, is the world of Death—though in our ignorance of truth we talk of leaving it as *dying,* and think that we can live only here, and that to be anywhere else must be death.

I found the gate at last. It was strange—or strangely wrought, I should say, of a hard, smooth substance that made me think of the horns of beasts. When I touched it an awe fell over me, and I would have paused and considered what I did, except that overpowering my awe and hesitation was a certainty that I wanted to go through. I could not have done anything else.

As I passed through the gate I felt different at once, and the feeling grew upon me as I ascended the rising ground beyond. It was as if a new lightness were ascending through me, from my feet, slowly, to my very brow and the crown of my head; as if *life* were rising in me, pushing out all *death.* And my friends tell me that in the One, who is All Mind, there can be no death; and that what I felt in entering their world were the delusions of mortality being squeezed out of my thoughts by the One, as I in my own bath have squeezed the clouded water from a sponge.

The slope on which I walked was clouded with mist as well, which the air moved about, engendering many confusing, though not frightening, shapes; but as I crested the hill, the mist parted in a kind of hollow about as big as the room in which I write, and there before me stood a figure of overpowering magnificence—I say magnificence because his clothes shone radiantly, even though he was dressed very simply. In his hands was a great sword with a blade of fire, which he held before him, upright, as though poised to bring it down upon me. Now I think rather that he was only making a show of doing so to induce me to turn and go back to the Unreal World—testing my will to remain there.

In my terror I sank before him; and though I knew he wished me to go back, I cast myself on the very ground in my despair, and would not go, thinking to myself, *Dear God, if Raphael be here, let me stay to find him; and if he be not here, let me perish and go to where he is.* And so I lay, face downward, shaking in fear, and indeed I think groaning and whimpering like a child, and waiting for the blow to fall.

But instead the wind came up, gently, and blew away the mist from the height of the hill; and sunlight fell upon me, soothing and rich and warm, and I could feel it, though I did not for a long time dare to open my eyes, but still lay prostrate and trembling with my fear.

Then two sweet voices came into my mind. I do not know how to put it any other way—it was as if minds were speaking to my mind, as my love's tongue in kissing me touched upon my tongue. I heard them say, "Who is this?" and "Oh, look— the poor thing! She trembles!"

Someone knelt beside me and put her hand caressingly on my shoulder. I thought to myself, *Was this the blow that I dreaded, made love instead of destruction by my prayer?* And another hand touched my other arm, and then I was helped to my feet.

I looked first at my comforters. Already (and I have barely begun to tell these wonders) all my powers of mind and language fail me. Who could tell how beautiful they were? They were two women, and though they appeared—unlike me—in the very bloom of youth still, perhaps five-and-twenty years of age, there was something about them that told me they were older and wiser than people my age commonly are. It was their eyes, I believe—so clear were they, so bright in luster (though as it happened they were dark in hue), so full of tender wonder and concern for me.

And though I to them was nothing, they exclaimed softly when they saw my face, as though they thought me beautiful; or perhaps it is the fact that in the Real World, the beauty given us—given all—by the One appears without disguise. In spite of this approval of me, they seemed to see that there was something different about me; and I remember they touched me again as if wondering if I was real and not some phantasm; and one lightly touched my breast, I recall, with the tips of her fingers, as if that would be the ultimate proof of my reality; and only that satisfied them.

"Why this fear?" said one of them. Though I know her name (or rather I should say her *qualities,* for a person's qualities determine her or his name there), I cannot write it in my waking language; so I shall call her Prima, since she spoke to me first.

"I scarce know if I dare be here," I said in answer.

But they laughed, sweetly and reassuringly, and the other said, "If you are here, you are meant to be here."

"And yet you must have come for a reason," said Prima.

"I have come seeking my husband—my *true* husband," I said.

"Ah!" she replied; and she and her companion exchanged a look that seemed to me both knowing and joyous.

"Is he here?" I asked at once, a wild hope springing up in me.

"I think not," Prima answered. "There is no man among us who is at this time waiting for his bride to reach us. But certainly this land is the place you ought to stay until either he comes to you or you decide that he is not meant for you."

At the absurd thought that Raphael was not meant for me, I laughed, suddenly and I think quite merrily. They instantly perceived the reason for my laughter; and the other woman, whom I shall call Altera because she was the second who spoke, persisted and said, "But sometimes, even oftentimes, we do not have the same partners here as we did in the world from which you come." At her warning I only laughed again, as a little child laughs, and my laughter was like a bright bubble of sound that burst on the air, and I could see that they were impressed by my perfect certainty.

Then I spoke, not as before, in the language of the mouth, but in the language they spoke, directly from my mind to theirs.

"Raphael," I told them, "is my husband, my *true* husband. From the time God made the world, the seed of my beloved's being slept in the deeps of time, until in this very aeon, when God made it to break its hard hull and blossom into the finest figure of man that ever was. He is as handsome as the wind that scours the stones of the high tower. His dark eyes are as dangerous to my heart as lances, and his smile is as bold as the fanfare of a conqueror. And yet he is all gentleness to me, all goodness; and beneath his single touch my body bursts into ecstasy, and I am become a woman as I never was before."

I may say that they stared at me for this outburst, and indeed I hardly knew how it came from me; and yet they did not think me strange, though at first I feared so; but instead they reached to me and touched me in a kind of affectionate awe.

"It is difficult to argue with love when it speaks in poetry," said Altera after a moment.

"You prove again that you come to the right place," said Prima: "This is the land and the city of the Image Makers. Here dwell all those artists who love the married state, whether they work in stone or word or number or song."

"And you are dressed as one of us as well," Altera pointed out. And looking down at myself, I found that though I had before been wearing only a thin night dress, like the one I wore when I first met my love, now I was arrayed in a lovely gown of a fashion unlike any I have seen in the Unreal World, except, in part, in picture books. It was a soft, fine cloth, a kind of silky linen, but of a very pure color, without a fleck of variegation, a hue rich as cream. It fitted tightly at the breasts and sides and over the stomach to the very thighs; and every seam and edge was ornamented with gold. The bodice of it was cut as low as an evening dress; and as I glanced down at myself, it seemed to me that never had my breasts been so beautiful, and all the lines of my body; and—a wonder greater still than that—I saw that my arm was here grown to a normal length and strength.

"You seem surprised to find yourself beautiful," said Prima with a laugh.

"And if I am so, I shall indeed be surprised," I said. "But however that may be, I am astonished at my arm. It was always stunted before, and weak; but now it is a true mate to the right."

"So it happens with true mates who come into this world," said Prima. "If one was weak in spirit or morals, he or she grows strong to match wife or husband."

"Then I may hope to deserve my husband here," I said.

"I think," said Prima, with another affectionate laugh, "that you will find your husband quite pleased with you.—Now, come away with us, and we will show you your new home."

"But this is not my home if my husband is not here," I said.

"Maybe he will come later," said Altera. "That sometimes happens. Even if he came to this world many years before you, he may not arrive at the city till sometime after you. He may need to learn certain things, by instruction or by journey. Everyone has different needs; and the One looks after us all."

"The One?" I repeated.

"That which you have called God," said Altera. "But that is a name we do not use here, because it is full of the confusion of the world you have come from."

"But tell me," I said, "what world *is* this?"

They smiled at me, again affectionately. "This is the World of Life," said Prima. "The world you come from is the World of Death. You might call the place you come from the *Beforelife.*"

"Then is *this* the Afterlife?" I demanded.

"They call it that, in the Beforelife," said Prima. "But here it is simply the world of life, the living world."

"But if this is the world after death," I cried in my excitement, "then Raphael must be here."

"If he is here," said Prima, "he will come to you, or you will in time conclude that he is not in any case right for you. Have no fear of that.—Now, do come with us."

And in the most affectionate manner, as if they had known me for years, or had been my sisters all their lives, they each linked an arm through mine and led me onward, telling me about the place I had come to, at times laughing as gaily as girls, at times as sweetly sober as matrons. They seemed to have appointed themselves—or to have been appointed, through some special attention of the One—my guides and guardians. But everyone in the City has been so to me: solicitous of my happiness and welfare, kind and tactful, freely answering any question I might voice, any question I might even *look.*

⬇ ⬇ ⬇

I have paused here, and sat an hour in silent contemplation of that place. My home! My lost home, my never-till-this-moment-found home. Only Raphael is lacking to make it *our* home; and even as it is, when I am there, I sense him, I feel him, even sometimes I smell the wonderful man-smell of him, and my blood begins to race in my veins. He *is* coming, he *shall* come to me there, I know it, though all my new friends are cautious.

I shall attempt to describe the place, but any account will be too hasty, shallow, coarse. The City is, before anything, not a place at all but a feeling and a knowing. When my friends put their arms through mine and stepped forward with me, and I turned my eyes from their kindly faces toward the scene before me, I *felt* at once that this place was right for us, for Raphael and me. I knew it, I recognized it, just as I recognized Raphael on that morning when first we met in storm and terror. If I could express any one impression of that glorious land in the feeble words of this language, on this dim page, written in the hand of imminent caducity, in ink that will fade with time, it would be that of *reality, solidity, permanence.* That world *is,* and it shall abide forever. And yet at the same time, the City is built of symbol and imagination; it is a structure raised by the mutual industry of thought and feeling of its inhabitants, by their love for one another and for the One. Here is the great paradox of our life: That *imagination* is real, and anything that is not imagination is a lie; because imagination partakes of the One, while the unimagined does not. And to know the City that imagination builds, one must have imagination. To the dull and prosaic folk of this world, the City would be invisible; and yet to us who dwell in it, its stone courts and spires are ancient and perdurable, and bear us up infallibly in our ascent toward higher things.

So much for the ineffable! I give over even making excuses for my failure to convey these mysteries. It seems a simple mat-ter, by contrast, to recount what my eyes saw.

She had gone on from there to describe the city of the Im-age Makers. Raphael had thought he knew that place; but reading how it looked through her eyes was a revelation. It was even more beautiful than he recalled it, or at least beautiful in ways of which he had known nothing. The attributes and practices of life in that world were equally vivid and strange and wonderful through her eyes. Here, for example, was her further description of language there, the mind-speech:

> To speak there is to sing forth the images of a dream into the mind of another. The flow of it is wonderful: it is as when a spring boils to the rim of its well and spills into a channel, cold and fresh, inexhaustible—there is no end to the images that the mind calls forth from the Mind, or that the Mind calls forth from the mind. As the images of a dream constantly shift and transmogrify themselves, as they transmute the iron and the dross to the gold and the refinings, so does language there sing each thing in its thousand allied forms. To say "Awen and her husband" there is to tell our entire history: our meeting in an hour of peril, our labor side by side, our laughter, our shared prayer and poetry, our lovemaking, our childbearing, our trial of separation. Indeed, when I say his name to myself sometimes, the flow of the spring is symboled in my body, for as my mind runs over with image, my loins melt and flow with desire.
>
> And these things appear not just as they happened, but in symbols that represent them. Our meeting is wind turning up wave, or a circlet of cloud closing on and capturing the peak of a mountain, or molten gold flowing into molten silver. Our labor together is a pair of horses running in common harness, or oars stroking in time, or twin bees ranging and foraging. Our laughter is brightness, upward bird flight, the swirling of falling leaves to the skirling of playful wind, or a falling freely in space without any fear of landing. Our prayer and poetry is the song of wild birds on a lake, calling for each other; or a falling star reversed and soaring into diminishment and vanishment. The images of our lovemaking—I hardly dare even think of them in this world, or I shall throw forth an aura of desire that shall make men for miles around stagger and turn toward this spot—or make women see Raphael in their minds and hunger for him. Our childbearing I see as the carrying of the moon by the sea, or as the bending and bowing and heaving of the branches of mother tree and father tree, or as bright water within cupped hands within cupped hands. Our trial of

separation is the tearing of cloud from cloud and the leaping forth of lightning; it is the veil of night sweeping over the land; it is a bridal veil blown and tumbled by the wind, torn and ragged with rents from the plucking grasp of bramble and briar; it is a desert, bare even of sand; it is an airy emptiness once filled a thousand fathoms deep by ocean and teeming sea life.

The alphabet there is rich beyond comprehending. There is no end to the characters it contains, or so I am told; and yet by merely being present in that world, anyone may read it without instruction. But the farther inward one lives toward the center of that world, the more meaning its characters have. Those in the Dark Lands just barely eke a paltry literal sense out of it; those in the deepest regions (which some call the highest regions, for reasons I as yet know not, as they are not *above* one in the sky) see endlessly deep sense in its runes and combinations. A single letter may indicate a myriad related things, through a method beyond any human ken. Frequently they appear in pairs, complementing one another, and express those attributes of the One that stand in complementary relationship, as Love on the one hand and Wisdom on the other, or Goodness and Truth, or Woman and Man, Beauty and Wonder. The letter that means my name also means *wife,* and not just *wife,* but—my joy to hear it, though I blush even in confiding it to these private pages—*wife excelling all her kind; and wise wife;* and *wife who wakes the ten thousand ways of desire, who fills her husband with both yearning and contentment, who melts and liquefies and draws forth the seed of her husband; wife who persuades to courage, fortitude, virtue; wife-poetess who inspires poetry;* and much more. The spiral within the letter is the sign of our slow path inward toward the Center; and even, they say, it is a sign of the gentle path the One takes outward to guide us in, though the radiance of the One is more commonly shown with bold and direct rays beaming from the center. The double bars of my letter-name are the doubling of my being in Raphael, or so I am to understand; the overall form teaches the way it is to be uttered, and, if I could understand it, it teaches the way I myself am to be uttered as a syllable of the One's voice to eternity.

What Raphael's name is to be in the Real World has not yet been granted me to know. He must arrive among us first, they tell me, and then his name will be perceived. I tell them that I hope that though old names are shed there, I will still be allowed to call him Raphael still, because that is an ancient and beautiful name that stems from the language of the Real World. It signifies *The One has healed* or *made whole; and the One has made two into one,* that is, *the One has unified or reunited.* But I can think of many more names I could give to him; indeed, when I lie alone and think of him, I feel as if my whole body and brain has become one name, his name, aching to be uttered. My friends tell me that if all goes well, someday he and I shall become together one name, the name of the One, likewise yearning to be spoken.

One of the key passages in her account—key in being a part that unlocked much of that world to comprehension—was her exposition of the importance of the imagination. It was a theme he had heard her enlarge upon from his first acquaintance with her, but this discussion of it was utterly different, almost shockingly different. She wrote:

The Real World is founded upon the love of the One; that is its primary basis, the ultimate reality, and all else but love must be lower in degree. But secondary in degree is imagination. The imagination of the One is the formative power that makes all the universe take its shape. We exist in the mind of the One, we are utterly real fashionings of the One's imagination. And we borrow that power from the One, though during most of our lives we scarcely know it. Indeed, most often we are prey to that power in us, because it rages without control, without the guidance of love; and love must come first, or the pure and perfect order of the One is not served, and we find ourselves living in a hell of our own imagining.

In the Real World, our powers of imagination are that much more perfect and real, because we are that much closer to the Center and the Only Reality. For example, from what

Prima tells me, we need only picture ourselves in a distant land, and we have gone there: we are walking its paths, conversing with its inhabitants, and yet never leaving the protection of the One. But that is only a fact of life there that seems particularly striking because of the limitations of the Unreal World. In truth I do not know, but perhaps we could do the same here if we were not bound into our illusions—if we could here set free the divine power to *see* that lies within us.

I do, however, know that we could do others wonders even here if we could use those powers that are freely granted us. Why are we cruel to one another? Or better to ask: Why do we not love one another instead? The answer is that we have never imagined what the consequences would be. It is like those dark moments in the first months of this sham marriage to Mr. Quinn when he used to claim what he believed to be his rights as a husband. I knew not whether to retch with the horror of it, or to be dumbfounded with the paltry nature of the act, or to be disgusted with his carelessness and blindness—sometimes I felt like sobbing at the violation, and sometimes I felt like laughing at it. It was the perfect *failure* of imagination, not only because it was broken in itself, but because it was not built on love. I know now that that act occurred *outside* of the Real World of love, whereas my lovemakings with Raphael were linked with the Real World, symbolic of our loving there.

Ah, Raphael! Your imagination in love was fertile and powerful, so that one look from you would be enough to unstring my knees, as I wondered what delight you planned for us; and though you inspired me always to new forms of love, I could never match you in ingenuity, and always followed you, an eager pupil, always ran after you in that, but could never catch up.

Without imagination we do not know what use we are. We do not know our own purpose: we revert to seeing and being an entire universe unto ourselves. We fail to know how serving others joins us to them, raises us out of ourselves, draws us nearer to the One. Only love and imagination can teach us that.

Without imagination we do not know even the first consequences of the beliefs we profess. Many a man and woman and child will admit a belief in life after death; but who lives as though life were eternal? No one. Every ache and pain and cross and trial terrifies us and burdens us and makes us complain; and where is our belief in eternity then? Our impoverished imaginations fail to teach us the use of those seemingly contrary events. Some even doubt the mere existence of the One because they see the Unreal World filled with suffering and misrule. They are like the schoolboy who begrudges his time at the slate because he cannot imagine any purpose in writing and figuring, who believes that nothing is of use unless it provides him with instant pleasure—so they cannot believe in "God"—whom they picture, with their limited vision, as a white-bearded man on a throne, the Ancient of Days—because he does not heap them with the gratifications of the senses or because he does not enforce good behavior in all as if we were automata.

Or let me put it a different way: I dare say that there are no people who do not believe in God, only those who fail to imagine Divinity.

And it is the very contrary that I see in the worship of the One in the city of the Image Makers. That worship is one long ferment of the imagination, offered in delight, offered in love of the One and of all humanity, because they are beloved of the One. I see it too in the skill and zeal of all as they work in service of the people of the city and of the many realms round about, even to the most distant borders of the Real World. Some serve by going into the Dark Lands and easing the self-inflicted sufferings of those there, by attempting to teach them about the love and the imagination.

And yet it seems to be strangely true that the imagination, once killed off, cannot be brought back to life.

Another remarkable passage ran as follows:

This past night (in this world) and day (in the Real World) has seen the most incomprehensible and yet most beautiful of all my experiences—I was going to say, "of all my experiences in the Real World," but instead I must say, of all the experiences in my entire life, with the exception only of the days of wonder that I knew with my Raphael on Vigia, which were and are to me veritable heaven.

I was with my friends and we were talking of the nature of the Real World. They met my expressions of delight at its beauty with perfect agreement; and yet they must for the sake of full truth add that the lands of the Image Makers, and all the lands with which we trade or which we can readily visit, lie on the margin of the Real World, and only the Dark Lands lie farther out. Toward the center are more realms, infinitely deep in extent. And it was mooted that I ought to go visit the next most inward realm, so that I might have some understanding of what it was like; though in fact, they said, none from our city would be able to comprehend much of it. I agreed eagerly to this suggestion, though I was also hesitant for reasons of humility; but when I learned that the way inward is through prayer—that the request must be made directly to the One—then I was, if daunted at the idea of presuming to ask, still reassured that if the journey was not proper, I would not be allowed.

Altera and Prima volunteered to accompany me. Accordingly we went, all three of us, to the temple of the One in the city and purified ourselves (as much as we could) in prayer and meditation. And so it came about that, after some time in such silent reflection, we heard a voice saying *Arise, my beloveds, and follow;* and we saw that a young woman had appeared before us in the temple.

Now, the sight of this woman, unforgettable as it was, and beautiful as she was, would have been enough to delight me for the rest of my life. In looking on her, I had the impression of complete *cleanliness,* as if she had just come from a bath of the soul, and was fresh and fragrant from the surface of her skin to the innermost organ of her being. Her eyes, I remember, were particularly wonderful: their expression was as kindly as that of a mother. Indeed, her shape, her fragrance, her speech, her movements, her expression were purely womanly. I kept thinking, *She is more* woman *than any woman I have ever known.*

We arose; at her beckoning we followed; and with our first step, it seemed the temple in which we had been fell away from us, and we trod a deeper realm.

I had thought the land of the Image Makers infinitely more real than this dull, unreal place in which I dwell by day; but in comparison to the land of the Image Makers, that inner realm to which we were taken (and again I say that it was only the first of many more inward realms) was infinitely more real still.

I falter now, because I do not know how to describe it. I have said it was more real; but here is the oddest part: I felt as if *I were not real enough for it.* I felt as if I were a mere dream drifting into it; and though I might have thought that was because I truly am a kind of dreamwalker in that other world, afterward Prima and Altera told me they had felt the same. It was as if I was merely an illusion and might turn to vapor and dissipate in that greater reality. I had the sensation that I could not breathe there—that its atmosphere was too good for the likes of me to inhale, as if the pressure of goodness and love were too great for someone as minimally good and loving as I am.

At the same time I was not frightened. It was impossible to be frightened there. Fear could not exist in that realm. Never, except in the arms of my beloved, have I felt so loved as I did when I walked in that place. Love irradiated me; love poured through all the interstices of my atoms; love laved, saturated, cleansed me. And it was as if suddenly I knew I was good, that I was inherently good because I had been made by the One, who is All Good; and all the petty evils that I had acquired were only laughable smoke, irrelevant shadow that vanished from my soul in the all-seeing rays of the Godhead.

For a moment I stood on that more realer soil. As I look back on that instant, I have the impression of a lawn and garden surrounded by a wood—but such a lawn, such a garden, such a wood as can never be told. It was, I now know, a certain storied garden devoted to the delight of love, but only the sort of love as man and woman have in marriage; and I have heard that it has an echo of its name that can be spoken in the Unreal World: it is called *Andramandoni.* Beautiful and unique as that name is, it is only a shell that does not convey how in that life the name of that garden bursts with meaning. I do not doubt that we were taken there because our guide knew of the passionate interest of the Image Makers in marriage love.

The colors of that place—oh, the colors—how to tell them? There were colors such as I had not only never seen, but never conceived. The palette of colors we have on this earth, which we think so rich and varied, was impoverished by one glimpse of that garden. The shapes of the plants were infinitely varied, too: some were green (in myriad shades), representations of love in topiary; some were male spikes of flowers, or deep female orchids; others were flowers of broad petals splashed with paintings of more such symbols. The paths and hedges formed lover's knots symbolic of the infinite intertwinings of soul and soul in marriage, and streams of sweet water ran likewise looping through the place, singing as they went. The very air there seemed full of flowers—I cannot describe how this was—the most I can say is that it was as if the very particles of the atmosphere were minute and perfectly translucent blossoms exquisitely carved of impalpable diamond, in constant agitation, like motes of fine dust hovering and vibrating before the eyes; and they shimmered, and one saw them, and yet at the same time they were perfectly transparent and invisible and did not hinder the vision at all; and to the lungs they were fragrant and intoxicating.

But in my case that glimpse of the garden in that more inward realm was too much. Even as I was suffused with love and goodness, I was stricken with a longing for my own beloved so powerful that I could not bear it. My whole body seemed simultaneously to stiffen and to loosen, so that I could not control it; I wept copiously, my breath burst from me in a sob; my cheeks and shoulders and front burned hot with a blush; my breasts were instantly engorged with milk and overflowed at the paps; my womb churned, and the liquid of love's delight ran out of my sex like a stream of tears. My vision grew dim, or perhaps it was that I was blinded by brightness; I fell down on my side in the sweet grasses of that place and gave a groan that seemed to echo to the very skies—for indeed at the sound of it, ten thousand birds that had been rustling and twittering in

the trees about the garden suddenly rose in flight, and the rush
of their wings was like whispering thunder. I knew that I must
go back to the city, that in an instant more I *would* go back, I
would be carried back, and that the One had known this outcome, but wished me to have that glimpse of the joy to which
I hope and pray my beloved and I are destined. As I lay there,
undone with love and longing, our guide looked down at me
with the sweetest expression of kindness and pity, and she said
the words that above all were those I wished to hear:

Ah, he comes, he comes, she said: *Do not doubt it.*

And he would come to her in that other world; and she would
describe his coming, even years before her own death in this
world and before his own journeys there began. There could be
no more irrefutable and even unsettling proof of the disjunction
of the passage of time between the two worlds.

Of course, the first time Raphael read her diary, he had no
idea what it would contain or how it might link to the events he
himself had experienced. It was also difficult to track the days
Awen spent in the Bright World, because she did not regularly indicate their commencement or conclusions; her account seemed
to flow along in one continuous day, occasionally broken by her
description of a night in the city of the Image Makers, which was
spent in dreams of him. And what was still more confusing for
him was that after a point Awen ceased dating her individual entries; and not long after that, ceased demarcating them at all. Raphael had the impression that this change was a reflection of the
increasing unreality of her daytime experience. She had begun to
feel that she was *really* living in that other world, and her daytime
return to this world was only an irrelevant and irritating interrup-
tion that must be borne as best it could, that her experience *over
there* was ongoing. As a result, it became impossible to determine
the period of years over which the diary had been written.

It was evident, however, that she waited for Raphael for the
equivalent of many years; that is, that her dreams *here* were for
many years filled with the experience of awaiting him *there*. That

time passed pleasantly enough, it seemed: she had many friends in the Bright World and useful work to do, and she reveled in that company and in her poetry. But every day and every page was filled with her yearning for him, so that he must weep in reading it, continuously, and thank the One for the love of this good woman time and time again.

Finally a change occurred; and this was how she told of it:

He has come!

I have felt him come into the Real World—indeed, his coming into that place is to my mind what his coming into my body was to my womb. I am awake there, more than ever before; and though before I felt in every respect alert and aware, now I am still more so.

It was a holiday, a holy day; but something called me away from the city, and I walked farther than I have ever gone alone, down from the hill, through the meads and the woods, up another hill and into a high meadow that looks out over the lands to the east. The morning was fine and fair: the air held that coolness and crispness that comes with the night rain, but a warmth was building in, soaking in from the sun, beginning to rise up and return in moist heat from the grasses and trees. I was looking for a sign, some sign of Raphael's coming—I know not what I thought it would be. I climbed to the highest point of that meadow, even scrambled onto a higher rock there, and shaded my eyes with my hand and peered east as if I knew what I was looking for.

And then it came—a pang, a thrill, a recognition, an awareness—and I knew he was in that world with me. I verily believe that he first entered there at that moment, though I know not how that could be so, since he died so many years ago; but time between the two worlds, as they tell me, is utterly disjoined; and if it is the plan of the One that he should arrive in such-and-such a manner, at such-and-such a time, then so be it. I only know that he is there.

I felt what is called his *aura*. My first response, as I swayed and tottered on the height of that rock, was to laugh aloud for sheer joy. It was he—and so wonderfully familiar—as if he had only left me in the house on Vigia a moment before to go for water or for firewood—and now had come back. In our time together I had always felt a new thrill of love and interest every time I saw him, no matter how frequent that occurrence became; and in the same way I thrilled with this aura, only a hundredfold more so. And after I had laughed for sheer joy, I wept, I held up my arms, I stretched my body upward and eastward as if I could have leapt into his presence, and I called out to him.

He did not answer—I am sure that if he heard, it was not permitted to him to answer. He entered the Real World at a different place than where I was, and though I do not know why, I know there was a reason, and I trust the One in that as in all things. There is something he must learn in journeying to me, and something I must learn in waiting longer for him.

But though I did not hear him respond, for a moment I was granted the sight of him. He was walking across a wide plain toward a white city; but not as one going home, only as a traveler making toward a habitation in order to learn where he was. I could see that he was dressed in the raiment of the Image Makers, so I knew (as I have always known, no matter what my friends say) what his true destination is.

Then the vision faded, and I went home to the city, singing—singing a poem that came to me as I walked; and I came among my friends again in such a dream of happiness that they knew not what to do. Later they told me they had never seen anyone in the Real World in such a state as I was—indeed, I believe I was communing with my husband's aura, and scarcely could hear anything anyone said to me. But after some time I was able to explain myself; and all were happy for me, though still they said I could not be absolutely sure until I met Raphael again and spent time with him.

This account was particularly remarkable because, inasmuch as it was written by Awen in this world, it retained traces of her memories of their time together on Vigia. Yet according to what she said, when she was actually present in the Bright World, she could retrieve few or none of her memories of those difficult times of their separation, just as was the case when Raphael had come to her in the Bright World and found she had forgotten much of that past life.

The report of her time in the Bright World now became a tale of intense longing. She went about her ways, spending her time as before, writing her poetry, or in the company of her friends and neighbors in the city; and yet she thought of Raphael every minute. If she was invited into a house, she took the seat facing the door, in the hope that he would walk through it. If she stood or sat on the common lawn, she looked toward the east and the mouth of the path that led from that direction. When she lay in her bed at night, she turned toward the door, propped up on her pillows, watching and hoping that he would enter, until at length sleep overcame and conquered her; and when she woke, her first thought was to feel in the bed beside her and to look again toward the door in the new hope that he might at that moment be opening it to greet her. Her days in the Dim World were spent in long walks as she sought to tire herself for a sound sleep. Then he came across this extraordinary passage:

> It came to me not long ago how my love and I have no place to dwell when he arrives with me. For some days before we are wed again here, he will need to stay with someone else, and Altera and her husband have said that they would gladly have him lodge with them; but beyond that we will have no place to go. So I have begun to build us a house, knowing with confidence how my love would like it to be, but ready as well to change it all if need be when my love and his imagination work upon it.
>
> I talked with my friends about how it ought to be done. On their instruction, I went to the temple and prayed. My prayer was an imagining; I built the house in images in my mind; I raised up a point of land from the lake, and laid the foundations of stone and mortar, and put up the walls, the doors, the windows, the roofs, the inner rooms; then I sketched out the gardens outside and painted them in, in their manifold colors.

All the while I prayed that what I proposed might be pleasing to my husband.

And the One favored my imagining.

I left the temple and went down to the lake; and lo, there was our house, raised up on a peninsula of land, so that we may have an island house apart and yet still be connected to our friends in the city. It was more beautiful than I had imagined it, because the One had raised it.

There was still more work to be done in it; so I went to the woodworkers of the city, and they came gladly to fit it out inside. I went to the market when traders were visiting from the places where furniture is made, and they gave me what I needed. To me it seems still strange that there is no money in that world, except in the Dark Lands; that merchants (for so they are still called) travel for miles to bring goods to others for the sheer love of providing them. I gave them my poems, in return, which they accepted eagerly.

I cannot say that my preparations do not meet with some concern from my friends. But I only smile at them and tell them that they will see when the time comes to see.

I had another thought, too. I had the workers in gold make an amulet of my name-letter. For a few days I wore it, even slept wearing it, so that it should imbibe my aura; and then I took it with me and walked between the hills to the east, following up the path that I hope my love will come down. There is a place there where the path from the east diverges, the one route leading to the city, the other to a maze of paths among the hills, a trap for those who presume to come to the city but have no true business there. On a tree by the way I hung my token, symbol of my care for Raphael.

I felt, as I did so, that Raphael saw me, looked on me, and that his heart leapt at the vision. I was even reluctant to leave that place—I would have spent my days by the path, hoping to see him that much sooner; but the knowledge came to me that this was not according to what the One had ordained, so I would not stay.

The history of her waiting was an evidence of her love that was as precious as his own memories. If he had had this account in his possession in those months when he in his turn was waiting for her and hoping she would depart with him, he would have had an easier time of it; for though he had had perfect faith then, and never doubted her love, he would have known that she had once endured something very much like what he was then enduring.

I wait—that is the sum of my existence. By day in this dim and unreal day-lit world I wait for dark to come so that I may go to that bright and realer world and live my true day and night there. And by day and night there, I wait for Raphael to come. Here I wait to wait; but there I wait for an end of waiting.

Waiting for the beloved—how many have done so before me, and will do so afterward, in the aeons of human time yet to come? How many young women, pretty or homely, have sat in silence or have sighed and stretched fretfully, looking out the door or window of their soul on a road that was bare of traveler to the very horizon? How many young men have tossed, in their waiting, on a bed that, though narrow as a board, seemed to stretch away empty beside them as broad as the plain that lies before the mountains?—So why should I complain? I am only one of countless millions, waiting; this is a fact of our common life.

Yet I do have a great advantage, for in that world I can feel the approaching aura of my beloved. On some days (in the Real World) the breeze from the east seems to bring it over the trees or along the shore of the lake; and I lie down in a bed of grasses or flowers and let it flow over me and am covered by my lover, and scarcely can hear the voices of my friends beside me. Or it drifts in the windows of the tower where I sit at work, and then for hours I write incoherently of love.

The waiting is all the more striking because when I am there, I can remember so little of our life together. My memories have been hidden, or perhaps even lost, wiped gently away from the slate of my mind. So I wait for a love I hardly *know*— or at least, hardly know consciously—until I come back to this world, and the recollection of our loss and pain floods over me again, and I weep for joy to think that I might still make good that loss.

I own that I am preoccupied, and in my way less useful, unless manifesting love is useful, and I do suppose it is. Oh, man and maid, look on my love and learn what love is! See what price in bittersweet longing a person in love will gladly pay; and hope to love so much someday yourselves!

And at last, in the final pages of the journal, he came to the account of their meeting, in the way that he knew and remembered well; and it was both intoxicating and maddening for him to read her version of that event.

On this night past—on this day past in the Real World— our waiting came to an end. I have seen him, heard him, held him and been held by him. Praise be to the One!

It was a spring holy day in the city, the one called the Celebration of the Marriage of Love and Wisdom. In the morning there was a great fair outside the walls on the height of the hill, with declamations of special poems and stories, performances of choral pieces, and displays of mathematical and scientific wonders; and one could wander from booth to booth and see what amazing things one's neighbors had invented or discovered or written in the past year. The hilltop was full of visitors, too, curious travelers from many cities—the Starry Folk and the Child Raisers and the Music Makers and the Weavers and the Lovers of Old Days and many more I did not recognize. In the afternoon many of the Image Makers went down the hill to the common lawn by the lake; and there the celebration continued, apart from visiting eyes, in the comfortable company of Image Makers only.

The Binding of the Pole was to take place. This is like the Maypole dance in the Unreal World, and I think that the two are related in some strange way. There they say that the Pole is male power and the binding by woven ribbon is the gentle guiding and containment of maleness into deeds of creation rather than destruction; for they say without such guiding, the male force would sink into itself and destroy all, just as the female force would be dissipated and enervated and vanish into nothing without the male. These are the two aspects of the One; and praise be to the One!

Now, I was chosen to play the Virgin Queen; because at this time among the Image Makers, I am the only virgin. It seems strange to be called a virgin, and at first I protested what I thought to be the truth against it; but they told me that when one enters the Real World, one is again, whether man or woman, a virgin. And so it was my task and honor and delight to lead the dancers as they circled the Pole and wove a gentle sheath of ribbon over it.

It was a most powerful and sweet symboling, and the ceremony and the dance affected me more than I can say. And the fact was that Raphael's aura was now so strong upon me that I was half-blind with it, and in the dance I was aroused by the mere sight of the pole above me, as in the old times on Vigia I had gone hot and moist with the mere sight of his maleness, and when the dance was over, my knees wobbled as if they had been made of India rubber, and I sat down on the grass.

I had been sitting there not more than a few minutes. Many of the dancers had drifted away, but Prima and Altera came to me. They told me that there had never been such a fine Dance of Binding before; and I must have looked strangely at them, and I know I replied to them in images that were incomprehensible, because they at once asked what was wrong—"Or *right*," as Altera added, for indeed they knew that nothing could be wrong with me in such a place as that.

And at that moment all the throng that teemed over the commons seemed to hush, even to the last child; and then a voice or two called my name. But indeed, there was no need for that, for his aura had come upon me like the lover's thrust. I rose in all haste to my feet and turned toward it, all my soul become a welcome.

And there he was

I have been overcome again in writing this and had to stop for a time; but I will press on, for the recording of that hour is sweet, though the memory drives me into dreams and breaks my effort short at every turn.

And there he was—he had already crossed half the lawn, and the crowd had parted to make an avenue between us. He was tall and straight, and though he was as handsome to my eyes as on the day I had last seen him, he was older by perhaps some ten years—yes, he might have looked thirty years of age. He was wearing a pilgrim's scrip and carrying a pilgrim's staff; but he had come home; and all who saw him knew it.

But what did I do then? It is one of love's sweet tricks and benefits to make us doubt our worthiness; and when I saw him—mad as it seems to me now—I *wondered if he would want me.* For what if *I* thought *him* my perfect spouse, but now in the Real World he thought otherwise? I plead in excuse of that moment of insanity the entire confusion of my mind and senses at seeing him; for to me, he is of all created beings and things the most beautiful that ever was; and I was struck dumb, and made stupid, and stood like a fool, breathless, wide-eyed, and I doubt not gone pale, and hardly even able to hope that he was come for me.

Then I saw, over the distance between us, that he had found my gift and sign to him and wore my name-letter around his neck. Then all doubt burst like a bubble, and I took a step toward him; and I remember (it was almost like my heart speaking) that someone said, "He has come, Awen! He is here!"

Still, I could barely believe it. The fear now came over me that he would disappear before I could touch him, seize him, hold him; and I went toward him—but such a walk! I had to think and will every step or I would have fallen to my knees. I felt, too, that my whole body had become a beckoning to him, and my hips wanted to roll with each stride, as if to proclaim my desire; and so I went by half-steps, as if I were hesitating, when it was all I could do to keep from running to him.

When I had come near him, suddenly it was as if my whole body were pressed against his aura, and I dared not go closer. I was by turns numb and aflame with longing for him, and I was afraid that if I went on, I would either faint or go mad with de-sire as I did when I looked on the Garden of Andramandoni; for Raphael *is* my garden of love.

How sweet just to look on him! Perhaps I could have stood there a thousand years and looked, and never needed more. It came to me that he was like a god; and though that might seem a blasphemy, the wise ones of that world teach that the One is Human and has or can take a form either male or female—indeed, has done so, though this is not the time to tell that tale. It is a deep mystery I do not understand—how the Divine can be Human; but I am certain that it is so. Perhaps it is that we are only human because we partake of that quality, which originally resided in the One and is lent to us. But I know that a man or a woman can represent one half of the One; and at that moment, so Raphael did to me. It was as if I were looking through a doorway into a place where he stood, and there was just room enough for me beside him, and he were summoning me to take that place; or (the thought came to me, and I probably blushed) that it was as if he were in the holy bed of our marriage, waiting for me.

But like a fool, all I could say was, "It is *you!*" It was not as if I had ever doubted it; I meant it only as acknowledgement, recognition.

Of course, he perfectly understood me, and he answered simply, "It is *you.*"

Then some of my friends laughed softly, in delight; and some began to weep. And as I heard that sound, I know I must have blushed; for my face felt hot. But I was saved from the embarrassment of being embarrassed of my embarrassment by a wondrous thing that then took place.

The staff that Raphael carried turned from dead and dry wood to living sapling, and from sapling to short green stalk, and the green stalk blossomed the kind of flower that in that world is called the *hearts-as-one,* because its petals look like two hearts joined.

And without an instant's hesitation—and the boldness and certainty of his action made my heart leap—he came those last few steps toward me and held out the flower.

I must have gone a little mad with my desire for him then—but truly, it is a wonder I did not do worse! For I took the flower from his hand, and I stripped my virgin's crown from my head and cast it on the ground, as a thing that had served its time; and I wove the stalk of the flower into my hair and in that symbol was no more a virgin. I imagine that in some places in that world, the ceremony of marriage consists of such an exchange.

Now I was grown bolder, for I knew perfectly that he loved me still; and I took his hand—it seemed an electricity raced up my arm as I did so—and I turned to my Doubting Thomas friends and I said, "He has come! Now you see him—do you still doubt he is my husband?"

They were humbled by the power of the One and stood in silence. Not a single one of them doubted any longer, I am sure of that. And to put the seal upon their approval, Prima ran up to us. She was in awe of Raphael, I think—and who would not be?—and she halted, and made the salutation of the Image Makers, as if she were asking his permission to proceed; and then she darted close to me and kissed me, and said, "We should have believed you, dear friend!"

Even while giving thanks to the One in my heart, I could not help glorying in my love. "But you believe me now, do you not?" I asked.

"Your husband is everything he ought to be," she said. And then she called a blessing down on me, and the crowd around us repeated it.

Then I wanted nothing but to be alone with Raphael. I wanted to go apart from all the rest, and I wanted to kiss him, and be kissed by him, and hold him and be held by him; and at the thought I could feel the heat burning in my cheeks, and I tugged him by the hand; and my friends all knew what I was thinking, and they laughed. But not harshly, for they could never be harsh; instead in a loving, kindly way, that said they shared in my delight, as much as they could.

And so we went away together, together at last, away from the festival, and my friends called blessings after us, until we were out of sight and alone. And I led him away up the margin of the lake toward our house.

I would have been, indeed, in a state of trepidation about whether he would like the house, even though we could readily change it to suit, except that I myself would gladly do so, for I knew that once we were together we would think as one. Furthermore, I gave the house very little thought, I confess—all I was thinking was how I could encourage him to hold me and kiss me, without seeming utterly brazen myself.

He asked me about my friends. He had sensed that they had had doubts about him; and I answered something, I hardly knew what, that was meant to be reassuring, and certainly now I cannot recall what it was; but I do know that he turned to me very seriously and said, "But you *are* my wife," as if rebuffing any suggestion to the contrary.

My heart gave another great leap of pleasure in me, just to hear him say it; and I went out of my head, I think; for instead of replying soberly, I teased him.

"I am not your wife yet," I said. "Do not hurry us along so wonderfully fast!"

And my teasing had exactly the effect I craved; because he insisted, "But you *are* my wife—we were married long ago."

I was still wild and said, "You *know* we are not married *here*." And I accused him playfully of teasing me, though I was teasing him, to provoke him.

Then—I could not help myself—I pretended to turn the topic; but he would have none of that, and said, "We were married in the Dim World—do you not remember?" ("The Dim World" is what he calls this Unreal World of death and failed imagination.)

He was so sweetly serious that I could not help myself—I slipped my arm around him as we walked, burning with the hope that he would stop and kiss me then; and he did put his arm around me—O, heaven!—but he did not take the hint further.

Then he told me more of our life together on Vigia. How it frustrates me now, and makes me laugh at myself, even as I weep for the puzzlement it seems to have cost Raphael—when I was speaking to him in the Real World, *I could remember almost nothing of our lives together.* What kind of dolt must he have thought me! Now that I have come back here, I long to cry out to him, "I remember it all! How could I ever forget any of it?" But there my memories were irretrievable, and I knew I loved him without the blessing of remembered incident to tell me why. But then again, I understand the wisdom of the One in this. When we go there, we grow better than the people we were here; and forgetting the pain and difficulty of this gray world helps us live better in that place. It is part of our regeneration that we look back on what we once were with incredulity, amazement, embarrassment, as something done by someone other than us, something we could never have done—and yet we did do it, or we would not have reached the point where we could look back and disown it. But too much memory would be a weight to us; and so the One has ordained that we shall gradually let go of our memories, even in this world.

As for Raphael's strange statement that he is only dreaming these things, I know not what to make of it. How could he be dreaming? He has died, passed on to that world, and *I* am the one who dreams; and yet *he* is the latecomer, and I have been waiting there for him for I know not how long. This is proof, if ever it was needed, that time does not work in the same way in the Real World as it does in the Unreal World. Perhaps he only believes he is dreaming. And to compound the puzzle, *he* was the one who told *me* there that I have dreamed of that world for years, though when I am there, it is as though I can never remember that I am dreaming. How did he know that?

And stranger still was his account of having a life *after Vigia*. Of having married Miss Grancomb! As I write that name I laugh aloud, remembering the day when I thought her my rival. Now the mere idea is too absurd to cause me a moment's qualm. But it cannot be possible—that he did not die at Vigia, but went on to live and marry her. I know that it is impossible. Not so, however, what he said about me—that I shall die at the hands of Quinn, that I shall be shot by him; *that* indeed is all too possible. But of the rest of it I can make no sense. *I* am the one who is dreaming this, and yet Raphael says that *he* is the one who is dreaming it; he is the one who has died, and yet he says *I* have died. And I cannot speak to tell him how things really stand, because I am, at least in memory, so addled when I am there!

We spoke of these matters as we walked along the shore; and I confess I was half-distracted, and more than half-distracted, for I could feel nothing but his arm around me, and see nothing but his earnest face, looking down into mine; and I watched his mouth more than his eyes, as I could not get the thought of kissing him out of my mind.

At last he told me—diffidently, as if he thought I would disapprove!—that he wanted to take me in his arms and kiss me. He said he was afraid that if I did not remember him, I would not want him to do so. And *I* in my turn grew afraid that he would talk himself out of it! I could not bear it anymore—I stopped, and turned to him, and put my arms around him; but even as I did so, I found that he had put his arms around me.

Then—oh, oh, oh! I laugh and I blush and I am giddy here at my desk just thinking of it—he held me so close and so tight that his aura completely enveloped me—it was absolute bliss, bliss absolute—I have never known anything so wonderful. It was as if his aura and mine became one for that moment. My breath at first rose out of me in a foolish giggle, and then I could not have done anything foolish for all the world, for he was looking down into my face with—such a look! It was full of a great, ineffable, transcendent love; and yet full too of delight and desire—I cannot say how pleased I was to know that I pleased him so. Now I *do* have to stop in writing this, and take a breath, and fan myself, and I feel I have gone all moist, and that I am shaking all over, at the mere recollection of that look. Of that look and of that *touch,* for he held me against him tightly; and I thought in that moment that *that* world is infinitely more real than this one. Sweet as all his touchings were to me in this mortal realm, they were nothing to that moment when he pressed me to him in that other world.

Rapturous though it was, it seemed to me too long that he held me so, looking on me; and all my mind and body called to him, *Kiss me, kiss me, kiss me!* And I ran my hands up the back of his head, to encourage him, I suppose; and then he leaned to me, and I raised myself on tiptoe to meet him, and at last we kissed.

And kissed again, and again, until we knew that if we did not stop, it would be too much for us. So he only held me instead, and put his mouth to my ear, and said my name over and over, and each time he uttered it a thrill went through me that was almost unbearable. I could tell that he feared to hold me too tightly; but such a thing could never be, and instead I begged him, "Tighter! Hold me tighter!"

And with a will he did as I asked, pressing me to him until I could barely breathe. And how sweet it was!

Here the journal ended.

When Raphael had read this, he stood from his chair. He crossed the room, reeling a bit at first; then he paced; then he put the book away under lock and key; then he went outside. It happened to be in the late morning and, for a man of property who can call his time his own, it was a good hour for a walk; and Raphael, avoiding all his servants and laborers successfully, reached the welcome solitude of the park.

Though he was grateful to have that message from the other world, he could not help wishing he had more; for he was strongly inclined to believe that there had originally been more.

But he could not absent himself from the journal for long, and soon he was back in his office. He reread the concluding pages again; and after weeping again, and living through that exquisite moment one more time, he almost accidentally discovered a final comment written on the endpaper inside the back cover. It seemed to be an afterthought, perhaps added later on the very day Awen had concluded the volume.

Raphael's story—about how Quinn killed me—makes me think—something that frightens me—but only because I wonder if it is blasphemous and ungrateful—and that is, what if I *could* die? Then I could be there always, and with my love. Who would not rather live in that world? And Raphael told me that I *shall* die. So be it! May it happen soon! May it happen this very day, or if not today, tomorrow!

No, I shall not go out to meet death; but if death does come to me, at Quinn's hand or anyone else's, I shall not fear its approach; and as the shot pierces my heart, I shall smile, and greet the love and reality to which I go with a laugh of joy.

Chapter 58

... They stonde all writte i thy boke:
my dayes were fashioned, when as yet there was not
one of them.

—Psalm 139:16 (Coverdale)

And this is the sixth month with her, who was called
barren. For with God nothing shall be impossible.

—Luke 1:36–37

The day after Raphael finished reading Awen's journal, he rode over to Madgelet Lodge, ostensibly to see how Bessie was settling in, but just as urgently, to see if she could tell him anything about any continuation of Awen's account in other volumes. For he was certain that those volumes had once existed—that there was more to Awen's experiences in the Bright World than just those events leading up to his reunion with her there. Had anything else been saved from the burning? Had she fetched anything else away?

Bessie, however, told him bluntly, in reply to his question, that there had been nothing in her possession but the one book. He thought there was some ambiguity in her answer, and too much animus and protest in it; and he interrogated her as intently as he could without actually insulting her with the imputation that she was not dealing openly with him.

He accepted that she did not have any other volumes, he told her; but could she confirm that there *had* been other volumes?

Her mistress had had dozens of books of her own writing, she said, but she did not know what was in them—poetry, some of them, and stories, she knew that much. But they were all bound the same, and she could not tell one from the other; she had been in haste at the time and had been able to take only one as a memento.

Raphael found this plausible—she could not have carried all of Awen's literary output with her. But he asked if she had looked into the books at all, chosen among them, intentionally taken the journal?

Yes.

And why that?

She was particularly slow to respond on this point, and her phrasing was very evasive, but it came down to the fact that she had thought the journal might prove indirectly useful in supporting her charge against Mr. Quinn. He thought she must have looked through it—she must have seen Raphael's name in it. In fact, he thought it probable that she had looked through Awen's journals before and knew what she was searching for.

But why, then, had she not offered it in evidence?

She claimed to have been unable to bring it with her—it was already hidden in the woods on the day of the inquest, and she herself had been brought directly to Oakage from Rush Hill to testify.

It was all very strange and unsatisfactory; but she persisted in her story that she had only taken the one book that he now had, even when he offered her a further sum of money.

He was disappointed, but in the end he held his peace. He had at last realized that he must await the working out of his strange history, and that nothing he could do would hurry it along or reveal it before the time the One had set.

Over the next few months, he went to Madgelet Lodge often—and now not only to see Lucy and her family as before, but also to see how Bessie was faring. Lucy confessed some concerns about her: she did not get on well with the other servants, mostly because she never ceased speaking of the excellence of her former mistress and comparing her to Lucy, who seemed to her a far lower order of being. She also said strange things, things that unnerved her fellow servants, and even some of the children on occasion; and though Lucy could never find anything disturbing enough in them to merit an outright reprimand, she made a plea to Bessie to keep them to herself for the peace of the household. Lucy, in the gentle dizziness typical of her, could not give Raphael a coherent example of these utterances, but from what he could make out, they were somehow connected with inferences about life and death Bessie had drawn from reading Awen's diary.

And read it she had; Raphael soon had no doubt of that, from hints that Bessie let drop in his company, especially when those clues were combined with things she had said on the first day she had visited him. Like any good lady's maid of the time, she could read—Lucy confirmed that—but she read with agonizing slowness. Raphael thought that perhaps she had spent most of the months of her long unemployment eking a meaning out of the notebook, and had only waited so long to sell it to him because, once she had begun it, she meant to finish it.

She seemed to think that the account it gave was part reality and part imagination—an accurate assessment, though she herself could never have understood how it was so: that is, because reality and imagination are one and the same. She would have said that part of it was true and part of it was made up in Awen's mind as a kind of lyrical retelling of the truth, an attempt to describe her illicit passion for Raphael in fictional guise. Most likely she gave great weight to the fictional; as Awen's maid, she knew better than anyone that Awen had had few opportunities for contact with Raphael in what Bessie herself would have called "real life."

And yet by the same token, she knew, as anyone living closely with Awen must have, that the book had been written years before her mistress ever moved to Norfolk. And this gave it in her eyes the luster of prophecy. Its otherworldly quality as well must have teased and puzzled her and made her wonder if Awen and Raphael had indeed met in some faeryland beyond space and time. She was in all likelihood a country girl—her accent proved as much—and had imbibed the superstitions of the countryside with her mother's milk. And if she did in fact think of the Bright World as Faeryland, perhaps there was some truth in that identification. For who knew if ancient tales of faeries and magic lands were not some confused human attempt to rationalize glimpses of the Bright World or the beauty that seeped into this world from that?

Bessie's intrusion on his life with Awen grieved him, but only lightly. He felt their love would stand up to, would scorn and rebuff, any attempt to demean it by spying upon it. The bold, knowing glances Bessie gave him at times amused him as much as they annoyed him, and any irritation he might have felt over them was soothed away by her occasional expression of sympathy.

One afternoon he went to Madgelet Lodge on a sudden impulse. He could not have said what drew him; but he later thought he had somehow received information through some portal of the Bright World. He found Lucy, happy as ever among her growing children, but wearing a little cloud on her brow as she labored in a note to tell her brother that his plans for Bessie were come to naught.

She sent the children out of the room with the nursery maid and then explained. "Just this morning," she told him, "she came down to me with her coat on and her bag in hand and said she was leaving our service. She asked for a letter of reference, which of course I gave her—I was, for your sake, dear Brother, more cheerful in my statements about her as a servant than I might have been, and I said all the good things I could muster together, rather hastily, on one sheet in ten minutes. When she had the letter in hand, she told me she did not like working in a house with children. If you can imagine her saying *that*—and to *me*, of all people. Yes, she certainly came to the wrong place if children annoy her.—Do you know, I almost think she only stayed to get a good character—that she never meant to be here long."

"Did she give any indication of where she is going? To Norwich, or to London?"

"Oh, I expect she is going to London. I think she wants to set up as a lady's maid again. She said something about that, too; she seemed to feel she did not have quite enough precedence here; and I must say, that was true; but she made no attempt to earn it."

"These lady's maids!" said Raphael with a sad laugh. "How they do put on airs! Well, if she will have nothing to do with us, we cannot help that. Still, I am sorry to lose touch with her, for Awen's sake."

Now Lucy was silent; and her gaze at Raphael, always so worshipful and loving, was now a little troubled. He saw she had something she would like to ask, but would not dare to do so without encouragement.

"What is it, Lucy?" he asked.

She blushed—though a woman of forty–three, with sixteen children, she was still a little girl where her brother was concerned.

"I know that we spoke of this before," she said hesitantly. "It was on that day that I came to Fulkothing, after Awen died. And I know that . . . I remember what you told me then." He too, remembered the conversation at once: she had asked him whether there was any truth to the rumor about Awen and him.

"And what is it that causes you to doubt what I said?" he asked, with a calm directness, in a voice without defensiveness or hurt.

"It is not that I doubt it," protested Lucy.

"Then what is it?"

"It is only . . . Did it never vex you that Bessie accused you of . . . being improperly close to Awen?"

"Did Bessie say something more during her time here?"

"She said . . . that Awen loved you more than anyone."

He had been standing beside her writing desk, where she was still seated, though she had turned toward him in her chair; and he drew another chair close and sat beside her and took her hand.

"It is true that Awen did so," he said, "and true that I loved her as I have loved no one else. But I shall tell you again, for your own peace of mind, that we committed no adultery. I have sworn to that in public, and I shall swear to it again any time the need may be. But I shall tell you more now than I told you before: That I would have gone away with her if I could have."

"And I did not tell you then, though I thought it indeed," she said, "that I would have forgiven you for that if you had done it."

She was wiping away tears, and she gave a little laugh. "But then again, I would forgive *you* for anything, Raffy."

"Lucy, dear," he said, "I think you did tell me that then, or at least hint at it.—But now you must hear this part as well. It was she—she who would not allow it. And now—though you may or may not believe this—I am glad she did not. She chose the best course, and I am grateful to her—as ever!—for knowing what was right and doing it. I was blinded by my love for her, but her love for *me* gave her sight, and insight, and even vision, that I did not have at the time. Now I know that we shall meet again, beyond the grave. Nothing shall stand between us then—no sin that others have committed on earth. And for that eternity of love I shall gladly wait, and I shall gladly work to deserve it if I can."

He was silent for a moment, and Lucy wrung his hand in hers, weeping again, but smiling at him still.

"There is more to the story that I cannot tell you," he said then. "Much more, much more. But in all of it there is nothing that would make you ashamed of me—of that I am sure."

"And of that I, too, am sure," she said.

They sat for a few minutes further, strangely happy in the mutuality of their grief. Then Lucy spoke again in a troubled voice.

"But there is no giving in marriage in heaven," she said. "Scripture says so—Our Lord says so. I have always thought it a cruel thing, but so it says."

"There is no *giving* in marriage," said Raphael, "because we choose our own partners there. That is what I believe."

She smiled hopefully. "Do you mean that Reuben and I may be together there still?"

He laughed. "Aye," he said, "and have many more babies there, if you like."

She blushed with pleasure at the thought.

After Raphael left Madgelet Lodge, he made inquiries at the local inn, where the coaches stopped. He found that Bessie had gone to London. He did not attempt to pursue her: in that metropolis she would be utterly hidden from him.

He guessed that if she succeeded in her plans, he would never hear from her again. But if she were ever in trouble, he thought, she would reappear on his doorstep; and he would always be willing to take her in, no matter what foolish thing she had done.

◎ ◎ ◎

It was not until a year later that Bessie fell into trouble again. He had gone to London to have some legal papers drawn up, on matters that shall be told in their place. He had been in town for three days—his business was done, but he was about to visit Mr. Lissome, for he had asked that agent to gather together any books by Reverend Clowes that he might find on the market. He was in fact on the way out the door of the inn with Jackman when he met the maid coming in.

"Bessie!" he exclaimed.

She seemed not the least surprised to meet him. She must have had her sources of information in Norfolk still.

"Might I beg the favor of a few minutes with you, Mr. Kerr?" she asked. Her country brogue had been papered over with the affectation of a London accent, and she wore an unusually handsome dress for a lady's maid. With these accoutrements she had put on a certain superciliousness as well. He could see that the absence of Awen from her life had not been good for her character.

"Of course you may have a few minutes," he said warmly. "Come—the landlord has a private room here; we shall step into it.—Jackman, wait here for me." He showed Bessie into the room he had indicated and shut the door behind them.

"You are looking prosperous," he said to her with a smile.

"I am doing well, sir," she said, warming a little as she saw the unfeigned pleasure he took in her well-being.

"I am very glad to hear it—very glad. I had thought we would tempt you to stay in Norfolk, but I see you have secured yourself a good place here in town."

"That I have, sir—with Lady Namberlin."

"Ah," said Raphael. His delight for her took a blow at hearing this name, which did not have good associations. Bessie's belief that he would be impressed carried her along, however, and she did not notice his disappointment.

"Well," he said, "how can I be of service to you, Bessie?"

Her face took on a hard expression, as if her determination to profit were forcing conscience to submit.

"You once asked me about . . . more of that journal belonging to . . . the late lady whose name we shall not speak."

He was so shocked by sudden hope that he could not reply; he only stared at her.

"Well," she said, when she saw he was waiting for her to go on, "I have found the second volume."

He did not bother to ask her where she had found it, for he knew now that it had been in her possession all along. She had only been reading it herself and saving it, as one saves money in a bank account against a time of difficulty.

"How much do you need, Bessie?" he asked her.

"I would not have you think I am grasping, sir," she said.

"Come, come, Bessie—we have been through all that. You need money for your own purposes, and I am glad to be able to help you. How much do you need?"

"I was thinking, sir—this being the last volume and all—that you might be willing to . . . help me out more than you did last time."

"Do not be shy, my good woman—state your price."

"I was thinking, sir, that maybe . . . twenty guineas would be useful."

He would have given any amount to have that book, but even in his eagerness he kept firmly fixed in his mind that it was important not to let Bessie know how much he would pay.

"Twenty guineas!" he repeated, affecting amazement.

She was at once frightened that she had overreached. "Well, sir," she said, "say twenty pounds." Then something else crossed her mind, and she said, "Nay, I shall stick to my twenty guineas;

and you shall be glad, Mr. Kerr, that it was a friend to you who had this book in her possession and was willing to part with it to you."

He guessed at once that there was some reference in it to an act of love between Awen and him, and she was threatening him with disclosure. He would not have been greatly concerned about that, even if he had not been intent on obtaining the book; no one would think an account of the Bright World to be anything but a novel of the purest fantasy—no one would ever guess that he had been there and walked those shores and woods with Awen.

"But what do you need that much for?" he asked Bessie now, taking the opportunity to probe for information about her circumstances. "Does not Lady Namerlin pay you a good wage?"

"Oh, she does, sir," said Bessie. "When she pays."

"Ah, it is like that, is it? Well, I shall give you your twenty guineas—and though I shall not pretend I am not glad to have the book, if the guineas help you, I am glad of that, too."

She was at once relieved and grateful and even a little puzzled at the evident depth and sincerity of his good wishes for her. *Poor creature,* he thought to himself. *To have lived for fifteen years in the company of someone who is as close to a true angel as this earth can see and not to have learned some heavenly graces from her! You have missed an opportunity indeed, Miss Fallows.*

To her he said nothing of these misgivings. They completed the transaction, for all the world as though he had been buying a pair of gloves. When he had the volume in his hands, he was so weakened by it that he had to sit down. It was as if it opened a portal into the Bright World, through which Awen's aura streamed into him, or as if suddenly he could feel her presence right there on the other side of the divide between them.

"I must go, sir," said Bessie then.

"One moment," he said.

She wanted very much to leave as quickly as possible now; he could see that, and he guessed why.

"You once told me that you only took one volume of your mistress's writings."

"I did, sir," she said in a defensive tone. "But that was because I had misplaced this second volume. I did not want you to be angry at me for losing it. The other day I found it again among my things—that is all; and I knew you would want it."

"Bessie," he said, "if you give me the rest of the books you have, I shall set you up in an annuity. You will never have to work again. How much does Lady Namberlin pay you in a year? Ten pounds? Fifteen? When she *does* pay you, as yourself have said—that is the rub. I shall give you one hundred pounds per year until you die; only you must give me all the books that belonged to Awen, and you must give them to me *now.*"

But evidently Bessie had no more. After Raphael saw her reaction, he fully believed her little store to be exhausted; for she went pale and rolled her eyes in a kind of agony at the thought of what she might have had if she had only stolen even a few more of the many volumes her former mistress had written.

"I *have* no more, sir," she said, in a tone of anguish. "Would that I did, sir!"

He considered her in silence for a minute longer.

"Well," he said, "if you grow tired of waiting on bankrupt elegance, come back to Norfolk and I shall find you employment again."

"Oh, I shall *not* go back to the country again," vowed Bessie with considerable maidish hauteur.

"As I say, if you ever grow tired of the town, come to me. If I am still living, I shall do my best for you.—Tell me, Bessie, do you miss your old mistress?"

At this question Bessie looked sullen at first, as if she did not like to admit the worth and value of her old circumstances; but then tears welled up into her eyes despite her, and she said, "I do, sir. She was good to me, though she was a simple lady, in her way."

"By 'simple' I take it you mean good, and virtuous, and kind, and forgiving, and patient, and tolerant."

"She was all that," admitted Bessie. And then she added, "But *I* am not, sir. I cannot be a saint like her. When people do me wrong, I like to pay them back—I cannot help it."

"And she never did you wrong, did she, Bessie?"

"No, sir. Of all the people I've ever known, she was the only one as never did me no wrong."

"Have I done you wrong?"

"No, sir. You've treated me better than I've treated you."

"Well, if that is so, I am glad of it." It was on the tip of his tongue to add a moral lesson about doing better to others than they expected; but he kept his silence on that point, sensing that the thoughts he had kneaded lightly into the inelastic dough of her understanding might work most effectively if they were left to ferment and were not pressed in overmuch.

He rose to his feet, still clutching the book tightly in his hand. "Do remember my offer, Bessie," he said.

She was unable to speak. He had never before seen her so moved, or guessed her to be capable of such grateful emotion. She curtsied, hastily and silently, and then left him.

That was the last he ever saw or heard of Bessie Fallows; but to tell the truth, as he stood there, after she had gone, looking down at the book in his hand in a kind of wonder, he forgot about her entirely for that time; and if anyone had spoken her name in the next minute, he would have had to struggle to recall who she was.

✯ ✯ ✯

He hid the journal within his shirt and wore it about with him for the rest of that day. His business with the bookseller he conducted in a half-dream, and even with some distaste; for who would care about the conjectures of an apostle like Clowes, writing at a remove from the truth, when he had in his possession the testimony of a witness to it? Still, he gathered all he could of any literature pertaining to the travels and teachings of the Wonderful, because he knew that in times to come he would want every scrap of writing on the topic of the Bright World.

He did not dare open Awen's journal until he returned to Norfolk. Once he began it, he would care for nothing else; and so he restrained his passion and his curiosity until he sat by the fire in his own study again, with the cat in the chair opposite, and the door locked and the servants forbidden to disturb him.

But then he read; and it was, for him, like falling into a trance, a dream of reality, though not real as the Real World was.

She told of that happy interval of days between his arrival and their wedding. There were many details he had not known and which were very welcome to him to learn. He recalled one time in those days when they had met Prima in the city, and she had taken Awen aside to speak with her.

We went out onto one of the terraces overlooking the lake—though I would only consent to go apart from Raphael on condition that I could still look back and see him sitting by the table inside; which I did from time to time, just as he stole long looks at me. Prima put her arms around me, and put her mouth to my ear and said, "How did you ever find this one?"

"That is a silly question," I said, laughing at her teasing. "You know that *he* found *me*."

"But in the other life, I mean. He was your husband there—you always said so. Do you remember anything of your life with him?"

"Not a great deal," I had to admit. "But since he has come to me, I have remembered more, and he has told me more. I saved his life, that is what he says. He was in a shipwreck, and at the risk of my own life, I rowed out to the wreck in a gale and rescued him."

"Ah!" she said excitedly. "It is a representation of your love!"

"Do you think so?"

"Do you not see? You saved his life; and life stands for the soul. You saved his soul from a fate that would have sent him to the Dark Lands."

"If I have done any such thing, then I shall give thanks to the One forever; but I think, or rather I *know,* that Raphael saved me."

But she would not listen to any such thing, and chattered away in my ear about the representation of it all; and we kept looking back at Raphael, to tease him; and he smiled at us in such a kind and humorous way that after a few more minutes, I could not endure to be apart from him by even as much as a few yards, but must go back and hang on him and pester him with kisses, which in truth he did not seem to mind at all.

From the evening of their wedding day until the time he had seen her in the city square, they had been apart, he going with a band of men to the Tower of the Groom's Waiting, and she to another place with a group of her friends. She described this gathering, and said something of the Secrets of Wives that matched the Secrets of Husbands, which he had been told by the men. He would have refrained from reading them, but for two considerations: one was that she said explicitly that she would set down only those that she had already known from her marriage with him in the Dim World; and the other was that he knew that when he went to join her in that other world, his memory of them would be lost to him.

We went to the House of the Bride's Waiting. It is on a rocky spur of the great hill on which the City has been built; and though it is no more than a mile from the City, I had never seen it before. Indeed, I did not know it even existed; and I suspect that until a woman is about to be married, she may not be able to see it. It is formed of a circular base of white stone—something more lustrous than marble—with columns set around its circumference. These columns support joined plinths of the same white stone, but that is all: there is no roof above them. Thus it is open to the air on all sides and overhead.

Inside the circumference, couches are arrayed, on which one may lie and look out at the moon and stars and feel the breeze rising up the land. Before one enters the place, it seems to contain too small an area for anything but this ring of beds; but as is often the case in buildings in the Real World, once one steps inside, one finds the interior is far more extensive than it appeared to be from without. (My friends tell me that this appearance is symbolic of the unexpected depth of our inner lives: we believe not only others but we ourselves are shallower than in truth we are.) In this greater depth of the interior of the House of Waiting there is ample room for a sunken garden at the very center. The moment I saw that garden I felt it to be familiar, but it was not until I came back into the Unreal World and regained my memories of my past here that I realized what it reminded me of: the garden on Vigia. It is far smaller, and not naturally formed—rather, it is built with great artistry, being hollowed from the very stone and supplied with rich earth and with provision for drainage. Its flowers are so lush that the air is heavy with their scent. Within the garden, which is also circular in shape, are stone benches, remarkable in themselves: they might really be said to be simply one bench, for they are carved from the living rock in the shape of an unbroken ring, and one must step over the seats to enter it. Around the ring is a space of turf only about a yard wide, which leaves the plantings almost pressing upon one on all sides with their nodding blooms. It seems to have been purposely made small, in fact, so that the bride and her friends will sit close together on the stone benches. From the first glimpse I had of it I thought of comfortable privacy and secrets shared among sisters.

We did not go down into this garden immediately. We had a light meal at a table in the upper temple—or rather, my friends had a meal, for I could scarcely be coaxed to eat anything, so elated and eager I was, for the morrow to come; and indeed *there* it does not matter if one eats at all, except for what the food and the act of eating symbolizes. Then the others led me down into the garden, by a set of narrow steps set into the round wall of the place, and made me sit among them; and for a few minutes they were silent, even oddly silent, as if impressed by the magnitude of the bond I was about to undertake and the change that was to come to me; and yet during this silence they were very close to me, some sitting beside me, some kneeling before me, some standing behind me, caressing my hair and shoulders and sometimes kissing my hands and cheeks and making much of me, all in silence; and some wept and some only smiled.

Finally I could not endure the mystery of it anymore, and I said, "What is it? You are all so moved by—some particular thing."

Then it was as if they spell was broken, and they laughed gently, and sat in more orderly fashion on the benches. When they had taken their places, they looked to one of the elders of the City (though she looked the youngest of us all), whom I shall call Principia; and she, having their attention, said, "My dear, we are here to tell you the Secrets of Wives."

"Ah!" I said—joyously, as I am sure they knew, for I had heard of these mysterious secrets, but could never prevail upon anyone to say more of them. They smiled at my eagerness.

"You are ready to hear them, I think?" said Principia.

"Indeed I am."

"Well, hear them you shall; but first you must make several promises to us."

"And what are they?"

"The first is that you must never reveal these secrets to anyone, except to another bride-to-be on her wedding eve."

"That I cannot promise," I said. "For I shall have no secrets from my husband."

They were very pleased with this answer, and smiled and nodded at one another when they heard it. I realized that it had been some kind of test.

"That is right, my dear," said Principia. "But he will not ask you these secrets. It is very cleverly managed, you see: He is even now in the Tor of the Groom's Waiting, being told the Secrets of Husbands. And before he is told them, he must promise never to ask *you* the Secrets of Wives, and to bind any other man to this same promise before he reveals his own secrets. So we must also require that you never ask your husband the Secrets of Husbands; and that when you pass on the Secrets of Wives, you make it a condition of the one you tell that she similarly promise."

"I see that this must be the way the One has ordered things," I said.

"Indeed it is."

"Then under those terms I can consent," I said. "But am I not likely to *guess* some of the Secrets of Husbands from time to time? And is my husband not likely to *guess* some of the Secrets of Wives?"

"Of course. Even if he does not guess them outright, he will know them without knowing he knows them; for he will see what you do and how you act toward him. Between him and you these will not be secrets, but unspoken acts of love."

Then they told me these secrets. They spoke together, as people sometimes do there, from their minds to mine—images pouring into my mind. I could not now recount the things they said, not because they were so numerous, but because they were so rich. There is no way to put them into words; even trying to understand them here is difficult, though in that world I will know them forever because I heard them once.

There were, however, some secrets that I recognized from my marriage with Raphael in the Unreal World, and I was glad to discover that I knew them already; those I can retell.

First of all, a wife must remember that she is not a lone and single person who happens to be living in the company of another lone and single person. She is one of a pair; and the pair must work together, before all other things they do, or they will never be anything more than lone individuals deluding themselves that they are married. Besides, the great joy and pleasure of marriage lies in working together, whether in the house or outside it, whether in the difficulties of life or the pleasures of the bed.

Second, a wife must be kind, no matter how vexing her husband may be. She will not accomplish anything good by being mean or by speaking caustically. She may force her husband to do what she wishes, but he will not respect her; and if she does not have his respect, then the marriage will not be a true marriage. He may indeed love her, or pity her; he may indeed obey her, or pretend to; but if he does not respect her, she may as well walk away from him, as she will only be fooling herself that she has anything real.

Third, and related to the second, is that she must never try to force him to do anything. There are evil secrets of marriage as well as good ones; the evil secrets are taught in the Lands of Darkness, and they are all about coercion and cruelty. A wife must arm herself against those evil practices. She may rightly and properly try to persuade him with reason and with loving speech; and indeed if she believes he is going wrong, it is her duty to give him her counsel, no matter how painful her doing so may be to them both; but she must never use means beyond reason and kindness—never, for example, trick him, or lie to him, or withhold herself, in mind or speech or person, to compel him to obey her. One common practice that a wife learns from the Lands of Darkness is to attack her husband, angrily and secretly and subtly, pretending all the while that she is being passive; and the worst part of this evil is that a wife may not even recognize that she is falling into it. In short, she must never domineer over her husband, but must consider herself his equal, even striving to consider him her superior; for if she strives to do that, she may succeed in at least seeing him as her peer. This is why the Apostle said that a wife ought to submit to her husband—meaning not to submit as does a slave, but only that she ought not to be utterly intractable. To avoid this, she ought to cultivate in herself an adoration for him, and show the strength of that feeling for him as much as possible. And he, for his part, will cultivate an adoration of her. Not that this adoration will in any way mar their adoration of the One; rather, it will increase that adoration, being a visible shadow of it, just as the visible shadow of a thing gives depth and reality to that object.

Fourth, she ought to take pains to remain desirable to him throughout her life. If he desires her, he will be more likely to respect and listen to her. If she abandons herself to gluttony and slovenliness, he will feel that she has abandoned him and their marriage; he will feel betrayed, and will be more likely to feel justified in looking elsewhere for love.

Fifth, she ought actively to set out to learn what he enjoys in bed. For most women, the pleasures of the bed are something they think of as *happening to them,* not something they actively engage in. Such a woman thinks her husband is responsible for arousing her and himself to the act of love; she lies back passively and lets him do all. But there come times and seasons in a marriage when the man is moody or discouraged, and he needs her to arouse him. If she has never learned how to do so, the bloom of their life in bed will wither and dry and die, and it will be very difficult to make it green again. In other words, she should not always be as unknowing as a bride, but discover and store up knowledge of what pleases him against the day they both will need it.

Sixth—and this is one of the greatest secrets of all, and the one most wives never even begin to grasp—she ought to be willing always for the pleasures of the bed, unless (as happens sometimes in the Unreal World, though not in the Real World) she is unable because of sickness or exhaustion or some obligation she is under. If she is willing to take her husband between her legs even for the briefest of delights first thing upon waking, she will grant him serenity for the rest of the day; if she will indulge with him in longer and deeper sport by night, she will confirm him in love for her more and more as time passes.

She went on to tell of how she and her friends spent another hour in further conversation and then slept in the House of the Bride's Waiting, on the couches that ringed the main floor. And then she wrote of their wedding; of that and the day-long celebration after it, and of how at last they had departed for their home; and when he came to her account of the end of that day, his heart beat both slowly and with furious pressure, and he gripped the book tightly; for this was what she wrote:

And so at last we were come to the same room, alone, and in the right time; and stood facing one another, at a little distance, still fully clothed in our wedding raiment. Our auras were burning bright around us, and throbbing audibly with something between a whisper and a music, between a sigh and a cry; and whorls of light spun up from my loins and his and off the paps of my breasts and whirled through air and fell kissingly each on the others' loins; and something like sparks or stars were shed from his eyes and lips and my eyes and lips, and waves of lightning light undulated forth from the curve of his shoulders and sides and the same of mine, and these sparks and waves met in the air between us and passed through one another, crackling faintly and then colliding with our flesh and stinging and warming it and raising a heat in it and prickling it; and these sendings of our auras plucked at us and tugged at us where our senses were gathered and sweetest, and so I could feel his aura tugging at my paps and at the lips between my legs until they grew as hard as young fruits; and my blood (and they say blood is the symbol of life and the soul) hummed shudderingly in my ears, and indeed, I thought I could hear his own as well.

And it came to me that I could give him the gift of disrobing first; and this I did, in love for him, eager to please; and I took off my gown slowly, to prolong his pleasure and to tease him in the doing of it, making myself naked by degrees until I stood before him, all my body exposed; and I almost felt rather than saw (for I could not take my eyes from him) how my aura was sloughing off dim shells of light in the form of my body and pressing them in midair against the similar dim forms that radiated from him; and as his eyes moved over my body, they roused it still more, so that when he looked at my breasts, I became as awake to desire there as he did in looking there; and likewise my wholeness, from head to toes; for he looked at all of me, lingeringly, until my whole body burned rapturously with his looking. All this latter while, I was brushing my hair; and as I did so, the One graced me with a sweet memory from our first life together, how he used to love to watch me brush my hair—indeed, were I clothed or not, but especially when I was not; and as each curve of my body shook and moved in that act of grooming, more and more the waves of light were shaken from them and sped to him; and I grasped in a minute or two of this how I might speed them to him all the faster, as one blows a kiss; and those aural sendings of my love fairly battered him with their sweetness, as one pummels one's beloved with blossoms.

Then I ceased brushing my hair, and put aside the brush, and waited for him in my turn, full of delight at being naked before him.

He took off his own wedding raiment—though not as I did, teasingly and in full awareness what a riot of pleasure I caused in him, but like a man; not hastily, but (I might say) like one more mindful of the business he is about, and intent on it, namely, to enter between my legs; yes, with his mind set on that. And he stood before me and the organ of his love was not only fully erect, but straining and throbbing visibly with the pulse of his blood and heart; and with each pulse it shed the shells of light I have described, but upward, in a long, slow trajectory from the end of his wand of love, toward me, arcing downward; and some of those rings and circlets of dim light grew wide and fell over me like coils of capturing rope, and some remained small and spattered with an audible rainy splash against the golden hair of my belly's angle, causing an electric tingle to run through my loins from lips to deep womb.

And with the pattering of that light against my sex, and with the sweet squeezing embrace of those gleaming rings about my shoulders and arms and waist, I lost my sense of self—I became a self with him. I wanted only to join him, and in so joining to become something more than I was or than he was.

It came to me then, as the rapture began to mount up in my body (and this before he had even touched me, but even while we still stood a dozen feet apart, looking at one another), that I had another sweet gift to give him; and that was in the manner of my lying down. And I went to the bed and turned back the covers; and I lay down on my belly, flat on the bed, turning my face away from him, but opening my legs. And it was as if to say, *You are welcome to me, my love;* and my turning my face away was a symbol of how he and I had turned our selves away from our selves and joined in one higher oneness symbolic of the One.

And he understood the invitation—how could he not? And he came to me and lay on me. How sweet his weight! All lithe muscle and sturdy bone and sweet organs—heart and lungs and eyes and brain beloved to me in every way. I could only have wished that weight upon me was ten times, a thousand times more, and so it would have seemed to me ten or a thousand times sweeter—if that were possible, for it seemed infinitely sweet and perfect as it was. And I opened my legs and moved and raised myself to him, and he entered me; and my loins embraced his wand.

And there leapt through me such a current of delight that I thought I would die, though in that world one cannot die. But maybe I did die—die to ancient loneliness and solitude, bisectitude and dimidation, waiting and postponement, sorrow and grief, forlornment and loss. If I became more than I was in that moment, yet I cried out with a cry that was a woman's cry, for at his mere touch and entry all of my ecstasy was loosed in a torrent in which consciousness nearly drowned.

I have died again, in the sexual sense, in the remembering and writing of this.

I wish I could tell what next we did—or what he did, for in that meeting after so many years, I played the symbol of the receiver. But I cannot mark out the individual movements, the comings and goings of it all. All I can say is that he made love to me for an unknown time after that, masterfully, taking his leisure of that event so long yearned-for. It was as if I were bound to a stake on the shore of a warm and fragrant ocean, and the waves rose higher and higher, slapping at me, leaping at me, surging around me, finally smothering me with sheer delight. As this wondrous tide rose, I grew dizzy, I wept, I cried out to him, I sobbed, I even think I babbled from time to time in a breathless whisper, a nonsense of endearments; and still he loved me, on and on; and every time I thought there was no more pleasure to be had in all of my body, he found more.

All around us the whole time there was the play of wild but soft and gentle light, sometimes of the purest gold, sometimes of vibrant color, glimmering in the dusky night. A breeze breathed over us to cool us in our warm work, bearing a scent of lake water and lavender and exotic oils—citrus and musk and bee's wax and coconut and what I have heard some call lang-lang. There was music, indescribable, wrought out of our cries and breathings, out of the frictions and slidings of our bodies, and it was like no hymn I have ever heard. It seemed that approving stars danced through the room and the earth trembled in envy.

When at last he joined me—then was a mighty reckoning made and paid between us; and I know that I gave him as much as ever he gave to me. As he lay shuddering upon me, stunned and gasping, I slipped about, turned so that I could hold him in my arms. Then I held his head against my breasts, and it seemed we had become a song, a single syllable of song, a single note and word, uttered by the One, and that we were flying over the abyss of time and the universe, flying toward the center and heart of the One; until the One blessed us with a deep sleep.

The reading of this account was scarcely to be borne by material flesh; for only in the other world could desire endure such provocation, much less fulfill itself. Trammeled by physical body as he was in this world, after he had finished this passage Raphael was deranged for some time by his longing for Awen; but his insanity took the form of stupor, and he lay unknowing and unseeing, reliving that moment inwardly; and during those hours, it seemed to him that Awen was with him, in his very presence, only on the other side of whatever barrier or veil it was that divided the Dim World from the Bright World. It seemed to him that in that realer world (superterminous with this world as it was, superpenetrating it and overlapping it, in its placelessness and timelessness) Awen lay at his side, even lay with her breasts against him; or that he was, briefly, nearly in the very body that he had in that other world.

But gradually the intensity of his reaction ebbed; and coming out of his unconscious state, he found that poor flesh had reacted in the only way it could, and that he had spontaneously cast his seed, and that in preternaturally copious quantity, while he had been unaware of his physical life. He changed his clothing and then stood for a time by the window, looking down on the broad hill before Fulkothing, a favorite view because she had once walked there, on the day when she had met him in the Paradise.

But his thoughts remained on her account of their lovemaking. He marveled that she had been able to see so much more than he had. She had experienced it far more deeply; she had seen spiritual representations to which he had been blind. Was that because he still slept in the material world during his visits to the Bright World? No—she had visited there at first under the same conditions, and yet she had seen and described these spiritual signs even then. It was only another proof that she was far in advance of him spiritually. And as he understood this proof, his heart soared with delight and pride in her. Someday he might be as wise as was she, he hoped; but in the meantime, it was enough to partake of her wisdom in the reflection that her love threw upon him. She was his wife; and never, he thought, had a man been more proud of his spouse and more grateful to be connected to her.

In his later reading in the journal, on another day, he found a further passage that encouraged him to believe that he would, in that other world, grow in his power to experience as Awen did. This entry was from a time, or a series of events, long after those of which he himself had known. For he now saw that this notebook contained events in time to come, written as though they were past; events that not only *had not* happened, but if the Wonderful was correct, still *might not* happen. These very notebooks were one of those things that the One would unwrite if Raphael failed to deserve his own wife; but it was comforting to him to see what he might yet accomplish, if he found his way properly.

Awen wrote:

> It is strange to think how it is not known in the Dim World that the act of love is of all acts the most holy, or at least that it ought to be the most holy, because it is the most symbolic of our joining those qualities we lack to make us images of the One. Perhaps it is precisely *because* it is the most holy that it is capable of becoming so horrible when it is profaned. Rape is, in symbol, the absolute denial of all Love, and so it is the absolute denial of the One. Only murder is worse, for that is the denial of life itself; in fact, it is the denial both of the One and of all things given by the One—as all things are.

And yet how ill-equipped we are to experience the holiness of that act. How does that deficiency come about? It can only be because as we leave childhood behind and progress into adulthood, where the overtly sexual part of our lives begins, we leave behind as well the very power that we need to make sexual love beautiful and deep, to make it consonant with our innerness. And by that power I mean the imagination; and by the imagination I mean the power of the mind to open itself to the infinite and abundant inflow of the Divine Mind and to render back images of eloquent beauty, whether of rich detail or elegant spareness. For we are nothing but the content of our thoughts; and that which we wish the world to be, we can make through the power of reflecting the Divine that constantly moves into us. The One creates and recreates us and all things at every moment, pouring into us its spiritual substance; otherwise neither we nor anything would subsist for even a fraction of an instant.

To bring to the act of love a mind open to the Divine that breathes into us on all sides from the Omnipresent One—to transmute that Divine into love expressed by our bodies— that is the work of *imagination* in love. My Raphael has always known that instinctively; but in the Real World, his abilities have grown and doubled and tripled and ascended, yea, by the exponential power, so that to yield myself in love to him is to surrender my little self to a oneness greater than either of us. At times when he looks at me with that look a lover gives his lover, and I know that he wants me, and I know that I therefore want him, I feel that strange mingling of fear and delight that a climber of mountains must know. To truly love, one must be thrilled by the terror one feels in the presence of intimacy. The wise have said that in the deeper realms, husbands and wives are bound together by a kind of force, a gravitation of desire, revolving around one another, spinning on a common axis, facing one another; because in one another they each face their wholeness and thus the One; and that for the uninitiated, this revolution would be, even for two who love each other as Raphael and I do, terrifying and intense. And yet we are told that he and I shall one day, as we are transmuted into new forms of spirit in deeper realms, achieve that binding force and find in it the ultimate delight, a kind of continual lovemaking and procreation, but infinitely more complex, involving as it does every aspect of our being. Then our minds shall be open wide to the inpouring images of the Divine, and we shall become *all* imagination, and create and procreate constantly as the One moves through us.

In her journal he caught beautiful vistas of their quotidian life (if that adjective could be applied to life there) among the Image Makers, in aspects previously unknown to him. He had never heard during his time among those people, for example, that they loved to sail on the lake as a pastime, and that at certain times of the year nearly the entire citizenry left its studies in the city to take to sailboats. She described one such event thus:

The wind came up very fresh in the afternoon—and all the city, having patiently anticipated this change in the weather for some time, greeted the rustle it made in the curtains at the windows and the papers on their desks as they would have started up at the voice of a friend returning from the absence of a year. From home and study they poured out into the streets; some thronged to the gates to meet the messenger from the shore who had been posted to watch for this alteration. "Fresh but favorable," were his words; and then we hastened out of the city and down the hill, with avid steps, carrying our gear— sail and tackle, knit and woven jackets, sailing caps and shoes. The boathouse was all a bustle, neighbors helping neighbors launch boats and step masts; and one by one the boats sprang away from the long quay, spread their wings, and flew off to the starting point of their appointed race. The wind was delicious—full of strength, but nothing fearsome; full of the scent of pine, arborvitae, balsam that it brought from far shores, and also of the clean fragrance of clear waters over which it had sped in its journey; and coolish, but not chilly, so that Raphael must wear the jacket I knitted for him, and looked (if I may say) the handsomest of all. But in the Real World a wife cannot have the petty pleasure of being the envy of other wives, for all love their own husbands too well; and so I happily enjoyed the looking at him, as our little boat sped along, knowing that no one could know how fine he is as well as I do.

Our race was for couples without children—our boats being lighter and smaller than the family boats. After much humorous striving and jostling, we were all lined up approximately on the starting line, and then at the signal set off up the wind. At first we must tack this way and that—and this, they say, is symbolic: that marriages at first go every which way but straight, and must fight their way into the opposition of what seems like circumstance, but is in fact the very wind that shall one day carry them down to completion. Raphael and I worked perfectly together, and between us we proved a canny crew; for we rounded the turn, though not actually first, at least among the frontrunners.

That—the long stretch home with the wind at our backs—was the finest part of the day. We sat side by side at the stern, with only the tiller between us (not sufficient barrier to prevent my love from putting his arm around me) and we flew before the wind so swiftly we scarcely could hear it in the lines. The afternoon light was blazing on all the waters to the west and casting a glow of mellow gold on the creamy sails; song and laughter carried to us from the boats of our loving friends, and we saw their smiling faces and returned their waves of greeting. And somewhere in that fine sail to the finish line, I realized that this part, too, was a symbol: of the race home to the perfecting of marriage, borne by a divine wind, and that all who reached the goal, whether first or last, are victors.

Shortly after the account of that day's sail, she wrote of her pregnancy. He had looked forward to this moment eagerly in his reading, but he could never have foreseen how it would come about.

After our return from our honeymoon, we prayed for our lost child to be given back to us, and then offered up that longing to the will of the One. I shall not say we have not thought of it since; indeed, we have often spoken of it. But we did so in the awareness that it was not within our own providing, but in the providence of the One; and we accepted the outcome even before we knew what it was to be.

Last night we learned something of that future. We had dined with Altera and her family, and returned to our house on the island shortly after sunset. We swam briefly in the lake and then went to bed, as eager as ever we were, in our days on Vigia, to join in love again, as if we had not done so in weeks.

Often of late we have begun our love with a kind of ceremony of intoxication: we lie face to face, or I should say body to body, kissing almost without pause, and touching each other with our hands; and this for time without reckoning. Time is so different there anyway, but in one way it seems we lie so for days, and yet in another it seems only a few minutes, and not long enough to satisfy us. And then by almost imperceptible degrees, and still close within my arms the while, Raphael mounts me and enters me and we become a rhythm of mutual moving.

That occasion was the same up to that point of entry and joining; but last night when he entered me all was different. I had a sense of vastness bursting into my loins, straining the very fibers of my sex; I cried out, not in pain but joy, and gripped my love to me the more tightly with my legs and arms, holding him against my sex with all my might. And I felt a great flow begin to move into me there; it was as if I had become an ancient land, a forest, through which a river a mile deep and a mile wide flowed in spate out of lakes in high mountain ranges heated by volcanic fire. I could tell that Raphael felt the difference also, for he gripped me both tenderly and tightly in his arms. He seemed to become larger in all of his body, not just his member, and in his embrace I felt like a fallen bird cradled with perfect gentleness in a protecting hand. And still the stream went on, pouring and pouring into me, infinite in richness, and I infinitely capacious to receive it; and only gradually did we realize that it was indeed the sensed symbol of a stream of seed.

And even while we were thus locked together in love, in that vast sowing and receiving, groaning breathlessly with delight, we next became aware that we were in some *other where*. We were transported inward, as I think now, into some deeper realm. The fragrant darkness of our room fell away, as did even the bed beneath us, and we were lying in a bed of— what shall I call it?—crystalline air, or say that we were lying on a warm wind, but supported by it, moving with great speed in the direction of the flow that coursed out of him and into me, spiraling as we went, so that sometimes up was down and down was up. There was a roaring music in our ears, like the sound of a cataract, and I believe it was somehow the sound of that torrent of seed entering me.

Then we stopped whirling and traversing. There were visions beside us and around us, strange ceremonies, deep events, which at the time we were barely aware of, for we were transfixed in the ecstasy of that sowing; but those external visions affixed themselves in our memories even though we did not fully *see* and *hear* them as they transpired, and we remembered them later as if we had seen nothing but their strange shapings.

We heard a strain of the hymn from our wedding day— nay, not a strain, but a single note—yet richer, fuller, rendered out of ten thousand seraphic breasts and throats. Hearing it we knew that it was the One making utterance through the One's own creation—it was the MAKING WORD of the One—it was the One's Word, uttered once in eternity. Taking up the theme of that wedding hymn, the vision showed us worlds being formed, and then forms of life springing up out of nothing, out of powdered rock and seawater, bitter salts and sweet sunlight. Those forms—at first mere motes of life—accreted, organized, became larger entities, and then it was as if a huge blossoming of life took place, and from those minute forms all other forms proceeded, following only the dictates of divine order, the laws and rules the One had given. Laws they might be, and yet there was freedom, endless freedom to be and to become within their scope; and some creatures failed, and some throve, and yet all was within the providence of the One; and finally, within this procession of beings, humankind arose. As it came forth, by degrees that were slow in epoch but telescoped in our vision into fractions of fleeting seconds, all of creation grew bright with a flash of joyous light, for here at last was a being that could give forth the One in symbol; for the One is human, though not mere human, not some spirit person sitting in one place and one time, but humanity infinitized, if such a paradox can be conceived. Or perhaps the great paradox is to think that we ourselves are a fractionation of Divinity.

Still more wonderful than the unfoldment of living form into humankind was that we saw the human form itself, once achieved, change and become a new form, still more unexpected, still more beautiful; and this is the future of humankind: to grow always, not only in spirit, but in form, into new beatitude of being.

Around us now we felt, more than saw, the chorus through whom the One had sung that hymnic note, looking on our holy lovemaking with solemn and joyous approval. They seemed to us airy beings, or rather beings made of light; or as if their blood was light itself and we could see it coursing through their veins, and as if they breathed light and we could see it filling out their lungs; or as if they *thought* light and we could see their thoughts radiating from their minds. They were beings of those inner realms, or so I believe. Thus shall Raphael and I be someday, if the One is willing.

And as we loved on, convulsed with the inpouring of the seed, one of those benignant watchers, a woman, came close to the side of our bedless bed, carrying in her arms a little baby wrapped in a gleaming blanket. As I became aware of the child, a pain lanced through my womb, sharp but still joyous—a pang of buried memory. In that world I cannot recall my child, except from time to time as Raphael (who remembers much more than I do) brings it back to my mind. But when the child was brought to us, I remembered everything, or at least all my *carrying* of her, for my *birthing* of her, terrible as it was, has been effaced from my mind there, I do believe.

And still we loved on, absorbed in one another, while the vision glowed at the edges of our understanding, storing itself in our minds to be later re-seen and comprehended.

The child grew—wriggled out of her divine nursemaid's arms, stood beside us, watching solemnly and curiously her own symboled conception—seeing who knows what symbol of the One made One. Into a woman in her own right she grew, youthful, tall, fair-haired, beautiful, graceful, loving, kind, sweet-tempered, wise—but playful, keenly interested in the ways of humankind and the One, and especially curious about all of the interwoven paths of the creatures of the natural world.

And we heard her speak; softly, as if not to disturb us as we loved: *My Father and Mother—I thank you! May the One bless you as you have blessed me. You brought me forth not once but twice from your seed and womb; may the One likewise give you rebirth into deeper realms of being.*

Someone else came forward—a youth. She turned to him as one irresistibly drawn. They joined hands; they spoke to one another in low voices that we could not hear over the still-resonant echoes of the Word, over our own love cries. They knelt together and prayed—it was a symbol of their marriage, as it seems to me, for thus had our own first wedding been; they rose and began to dance. And lo, as they danced, we saw all time passing, passing *for* them, *in* them, *around* them. We saw their many forms, representing the One: working together, playing together, loving together, bearing their own children; then we saw them transmuting slowly into beings of the inner realms, ascending closer and closer to the Center where dwells the One. And that seemed our own story as well, our own progression to what we are to be; and there were times I did not know if my daughter was I or she, for she was she but symboled me.

Finally we realized that they (or was it ourselves we saw?) were returning to the One, and yet not returning, never finally returning; and we knew that all life is an infinite stream pouring out of the One and returning to it without cessation. Our lives in eternity are a constant return. Praise be to the One!

(At this moment, writing this, I think of death and I laugh. What is death? It is not even as much as when a child falls down and weeps a few tears and then runs on to rejoin his companions, forgetting the event that gave him, for a time, overmastering pain and sorrow.)

Now the vision passed away from us. We were in our own bed, lying locked in fierce embrace, I impaled upon his manhood, he engulfed by my deep womanhood; and final ecstasy broke through our bodies in a mighty storm, and I tilted back my head and cried out as though I had the breath of that myriad chorus all in myself.

Then it was over.

We lay thus grappled together for—hours, was it? What is time to lovers? When at last we could move, we found we lay in a veritable pool of our own love, and the deep flowings we had felt when in the act had some corresponding and symbolizing reality, considerable, though lesser than in the seeming of the symbol. But to discover such effects is the merriment of lovers; and moving again, sitting up together, speaking in soft, kind voices to one another afterward—this is a bliss of a different kind, very sweet, not to be missed. We were very quiet then, still filled with awe of what we had felt and seen; but slowly we began to speak of the visions, to re-image them together and achieve a harmony of memory.

And so in the Real World I carry now in my womb the making of our child. Even here, as I sit at my desk writing this, I glow with the joy of it, and I feel almost as if I were pregnant with her again.

But *there* I shall know I am so. I shall feel her soul in my womb, clothing itself in its substance. Raphael shall know it too, as perfectly as I do; for she is his as much as mine.

Again and again I say: May the One be praised.

For many days after he read this, Raphael went about in a holy daze. All felt it in him: it was as if he could bless man, woman, girl-child, boy-child, with a smile or word. People looked on him with wonder, lingered near him, even followed him sometimes, longing vaguely for some further speech or a touch from him.

Even Veronica, who had shown herself quick to jealousy whenever his thoughts and feelings were preoccupied with Awen, was struck with awe at his transcendent happiness. She was perturbed and humbled; she did not know whether to seek his presence or to stay away from him. When she was in fact with him, which generally only occurred at meals, she watched him furtively, filled with both hurt and wonder.

It was as if Raphael's reading of that account were concurrent with its enactment or reenactment in the world on the other side of the barrier. There, he felt, he and Awen were experiencing it all again; and here, he felt her close to him, always. If he sat, her chair was drawn up beside him just on the other side; if he lay down, she lay down beside him, just over there; if he walked, she walked with him, only in a world more real than this.

She had written more, much more, about their later life together. As she continued, sometimes her entries became almost incomprehensible, so lyrical were they, or filled with accounts of symbol. Of her pregnant state, for example, she once wrote:

> Sweet to *become* belly, all heavy before, posture changing to the perpetual swayback of love's offering mood; gravity drawing down on me *through* my womb, whether walking or sitting or lying.
>
> Sweet to feed the weaving of our child's substance from the substance of my own blood, a rich red rapids of irrigating nutriment.
>
> Raphael, ever-present, even when not in our presence; his aura enveloping us, warming us, tenderly cushioning and protecting us; as if his hands are under my heavy belly, holding it up to ease me.
>
> Lying on our sides in lovemaking, he behind me, in symbol his new seed showering on the womb, fostering it, guarding it.
>
> When we are together apart from others these days, his manhood remains erect without ceasing, in every ordinary occupation; and our friends tell us that this is always so, because it is the male state that matches my fertility; and the wise here say that in the inner realms, this state is perpetual, because there we are fully awake. Likewise my sexual organs are engorged almost continually.
>
> Hand in hand with Raphael I walk in our garden, my robe open so that the sun may shine on my breasts and belly—shine

on, O Sun, symbol of Divine Love; for some say that in the Real World you, O Sun, *are* the One, you are where we may look (though we cannot endure to behold you) to see you irradiant above us all.

I am *become* garden, *become* the place where Raphael and I walk; inside me grows the Tree of Life, its great single fruit pendant from my inner organs, my inner soul; and our child grows just as life grows out into the universe from the inner realms, from the self-seeded womb of the One.

I am *become* the female of the Divine, in symbol, become the symbol of the creating All.

Now he did not devour her account as rapidly as possible, as when he first began; instead, he nibbled at it, as one eats a vastly rich dish, a little at a time, savoring it, and half-afraid it might be too much for the palate and stomach of his brain. Then, too, he was nearing the end of the notebook; and though he knew he would reread it all time after time before he passed out of this world into that one, still he luxuriated in the freshness of encountering his own future history for the first time.

In the final passage of the book, she related the experience of giving birth. It was nearly too much for him to bear; and in fact in the middle of his reading it, he was interrupted by a knock at the door from Mrs. McQuillit, who had heard him groaning mightily in his study and feared he was hurt or unwell. He made what assurances he could, but in truth the reading had taken him far from any state of mind that might be considered ordinary.

Awen wrote:

Today was the day of my bearing. I was walking by the lake with Raphael when the knowledge came on me: I knew it, and at the same time, my water broke, pouring out of my womb and rejoining the lake of waters at my feet. A pang of joy and a pang of grief went through me simultaneously, for I would happily and willingly have carried my child forever; but such is not the order the One has established. Raphael picked me up—picked *us* up, I should say—and carried me back to the house. He put me down tenderly on the bed, and then he summoned Prima and my other woman friends. But he did not leave me, as happens in this world; instead he stayed beside me throughout all the labor.

And no sooner had the first sweet pangs come upon me than visitors arrived. You would think that one would prefer to be in private, without strangers about, during such an event. But these were not unwelcome strangers. They came in couples, all of them. They were more beautiful than any people I have ever seen; you would say that they possessed a high, austere beauty, except that it was at the same time soft and bright with love and kindness. They were both messengers and witnesses: messengers bringing us the good will of those in the inner realms; witnesses, as they said (or somehow told us wordlessly), to the birth of the child of two lovers and spouses already a legend among them.

I know not how to describe that work of bearing except to say it was the ultimate of our lovemakings. Though Raphael was sitting beside me, holding me in his arms, the muscles of my body and womb worked as though I was in the surges of ecstasy in our love together. In increasing toil I ascended closer and closer to my release; and when I brought forth our child, I felt an ecstasy beyond all my former knowledge—became, they told me afterward, Delphic in speech, raving a mixture of cry, groan, song, poetry; and Raphael said that in literal fact visible symbols fell from my lips in miniature images and letters formed of glowing light.

At this writing I can still recall everything I saw in that time, but I cannot express it. I was carried into the inner realms again, I am sure: everything was *still more real* than the Real World. My aura in that inner place had merged with Raphael's, though we were still blessedly distinct; and out from between my legs, as out of the gate of time, came forth our child, mewling and bawling; but I understood her crying like a kind of speech. She told me of being in my womb, as in the making-womb of the One; of darkness, warmth, hearing distantly the resonance of our voices and feeling immediately the resonance of our love. I told her again of our love, weeping it to her; and it was a simple matter to tell her perfectly, because in that moment of giving birth, I had become perfect love in symbol, and perfect wisdom, symboling it in the high drama of the birthing.

And I understood for a moment why the tragedies of our earthly time so appeal to us: they are one half of the full joy we feel in the Real World. They are the riddle without resolution, the great puzzlement that yet soothes us because it reminds us that *somewhere*, in the mind of the One, there is a resolution and a joy that completes the pain and makes it whole. I bore her here in the Unreal World in anguish, grief, agony, strife; I bore her in the Real World in fullness, wholeness, ecstasy, knowledge, certainty, peace, joy. Indeed, I do believe there is no pain *here* that does not have its complement of ecstasy *there*, and having experienced that, our worldly misery suddenly makes sense, and does so in ways we cannot know here, in ways too mighty for me to express in my words, though in bearing her I understood them perfectly, if briefly.

Then she was with us. Our visitors told us what her name should be, but I cannot express it in the words of this lesser world. It means countless things. Some of its meanings tell where she has come from: "daughter of the great wife," as well as "daughter of the hero husband," "child of world-walkers," "daughter of the dream," and "the reborn real." Other meanings describe her character—and of these there are especially many, but some examples are: "she of the hungry mind" and "eager-hearted one" and "she whose glance is soothing." Other meanings hint at her future: "she whose arms draw down a husband from the sky" and "she whose very tresses are rest and peace" and "help of the frightened." Others tell her pleasures and joys: "laughing-footed runner" and "dancer of symbols" and "singer of perfect hymns" and "she who brings delight to the bed" and "weaver of tales" and "sea swimmer." There are other meanings that describe even the appearance she shall someday have: a few of these are "tall beauty" and "having eyes of blue starfire" and "having a waist like the nodding grass stalk" and "she whose breasts glimmer like water in the moonlight."

My helpers saw us washed and dried, and then, with our holy visitors, left us with an abundance of blessings. I held her in my arms and she nursed, while Raphael held us both within the circle of his arms. As the milk flowed out of me, we could see bands of light spiraling around my breast, from chest to pap; and the scent of it was wonderful, the essential embodied scent of all motherhood, lavendrous and saponaceous, sweet as crystal honey, soporific as poppy. Then she and I drowsed, and Raphael watched over us, holding us still; and I drifted off to sleep listening to his prayer of thanksgiving, mingled with his endearments for me and our daughter, and his sweet praises of me, which made me prouder than ever to have his love and still more eager to deserve it.

And as I write this I long to say: Have no fear, ye mothers and fathers in this dim and narrow world, who lose the child of your delight; for ye shall hold that child again in your arms, more living and happy than ever.

When he had come to the end of the second notebook, he began to read it over again, as he had in the case of the first. On that renewed reading it seemed even richer to him, as if its content had changed in the interval. For all he knew—and truly, he had witnessed many strange things in his life—it actually *had* changed: he thought that perhaps the One reweaves time and history even while we live in it, and the hues and fashioning of the very garment of knowledge and certainties, of facts and events, in which we think ourselves so splendidly and proudly raimented, changes without our even noticing.

The journal was indeed full of a holy certainty about the workings of the universe that he strove with difficulty to grasp. As always, Awen led and he followed, "late, but in earnest." For he, left behind as he was in the Dim World, could not be sure that he would find her again in the Bright; and though her every word spoke the rightness of their union there, he remained constantly aware that if she was right—and this was a lesson that the Wonderful had also taught—what he did here would determine his fate there. And so he looked about him freshly, in the place where he was, to see what he might do here to mend the suffering of others.

Chapter 59

My mind soon grew calm, and I began the duties of my new position, somewhat instructed, I hoped, by the adventure that had befallen me in Fairy Land. Could I translate the experience of my travels there, into common life? This was the question; or must I live it all over again, and learn it all over again, in the other forms that belong to the world of men, whose experience yet runs parallel to that of Fairy Land?

— George MacDonald

When Raphael read of such a glorious future, how could he be irritated by the petty difficulties of the Dim World? He surveyed the daily chaos of life around him, both near at hand and on the vast stage of politics and nations, with a serenity unattainable and even unthinkable to him before. He understood this better from his reading of Swedenborg: The physical world was only a playing out of good and ill in the world of spirit, and events here were only a shadowplay of a deeper struggle between good and evil, seen in silhouette on the curtain of materiality.

The Bright World, then, was part of the actual *cause* of the Dim World. The denizens of the Dark Lands, attracted to evil people here, clustered around them, just inside the barrier that separated the two worlds; and though they could not physically impinge upon the Dim World, they bent the thought of people here to worse courses. Likewise the good here were encouraged in their goodness by the good there. He had no doubt that, though he could not see the good folk who assisted him, they were just on the other side of that barrier. He often felt the presence of

Awen—good, peaceful, confident, loving—all about him, and the presence of his fellow Image Makers; and how, feeling that presence so strongly, could he harbor ill thoughts or do anything less than act with loving care of others?

In particular he became even more mild toward Veronica—whom, as a token of that mildness, he called by her given name, and his voice in speaking it was gentle. For the great mismatch that had tied him to her for this brief span of life was now revealed to him as beneficial: every moment it taught him the value of his true marriage. He had often in the past blamed her for her cruelty to him; now he felt only compassion for her.

Indeed, his voice when he spoke to her now lost all that lurking irony that is so toxic to the relationship between people who have been unfortunately yoked together. It was full of love instead; and though it was not the kind of love that spouses feel, it was nonetheless genuine, a love of her as a manifestation of the One and of a love of the One through her. It is likely that in this respect, he gave her more love than most husbands do who owe full love and allegiance to their legal wives. He wished for her that someday—and it would have to be in that other world—she might know, with someone suitable to her, some part of the happiness he knew with his true spouse.

Though he did not notice the reaction of others, others noticed his reaction to her; and knowing the trials he had undergone, they marveled at his lovingkindness. Some said he was soft-hearted to a fault and should have met her cruelness with cruelty of his own; others sensed some higher love at work and called him a saint. But he was no saint. He was only doing what he believed the One expected of him and what it was right and loving to do; he was only being obedient to the One.

In looking at the duties he owed others, he confronted one that in his day was paramount, though in ours it has fallen into disuse. He was the master of Fulkothing Hall, and of Dareweather, heir of the lands and wealth of the ancient Kerrs, and, by marriage, owner of Wapstrake Hall. He had no heir himself, except for an obscure cousin who did not even bear the name of Kerr. And this failing in the matter of offspring was a dereliction of the duty he owed to his family, and in particular to his father and uncle. The solution was not far to seek, and now he took it upon himself to find it.

It was the custom of those times, where an entail upon a property allowed it, for those circumstanced as Raphael was—childless heirs, that is—to adopt a relative's son and raise him to inherit the name and estate that otherwise would have passed to a remote branch. His sister had, among her large family, a boy who seemed destined for this role. Not only had he been christened Raphael, but he had especially endeared himself to Raphael for having been a favorite of Awen's when she visited with the Keiths at Madgelet Lodge. And so Raphael determined to adopt little Rafe, bring him into Fulkothing Hall, and make him, in all respects but natural birth, his own son.

Grief and mourning oftentimes engender an invincible loyalty, and Raphael had been paralyzed in redressing his lack of an heir in large part by the thought of the child he had lost. But the account that Awen had given of their daughter's rebirth in the next world had freed him of that grief; and so it was that he made his decision about Rafe with a lightening of the heart. There remained only the obstacles of demonstrating to Veronica that her opposition would not be brooked, and of persuading the boy's mother and father to part with him. The latter he had some good hopes of: it was too handsome an opportunity for the lad, an opportunity such as no loving parent could refuse, particularly in those times, in which custom sanctioned the arrangement. He intended to soften the blow by settling sums on his other nephews and nieces as well, which would enable the boys to begin careers in the army, the law, or the church, as it suited each, and allow the girls to marry into far better circumstances than they otherwise might have.

As to convincing Veronica to at least tolerate this adoption, he was less sanguine. The last thing he wanted was to allow her to make the boy's life miserable. She was jealous enough of Lucy's fertility; to see one of that mother's abundant brood take the place of the child she herself could never have would be, he guessed, deeply painful to her. But he must make the attempt to reconcile her to it; and accordingly, one day after breakfast he asked her to come with him into the sunlit parlor; and when she had settled herself, he turned to her, and in the mild voice that characterized his dealings with her now, he said, "Veronica, I have come to a decision. It is one that most closely affects you; and I wish to communicate it to you in such a way that you understand that though I respect the pain it may cause you, I shall not be turned back in regard to it."

She looked at him with grave dislike and perturbation at this commencement. It did not seem to be the announcement of a proceedings for divorce, but after what she had done, she could never be sure on that point. He went on immediately to remove this idea.

"I intend to adopt Lucy's son, Rafe," he said, "as heir of Fulkothing Hall."

It seemed she had never considered such a possibility. She was utterly shocked; she sat back in her chair, blenching.

"It is the natural and proper course of action for those situated such as we are," he added.

"Never!" she said, finding her voice with difficulty.

"I shall ride to Madgelet Lodge this morning to speak to Lucy and Reuben," he said calmly. "I do not know whether they will take to the idea, but I have hopes they will. The work of the lawyers will take some time; but it is my plan that he shall come here and live with us as soon as his parents deem appropriate and convenient—live with us as if he were indeed our own son. It is my belief that it is best so—that if he is to form the love of Fulkothing that is appropriate to the new patriarch of the line, he ought to live here, to grow up here."

"I shall not allow it!" she said, through teeth nearly clenched together.

"You shall not deter it," he replied. "This is my duty, and I shall not be deterred in it."

"Your *duty!*" she exclaimed. "Hypocrite! You do not do this out of *duty!*"

"I freely confess," he said, "that it means a great deal to me to have a child to love *here.*" And by the word "here" he meant something Veronica could never have imagined.

"And what of *my* feelings?" she demanded.

"Veronica," he said quietly, "you are most welcome to love this boy as your own."

She actually writhed in her chair as though in a paroxysm of disgust. "Love *a child not my own?*" she exclaimed. "Love one of the children of—of a woman who—"

"Be careful what you say," he warned her gently.

"But you *know* I cannot stand your sister! You do this on purpose to spite me!"

Lucy had, in imitation of her brother, for many years tried to love Veronica, and Veronica had always rebuffed her approaches. Between them now was only an icy disdain of Veronica's side and, on Lucy's, a fading but still earnest willingness to keep trying despite many wounds. Raphael knew he could not conquer Veronica's unthinking dislike of her, so he spoke instead of the boy's own virtues.

"Rafe is my nephew, as I was the nephew of my own dear uncle and aunt, who made me their heir. He is very little, it is true; but so far as we can judge his character, he is a sweet-tempered, intelligent, and honest boy who shows much promise to grow into a good, useful, and kind master. You might love him very much if you would reconcile yourself to this necessity; and necessity it is."

"How so?" she protested; but now he heard in her voice a hint of that self-awareness she seemed to experience at rare intervals; and not only did she at this instant know herself as she seldom did, she knew she was in the wrong. "How is it a necessity?" she demanded.

"Because we ourselves do not have children," he said quietly.

"That is not my fault!" she cried, in the bitterest tone of self-defense.

"I know it is not, my dear," he said. "It was the will of God." And he thought, but did not add aloud, that the barrenness of their marriage symboled the aridity of the love between them. He and Awen, by contrast, had conceived almost at the first touch. "In any case," he went on, "the fact remains that we have no recourse; so we shall adopt this boy and—I can only speak for myself, but I shall love him as a son. Or perhaps I should say as a future son-in-law, as if he were to be married to a daughter I shall have in some other place and time."

"Well, *I* shall not love him!" she cried.

"You will be kind to him," said Raphael, "or you shall be excluded from his company, and thus from mine. I will not have him growing up in fear of your ill-will and abuse."

"You would make me an outcast in my own house?" she exclaimed.

"If I must, I shall."

"What, lock me up in solitary confinement?"

"I would only compel you to take your meals apart from the boy and me, that is all. You and I seldom see each other except at meals in any case."

Then—perhaps in sheer vexation, though he was inclined to think it something more—she burst into tears. She gave up protesting; she gave up trying to explain her thoughts; she only wept, in anger and in shame, in shame and in anger. Indeed, those two emotions had always been the warders that imprisoned her in the solitary confinement she feared so much—the solitary confinement of her own tormented mind.

And he pitied her; and he spoke both soothingly and yet honestly.

"I know it is not easy for you," he said. "It cannot be easy for a woman who wished to have children to see her husband bring into her house, as his heir, the child of a woman who, as it seems, has too many children. But you must understand that it is no reproach against you. I am only facing the fact that we are without an heir, that is all; I am only seeking to redress that lack. And you might, if you will, look upon this not as a slight but as a God-given opportunity; an opportunity for us to have a child of our own at last. A child to love! This is what we wanted so long, both of us. It was, aside from our love of Fulkothing, really the only love we had in common—our longing for a child. Let this be the fulfillment of that. Our lives, I do believe, would have been very different if we had had children. We would have been kinder and better to one another. Let this boy be that child whom we were, in the wisdom and mercy of God, denied in our own earthly union. I *know* I shall love him; and I invite you to do the same."

But she would not answer him. She wept on; and it seemed to him that something in her had broken at last under the strain of her life's failure.

When he found he could not console her, he gave orders for the carriage to be brought; and though he offered her a place beside him in it, in the end he had to set out for Madgelet Lodge without her.

ʘ ʘ ʘ

Reuben was not at home when Raphael arrived; but he was expected back within the hour, and Raphael said nothing of his plans for that time. Lucy seemed to sense that he had something of importance to say, and took him aside from the children, and sat with him for that interval in the parlor at Madgelet, perhaps unconsciously hoping that if he was not beset by little Keiths, she would hear what was on his mind. When Reuben came in, she ordered tea brought; and they sat together over it, the three of them, in the amiable companionship of long mutual respect. Lucy's demeanor in these times when she had Reuben and Raphael to herself always amused her brother: they were her two most favored in all the world, and she was ineffably content when she was with them.

When they had spoken (inevitably) of the children, and of Titus, and before the conversation could slip into the men's world of politics and the assizes and business, Raphael said, "Well, there is something I have come to talk to you about, if you will hear me."

They both became very serious, almost frightened, and Lucy, who was sitting on a sofa beside Reuben, groped for his hand and held it.

"Perhaps you guess what it is," said Raphael, smiling gently.

They did not know what to say. Lucy managed a brave smile.

"Yes," said Raphael then. "I am hoping you will allow us to adopt Rafe."

He had not surprised them, certainly, but they were stricken all the same.

"If it does not seem presumptuous, dear Brother, " said Lucy, "I must say that we have been afraid you were going to propose this."

"Now, now," Reuben said to her, "remember what we agreed, dear."

"Are *you* remembering?" she asked him, with a kind of plaintive affection.

He smiled. "I am trying to," he said. "I know it is not easy." He put his arm around her shoulders and drew her close to him; and she shed a few tears, though in other respects she remained composed.

"Of course you know you will still see him," said Raphael. "It will not be that much worse than sending him to school."

"That is what we have told ourselves," said Lucy.

"And I promise you—if it is of any concern—that I shall not let Veronica's moods trouble him in any way, even if it means I must banish her from the table."

They said nothing in response on this head, though he could see that they had talked of it between themselves. He went on to explain his other plans for settling sums on the other children, and he woke their gratitude; this was beyond their expectation, and it gave them no little relief.

Then he said, "You have thought about Rafe coming to live with us. Then you must have decided something—you must have agreed between yourselves that this would be best for him."

They were unable to speak, but Reuben nodded for them.

"You know I shall love the boy as if he were my own son," said Raphael. "And you know that I shall not require him to love me as if I were his own father. It shall be as it was for me with Uncle and Aunt: their love for me was an increment of the love bestowed on me, not a decrement of the love of Father and Mother."

"I shall write him every day," said Lucy.

"Whatever you think is best," said Raphael.

"Unless it is disturbing to him," she added.

"We shall learn what is best for him," said Raphael. "I shall never stand between you and him, dear. You know how important it is that one of your children goes on to be master of Fulkothing; and I think he will grow up to be a good master."

"Oh, yes," said Lucy. "He has that in him, more than any of the other boys."

"And your idea of assisting the others," said Reuben, "that is very wise, Brother. They will be able to get ahead splendidly, if they have a chance."

"And we shall look out good livings for those who want them," said Raphael. "And we are not without connections from of old in the church and the army and the navy. I think we may do very well by all of them if we take thought."

This was very pleasing to Lucy, and she wiped away her tears for the time being.

"Then ought we not to ask Rafe himself?" she said.

"Yes," said Raphael.

The little fellow was summoned; he came in happily to see his uncle, of whom he was genuinely fond.

"Come here to us, my boy," said his father. Rafe did as he was told.

"Now, my boy," said Reuben, "we have some news for you."

Rafe's eyes opened expectantly; he was perhaps thinking of the baby duck he had asked for.

"You are to be master of Fulkothing someday," said Reuben.

Rafe looked mystified, then dubious; he could not think of anything to say.

"Remember how I told you once about your Uncle Raphael's having been adopted by his uncle and aunt, and going to live with them at their house?"

"Dareweather, it was," said Rafe, brightening with the recollection.

"And they were very kind and good to him; and all the family was together again at holidays and had a jolly time."

"I do remember, Papa."

"Well, that is what your Uncle Raphael proposes for you. You are to go live at Fulkothing Hall, and someday you shall be master of the place."

He had spoken magic words. "Live at Fulkothing Hall" was enough to capture the boy's attention entirely. It was as if Reuben had told him he was to live in Fairyland, and ride a steed caparisoned with a golden saddle, and angle in silver streams for jeweled fish—glorious, and yet also not quite comprehensible or believable. He began to step about from side to side, almost to frisk like a new colt.

"Fulkothing!" he said. "I am to live at Fulkothing? With Uncle Raphael?

"Yes, dear boy," said Reuben. "It will be ever so much good fun. But you must be a good boy, always."

"And are you coming with me?" said Rafe suddenly, struck with this new question as he noticed the strained happiness in their expressions. "Mama? Papa? Are you coming too? And Joe, and Orlando, and Peter, and Jane, and Amanda?"

"We shall visit you often," said Lucy urgently, as if she were trying to get in some contribution to the discussion before she broke down in tears. "And you shall come back to visit us here. But you shall live at Fulkothing, and your Uncle shall take the very best care of you."

Then the little fellow turned, marched over to Raphael, and halted before him.

"Will that Mrs. Quinn be there?" he asked.

Raphael was speechless. He looked from the boy to Lucy.

She too was surprised, but she attempted an explanation. "He has so often heard me speaking of her with the other children," she told Raphael. Then she said to Rafe: "No, dear, Mrs. Quinn has passed on."

"Oh," said the boy dubiously.

Before Raphael could stop himself, he told the boy: "She *will* be there—only just on the other side of the barrier, in the other world. She will know of you and love you as if you had been her own, just as she loved you when you were a very little boy."

The boy thought about this for a moment.

"Is she here now?" he asked.

"God bless you," said Raphael. "She is right here. If you listen for her, if you let yourself notice her, you will feel her presence right in this room with us."

"I thought so," said Rafe.

And so it was Raphael whose emotions broke first. But he made a brave show of it for the boy's sake; and sat him on his knee, and told him what merry times they would have together at Fulkothing, and how his brothers and sisters and mother and father should come play with him whenever they liked.

℗ ℗ ℗

In the end it was decided that Rafe should move to his new home in a week. Too much longer and he might have had too much time to regret the transition; and anything shorter might have been too abrupt. Furthermore, Reuben and Lucy had been decided that they should not both accompany him, as it might also in that case seem too sharp a break if he had to bid them farewell in the same place and time; so his father said goodbye to him beside the carriage at Madgelet Lodge, as if Rafe were merely going to visit his uncle for a week, and his mother went with him all the way to Fulkothing.

For a little man of five years of age, Rafe was an unusual creature. He was in every respect a boy: that is, when the object in view was a kite, or a fishing rod, or dogs, or horses, or a hunting meet, or a country wrestling match, or a game of cricket, or in general anything mechanical or sporting, his eyes grew wide and his breath came short with excitement, and he bounced on his short legs as if he could not contain himself, and more often than not ran about in dizzying circles of sheer pleasure. And yet life with his mother and his many sisters had civilized him: he found repugnant those qualities that boys who have no other company than boys often develop. In particular, he was not cruel to animals or thoughtless to servants. Though his sisters sometimes teased him, he steadfastly refused to tease them in return, as though he already thought it unmanly to harass the opposite sex.

He not only transcended the commonality of boys, he had, in very mundane ways, shown qualities that put him morally above children in general. For example, he was not greedy for cake, though he particularly loved that commodity; and he had in fact on one occasion been observed to give the last and most precious bite to his sister, when she had dropped her own on the floor and it had been gulped down by the dog before it could be rescued. This generosity was a striking proof that he had escaped the solipsism common to early childhood. Little Rafe knew there were others in the world besides himself, and that is indeed a knowledge that many do not acquire before they reach the grave.

Over all, he was a combination of boyish blindness and adult thoughtfulness, of childish haste and mature gallantry. His extreme youth gave highlight to his care for others, and his precocious maturity put his childlike qualities in sharp relief. One had the sense that he was trying very hard to be kind and to do what was right, and that he made this attempt out of an inherent recognition that goodness was valuable in its own right, and not for its consequences. He was not petty in anything; and adults soon saw this quality in him and gravitated to him. He had his little woes and disappointments—when the aforesaid kite escaped from him, or his fishing line broke just as he was landing a glorious trout—and he related these, and felt them, indeed as if they were high tragedies worthy of treatment by the Greek dramatists; but he then went on to accept consolation, and ultimately, as it seemed, both to hope for better times and to bethink him that his own misfortunes were trifling.

When the boy arrived at Fulkothing, he was excited and seemed even to feel his change of status as an honor rather than as a painful separation from his parents. Lucy and Reuben had prepared him well with reassurances that he would never be far from them; and it helped greatly that he loved Fulkothing with a passion. To him it was as grand as the King's palace; and to go live there, and to someday be master of the place, was a chance he greeted with a humble gratitude and delight that was very touching to Raphael.

Lucy stayed but an hour. It was perhaps the bravest thing she had ever done when she kissed Rafe goodbye with an appearance of complete happiness, consigned him to the company of her brother, and stepped up into the carriage to ride away. She waved from the window, and the boy waved gaily back. He knew that she was to return at the end of the week for a visit, and at the moment that did not seem so terribly far away to him. But when the carriage started into motion, for a moment his happiness wavered and nearly collapsed.

"Now, my dear boy," said Raphael quickly, "what do you say to our taking a walk about Fulkothing, so you will know where everything is?"

"I should like that very much, Uncle," said Rafe, his near descent to despair canceled in mid-plummet, replaced by an eagerness bordering on rapture.

Raphael had accordingly taken him by the hand, and they had turned about to head away into the gardens; when suddenly Veronica intruded on Raphael's notice. She had been present during

Lucy's brief visit, but had said nothing. For some reason—he doubted it was politeness—she had come out of the house when Lucy was leaving. He had expected she would go in immediately, but she was here still, watching with that old expression of mingled anger and shame—this time at what she felt to be his neglect of her.

"Will you come with us?" he asked her, almost before he knew what he was saying. He expected her to refuse point-blank and to retreat into the house in a huff; but instead, after hesitating for the briefest moment, she took a step forward.

The boy instantly put out his free hand to her. It was the most natural thing in the world to him that this lady would want to hold it as they walked, for he had walked in this way with his parents many times. Much to Raphael's wonder, Veronica came to Rafe and took that hand; and so they started off together.

Raphael chatted with the boy with genuine enthusiasm. He himself loved Fulkothing, loved everything about it; and he re-membered very well all the particular features of it that a boy would love—the old hollow tree into which one could tuck oneself when playing hide-and-seek, the fishing stream beyond the pastures, the great ledge of rock in the park that could, in a child's imagination, serve as the stern of a ship or the wall of a castle—and he recalled perfectly the similar uses of the hay barn, the dairy, the gardeners' shed, the brewery, the hen house, and all of the many outbuildings of a great estate, each of them special to a curious boy in its own way.

To Raphael's continued surprise, on this grand tour Veronica clung doggedly to the boy's hand. She said nothing, however, and she seemed very awkward, even rather shy. Raphael knew for a fact that she was seeing many of these sights for the first time— she had never in her life been in her own henhouse, he was certain of that, or her hay barn; nor had she ever climbed the stile by the cow paddock. She was in poor condition even for this easy a walk, and her breath came short, but she would not quit them; and as she neither said nor did anything to spoil the boy's appreciation, he himself made no objection to her company.

Finally he saw that the boy's little legs were tired, and he carried him home on his back. Lucy had told them that Rafe customarily took a short nap in the afternoon, so Raphael tucked him into a blanket on a sofa in one of the parlors, and promised him cake with tea when he woke up. "You must come to me in my study when you have had your nap, my boy," he said; and the child promised to do so with an eagerness belied somewhat by his sleepy eyes and nodding head.

Veronica had followed them even to this little ceremony, though she hung back at the door of the room. She seemed not to want to speak to Raphael; she went away from the room before him; and having business to do, he went to his study, puzzled a bit at her behavior, but willing to abide the outcome, and soon forgetting her in the midst of his own occupation.

About half an hour later, the door of the office opened. He looked up, thinking at first it must be the boy; but instead it was Veronica. She came in and closed the door behind her.

She looked angry; but then again, she usually did. He sat back in his chair and waited.

If she was angry, she was irresolute. She stood where she was, rubbing the palm of one hand against the back of the other in a distracted fashion, neither looking full at him nor looking away.

"What is it, Veronica?" he asked finally.

She did not speak immediately; but she advanced into the room, haphazardly taking up a position at the side of the desk at which he sat, again not facing him.

Suddenly it all came forth.

"He must be *mine*, too," she said in a hoarse, anguished voice. She turned her face to his, and for once the tears flowed from her eyes without shame.

"Yours?" he said, feeling rather stupid as he uttered the word, but not believing what he was hearing from her.

"Yes," she said reproachfully. "You cannot just bring him in here and be everything to him. If we are to adopt him, then . . . I want to be his *mother*. Or at least, I want to be his mother at Fulkothing.

Just because I could never have a child . . . is no reason to think that I have no rights."

The tears were dropping fast, her lips were trembling, and her voice was shaking with resentment and something very much like fear—fear that Raphael meant to cut her off from the boy.

"It is not fair!" she added. "I have never deserved *this* wrong from you—whatever I may have done to you."

He stood very abruptly from his seat and went to her. In former times, before Awen had returned to him, he would have taken her in his arms, even though she would have stood within his embrace as stiff and loveless as a fencepost; now he did not attempt that consolation, but he spoke to her just as kindly as ever he would have.

"My dear," he said—and there was feeling in those words, they were not the usual commonplace title of address of those times—"I had no idea that you felt this way. You were quite opposed to our adopting him."

"Well," she exclaimed bitterly, "I cannot stop it now, can I?"

"Hush, hush," he said soothingly. "I am not trying to keep you from the child, or keep the child from you. No one would be more delighted than I if you should take the child into your heart and treat him as a mother."

"I *shall* be a mother to him," she said angrily. "I shall love him, and be kind to him—you shall see."

"My dear—you misunderstand me. I could not be happier than if you did so."

"Just because—" she began again; but her reproach was aborted by a sob.

"Do not exercise yourself, my dear," he said. "Do not imagine disapproval or objection where they do not exist."

"Just because there has not been much love between us," she managed to say, "do not imagine that I am not capable of love."

All he could think was how pitiable a wreck she was, compared to Awen.

"Come," he said, "you shall see. Love him, and he will love you like another mother."

"Then let me be with him when he wakes," she said.

"Of course, my dear, if you would like."

"And I will pour his tea and pass him his cake."

"Of course, my dear. You have no idea how delighted I would be. Let us make our home welcoming and comfortable to the boy in every way."

"And when I die," she said, in a voice now so hoarse and stifled with emotion that she could barely make her words audible, "then he will think of me and love me a little too, as if I had been a kind of mother to him."

"Of course he will," said Raphael. The spectacle of this lonely, wretched, angry, and proud woman clutching at these straws of comfort as she faced the inevitability of death was deeply moving to him. He almost said, *But fear nothing, because there is another world where you may, if you wish, find a happiness in life, and a goodness in yourself, that you cannot find here.* But he knew she was not capable of believing such a thing.

She went on for quite some time. Usually when she had begun one of these crying exercises, she would go on for at least an hour before she had repeated herself a sufficient number of times to sate her appetite for self-pitying complaint. On this occasion she exhausted herself in about half an hour; and she had just dried her face for the last time when there was a tentative knock at the door of the room.

Raphael opened the door and found Rafe there, still a bit sleepy, but very cheerful. "Please, Uncle Raphael, sir," he said, "may I have my tea and cake now?"

"Your aunt has just been telling me," said Raphael, "how very glad she is that you have come to live with us. Let us all go to the parlor, and she will do us the honor of pouring our tea, I think."

Rafe looked at his aunt, and with the perfect sympathy of children, knew that she had been crying. He came and took her hand spontaneously. "Come, Aunt Veronica," he said. "Cake will cheer you."

He led her away to the parlor then, as if he had lived all his life in the house; and Veronica allowed herself to be led. Raphael followed, his feelings a mixture of relief and wonder.

Veronica rang for tea, and they sat down like a little family, the boy in an enormous, oversized armchair in which he looked comically small, his feet sticking out from the seat cushion before him.

"Did you sleep well?" Veronica asked him.

Raphael was further amazed. A solicitous Veronica was outside his twenty years' experience of her thoughts and feelings.

"Very well, thank you," said the boy. "I dreamt of Mama, but I did not mind; she kept telling me it was all right that I am to live here now."

"Indeed it *is* all right," said Veronica. "For one thing, your aunt is very glad that you are here; and for another, Fulkothing Hall is a splendid place for you to be."

"And I am not so very far away from Mama and Papa and Annabelle," he said.

"Not far at all," agreed Veronica. "And you are to have a puppy, do not forget." Raphael had promised the boy his own dog while they had been walking earlier. It was surprising to Raphael to hear Veronica reiterate this now, as she had never liked animals.

"That will be a great comfort," said the boy, in one of those flights of precocious self-reflection to which he was prone.

"Your uncle," she went on, "will do all the things with you that boys like to do outside; and inside, I shall do all the things that women do: I shall always be here at teatime, and cut the cake; I shall tuck you in at night and give you a kiss; I shall keep an eye on your schoolmaster and your nursemaid to be sure they are fair to you. But I will be your aunt in other places too: on good days we shall have picnics; and sometimes we shall travel to Norwich and even to London."

At this prospect of his future, the boy sat up in the great chair and looked with new eyes on the woman before him. Hitherto she had seemed remote, inaccessible, even cold, and she had seemed in particular to be less than friendly to his mother; but Raphael could see that Rafe was now thinking he might need to reconsider his assessment.

"May we take Mother and Father and everyone on a picnic?" he asked tentatively.

"Of course we may," said Veronica. Raphael raised his eyebrows in another long moment of surprise. "Did you know," Veronica continued, "that your uncle was adopted by *his* uncle when he was a boy like you?"

"Yes, Aunt; I have heard that."

"He can tell you of the many good times he had in Dareweather, where he went to live, and the hunting and fishing there. When I first came to Hertfordshire, which is where Dareweather is, the first time I laid eyes on him was when he came into the parlor there all muddy from a day's shooting, carrying several brace of birds, and bristling with guns."

The boy laughed at the picture, as she had intended he should.

"But he cleaned up and became most presentable," she added.

"And is that why you married him?" asked Rafe. "Because he was a good shot?"

"No—I married him because he became presentable when he cleaned himself up."

The boy chuckled affably; the picture of his uncle as a boy with dirty face and hands was amusing to him.

"I should like to be as good a shot as my uncle," he said; and then, apparently feeling that this statement required some explanation, he added, "Papa is not fond of hunting."

"Your uncle shall teach you everything you need to know," said Veronica.

The boy looked at Raphael blissfully and proudly.

"Then if the cake here is good, and if you will love me too, Aunt Veronica," he told her, "I am sure I shall be happy."

☙ ☙ ☙

Veronica made an odd mother. The old adage says that good habits build good character; from which we are to infer that the pretense of loving eventually makes one a loving person. She had never really loved anyone but herself, and even at that she had done badly; so when Rafe arrived, and she began studying to be loving, she certainly tested the truism, and had at best mixed success in proving it.

But Rafe was the best substitute she would ever have for a child of her own. More than that, he was the one male in her life who did not become entangled in her mind with the crimes men had committed against her. Whereas her animus against Raphael, and against all men who reminded her of her father or uncle or whoever had so hurt her long ago, was now a given of her life, and she actually enjoyed the rage and anger it caused in her, Rafe did not evoke that hatred. There was good in her, as Raphael had always believed; and now she allowed it to come to the fore.

Raphael himself at times found this dual standard irritating, for he believed himself to be as innocent of guilt as Rafe. If she had been able to love him without associating him with her abuser, their life together would have been considerably more happy. But now, in his love for Awen, he had ample reason not to concern himself with that, and in general he looked on the irony of her affection for Rafe with an interest purely remote and academic. Sometimes he thought, too, that she was trying to make amends to him by loving the boy. And it was, in fact, the best, and indeed the only, way she could have offset those many subtotals of cruelty she had inscribed on the balance sheet of their relationship. Broken as she was, she could only make amends to Raphael by being kind to someone who was not Raphael; but he would accept this as the best she could give.

There were several truly wonderful things about her care for the boy. The first was that from the time he arrived at Fulkothing, she thought of little else but his presence there. When she was not actually in Rafe's company, she was thinking of him, planning for him, and planning not just that day and the next, but his future life. She was given, for once, a focus outside herself, and she grappled herself to it with a desperate relief; for egotism is boring even to the egotist, and the ennui of the selfish is a sentence to life in prison. Nor did she simply spoil him. She saw to his welfare with a judiciousness she had not shown in handling her own affairs. She did not give him too much cake or tea; she did not allow him to stay up late; he was forbidden wine; he was kept from the company of coarse persons (in fact, she refused to see some of her former friends for this reason); she balanced his hours of study and his hours of recreation intelligently; she blessed his tramps about the country with Raphael as part of his growth to manhood. She even had a tentative affection for Rafe's dog, once she saw how much the boy himself loved the creature. She said that a gentleman *ought* (perhaps this was a reflection on Raphael) to have a knowledge of music, and she herself taught Rafe to play the pianoforte, and to play it well. She proved a very effective and even kindly teacher. Raphael himself enjoyed being in the room during these lessons, because it pleased him much to see this gentler side of her personality—it vindicated his early love for her, and that meant a great deal to him, even if that love was now, and in view of Divine Providence always had been, thoroughly moot.

It was wonderful as well how she spoke to Rafe. She sat close to him, watching him intently with her beautiful eyes, and he seemed to glow under that attention, for his busy mother had never had time to give it. She wanted to know everything—where he and his uncle had ridden or walked, how many and what sort of birds they shot or fish they had caught; what sort of dreams he had had at night; what he thought of his playfellows in the neighborhood; how he had dined during a visit to his parents, and even what Annabelle and his other siblings were doing; the funny tricks his dog had performed; how he liked his new pen knife; and on and on, always, in a kind of perpetual, loving quiz, except that it was she who learned from it. She did not merely ask in order to converse; she stored up the information fixedly in her memory. In truth, in time she knew more of the facts of the boy's life, and his wants and desires, than Raphael himself. It was as if she had flayed her own soul, heedless of the pain, and were writing the boy's biography, his book of life, on that parchment with a steel nib and acid ink.

Another effect of this consuming interest in the lad was that now she and Raphael had something about which to converse. When Rafe was not present, they fairly prattled about how wonderful the little fellow was, and about his entertaining sayings and deeds, and how they ought to do this for him or that. In respect to his future, Veronica actually persuaded Raphael to change his mind from time to time, so thoughtful were her considerations on the matter, and so effective were her persuasions concerning it. In this he came to depend upon her opinion as never before, and as in no other matter.

A further small miracle was that, with this mutual interest, she now was able to speak with Lucy without envy and condescension. She even sought Lucy out on occasions when the two households came together, and spoke to her about Rafe for almost longer than Lucy had time to listen. From time to time in these earnest sessions, Lucy would turn to Raphael and look at him with wondering eyes; and he could tell that she understood at last that he had not been chasing an *ignis fatuus* in trying for all those years of marriage to win his wife's love—that Veronica was, despite all past evidence to the contrary, capable of some sort of affection.

There are many women and men to whom the accession of a child in their lives is a matter of indifference. There are many others who live good lives singly and need no child to become good. But there are some who remain broken until their love for a child makes them whole again; and such a one was Veronica. The repair of her shattered personality was imperfect at best, for she had lived too long amidst its shards to endure to be whole again—such a condition would have been frighteningly unfamiliar to her—but in her maternal affection for Rafe she achieved more true humanness than she ever would have found otherwise.

Her new *raison d'etre* became evident in a further increase in the care she took of herself. She knew, somehow, that it means much to a boy to have a beautiful woman in his life. She wanted to make the boy admire her, be proud of her, and she consciously worked to bring that about. She had begun to make some repair of her physical form after Manwaring had been driven out; now she continued that effort with a new will. She began to take more exercise, walking out with Rafe and Raphael; and to some extent she regained the figure that had been so beautiful in her youth. Her face, too, now that it was lit with kindness, won back in earnest some of the lost beauty it had possessed on false pretenses in her early years. She resumed the great pains she had once taken with her dress and her hair, but even in this she showed an unaccustomed wisdom: she might have frightened or repelled the boy if she had resorted to quantities of makeup and to the whims of fashion current in her girlhood, now grown quaint, or to the extremes of contemporary *couture;* instead she aimed at a simpler and more natural appearance, and succeeded in achieving the sort of looks that appealed to him rather than puzzled or disgusted him. Raphael indeed sometimes wondered if she had not learned something, if against her will, from the effect of Awen's simple beauty. And the boy did come to think her quite handsome.

Chapter 60

Ἔνδον σκάπτε, ἔνδον ἡ πηγὴ τοῦ ἀγαθοῦ καὶ ἀειάναβλύειν δυναμένη, ἐὰν ἀεὶ σκάπτῃς.

Delve within. Within is the fountain of good, and it will always flow if you will always delve.

—Marcus Aurelius

Husbands, love your wives, and be not bitter against them.

—Colossians 4:19

It is a commonplace that as life proceeds, we lose more and more our sense of elapsing time. Often we find that the letter that we remember as having arrived only last week is now dated a year previous, a year in which it has lain unanswered, unattended to, much to the distress and bafflement of our younger correspondent. Time slips along silently and quietly, at a pace beyond our apprehension, constantly gaining speed and strength against us, so that there is always more of its river behind us than we think.

Raphael's personal life followed the same rule of increasing acceleration. Rafe's time at Fulkothing seemed a mere flicker in the memory of his adoptive parents: in fact, he lived with them fewer than ten years before he must, following the custom of his time and his class, go away to school. From Eton he went to Cambridge, where he distinguished himself in mathematics, taking high honors. Like his uncle before him, he returned to Norfolk, for through Raphael's generosity, he was a man of means. He chose a dwelling midway between his adoptive and his natural parents, and within a year he had married. Raphael highly approved of the young woman, and believed that she and Rafe stood a good chance of having made a marriage to last for all eternity. He saw how their love had grown in much the same way as had his and Awen's on Vigia: they had first found one another's conversation of great interest; they had increasingly desired to be together for the sheer pleasure of sharing their thoughts; gradually that yearning had become fondness, and then that fondness had become mutual desire. Veronica was less certain of the girl, perhaps for the same reason Raphael delighted in her: because in many respects she called Awen to mind, both in her appearance and character. But the birth of a grandchild within the next year reconciled Veronica to the necessity of liking her daughter-in-law. She was able to extend the mothering she had learned in caring for Rafe and, in the few years in which she shared the lives of Rafe's children, she was a source of love they always remembered.

Over these years Veronica became more mild, especially toward others. She learned from Raphael himself something about being kind, though her charity remained primarily imitative. She was likely to flare up, to sulk or scold, when she saw him practicing generosity or charity to anyone but Rafe.

Yet still, she came to know herself better. She could see her faults, to some extent; sometimes she even spoke of them, and a few times even apologized for them. But she could not overcome them; her regeneration proceeded no further than an awareness that she was broken.

Nor did she ever reconcile herself to the memory of Awen. Once when a neighbor spent ten minutes during a visit to tea in recalling the strange Mrs. Quinn who had briefly been part of their lives years ago, Veronica had to leave the room to prevent their guest from seeing her fury; and she inflicted two weeks of brooding silence thereafter on Raphael. He suspected that she felt Awen's continued spiritual presence in his life—vicariously, not directly as he did.

He found that he could invoke Awen's spiritual participation in his life in three particular ways. One was to write. In addition to his credo, he wrote a memoir of his love for Awen and of their strange path through life and death together, and her presence infused every word. He wrote his imaginations of the world to come, and it was as if the very fertility of her imagination bore the fruit of his. He wrote an imaginary and symbolic cosmology and history of the world, in poetic terms, that told of the wholeness of the One and the creative dichotomy of male and female.

Another way to feel Awen's presence was to let himself slip into reverie. In daydreams she came into the Paradise and sat down beside him again, leaned against him, spoke with him; as he was drifting off to sleep, she came to his bed and they made love.

And the third way was in doing good; for he felt her delight and approbation in every kind or worthy deed he accomplished. He felt, too, that he and Awen had been chosen by the One for an extraordinary destiny—to live, as it were, a double life in the Dim World and the Bright World at the same time—to prepare themselves for a life in eternity together as no others before them had been allowed to prepare themselves; and that it behooved him to choose the One in turn by doing the work of the One; which were works of love to his fellow humans.

He took his cue for these works from his experience with Titus and with the Drayer family: he started a hospital for the insane, in a quiet and secluded vale about five miles from Fulkothing. He quickly realized that he would not be able to help all who were disturbed in their minds: some had illnesses he did not understand, or had suffered physical damage to their brains, or were violent beyond all control. But it was simple to recognize those who would be amenable to the treatment he had to offer.

Simple, because as life continued, he began to see more of the operation of the Bright World on this. Its influence was, as Swedenborg had seen long ago, everywhere. No human here made a decision or thought a thought that was not influenced in some way by the near presence of those on the other side of the barrier. Those thoughts and feelings were constantly flowing into the dim world; and because place in the Bright World was so fluid, by merely thinking a particular kind of thought—kind or concerned, hostile or resentful, or any of the spectrum of human affections, in the old sense of that term—the people of the Bright World who resonated with that thought or feeling were instantly present on the other side of the veil, pouring their sympathetic thoughts and feelings into one.

For example, at Rafe's wedding, Raphael sensed many people from the city of the Image Makers clustering about the bride and groom, enriching their joy and happiness with their own sympathetic feelings. And just as Rafe and his bride knew nothing of this, neither did those in the Bright World know how close they stood to the newly wedded couple.

So when new patients were brought to him at Muse House (the name he gave to his hospital), Raphael knew at once whether he could help them. If the barrier between the worlds had broken down in their minds, if they were beset by those from the Dark Lands, he could sense those unwanted companions beside them.

He was able to give them instant relief by driving away the evil ones; and by keeping them on in his hospital, he was able to foster a slow turning away from the fear and submission that had kept them in thrall to those ill spirits for so long.

There were, of course, many who brought their loved ones to him for care who were bitterly disappointed when he must turn them away. He could not explain to them why it was necessary to do so. Eventually their disappointment grew to affect him so strongly that he started another hospital to help the "untreatables," as he had previously called them. It was necessary to use a different method there, but it was still based on kindness, which was in that era a radical treatment for the insane. When he grew discouraged in this, as he did from time to time, he quoted these words to himself: "Heal the sick, cleanse the lepers, raise the dead, cast out devils: freely ye have received, freely give."

One point that Swedenborg made was troubling to him for a time. Those who do good *solely* with the view to living well in the other world must fail. It is the intention and the purity of the intention that matters, not the act. And how pure, he must ask himself, were his intentions in his good actions, when not a moment passed that he did not think of Awen and of returning to her side? It seemed that having once glimpsed the reward of good action, it was impossible not to incorporate a longing for that reward in his intentions; and the same must be true for anyone who had a glimpse of the eternal consequences of love for one's fellow human beings.

If Swedenborg raised the question, he also attempted to answer it, by putting it to some dwellers in the Bright World:

> I asked the two angels, "How can we know whether something we do arises out of our love for ourselves or out of a love of being useful? Everyone, good or evil, does things that are of service to his or her own particular community, from one kind of motive or another. Imagine that there is some society in the world composed completely of devils, and another composed completely of angels. I would go so far as to say that the devils

would do as many useful things for their society out of their love for themselves and their own splendor and glory, as the angels would do in their community. Who can say, then, what motive prompts any particular useful service?"

To this the two angels replied: "Yes, devils perform services for one another on their own account, or for the sake of winning fame and honor or wealth, but angels do not act on that basis. Instead they perform services for others out of the love they feel for their people. We ourselves cannot distinguish between them on the basis of their services alone, but the Lord can. All who believe in the Lord, and avoid doing evil because evil is wrong, serve the Lord's purposes when they act; but those who do not believe in the Lord, and do not avoid doing evil because evil is wrong, serve their own purposes and act on their own account. *That* is the difference between the service of devils and the service of angels."

This was reassuring, but for a long time Raphael retained some nagging doubts. In the end, after much inner struggle over this puzzle, the solution to his dilemma grew out of his continued experiences with Veronica.

For it is a fact that when one is in the right frame of mind, service to others is a joy. It transcends the petty rules and structures of the particular relationship in question. Not only had Veronica abused and betrayed Raphael over the years, she had simply failed him time after time in the necessary obligations of one human being to another: she had failed to do or even to wish him good. If Raphael had remained fixed on this betrayal and failure, he would have felt justified in doing her an equal harm. But he did not; he looked beyond that particular situation and relationship to a model of a better one. In essence, he *brought into his relationship with Veronica the love that he felt for Awen.* And that love for Awen was, he gradually realized, a love that he *brought into his relationship with her from the love he felt for the One.* The image he saw in his mind was that of a cascade of love descending from on high, falling into the broad and beautiful pool of his true marriage;

whose waters, overflowing in sheer superfluity, ran through further channels everywhere else throughout his life; and even to his relationship with Veronica. And as that love descended and dispersed through his life, bringing its cool, clean, nurturing power to everything it touched, he felt it as a joy, no matter where it ran.

When he met Veronica's pointless anger with mild words, or when he gently persisted in doing good to her, he felt a powerful joy in that act. He *knew* he was meeting her confusion and pain with a greater love than his own; and in doing so, he became a vessel for that love, contained in a larger vessel of love; and being thus *in* love, he could not help but be *in joy*.

Such joy is a simple gift. To obtain it, one need not have struggled as Raphael had. One need not study theology or philosophy, nor attend university or church, nor have any words at all to articulate where the joy comes from or why it is present within one. The roughest of men may feel it, if fleetingly, and the harshest of women; but good men and women feel it often, and more and more as they seek it out; and it buoys them, it gives them an implicit and satisfactory answer to the great question that haunts and torments any thinking and feeling person, which is: *Why bother living?*

And he would have gone further in explaining this philosophy of living. He would have said that anyone may feel this joy, by being loving toward the spouse or the parent or the sibling who is difficult, or toward the problematic man or woman erroneously placed by circumstance in a position superior to oneself.

He would not have said that service to others is without exception. In his credo he wrote of that exception:

> One must never serve evil. Some men and women do serve evil, and we must never serve them, never extend and perpetuate what they do. But the spouse who is broken and confused and unable to love, that person we can love and feel some joy in loving.
>
> Perhaps some limit will be decreed to our love for that difficult one. He or she may spiral into the Dark Lands, or tear

apart the connection circumstances have made. Perhaps love will lead us away to a different place. But so long as we do stay, the love of the One is available to sustain us.

This, then, was the answer Raphael found to his dilemma: The joy he felt in doing good taught him that his love was acceptable to the One. It was a clear and certain sign.

☙ ☙ ☙

In 1841, as she was nearing the age of seventy-two, Veronica suddenly began to decline. She had been growing weaker and had been subject to a great deal of fatigue in the preceding few years, but now the downward trajectory of her health grew quite steep. She lay in bed, at times nearly paralyzed with exhaustion; and yet she fretted—or at least mentally, for she did not have the energy to move about restlessly in the bed. The reason was not far to seek: she was abjectly terrified of death.

In the years since her confession of agnosticism in St. James's Park, before they were married, she had made no progress in her understanding of the Divine. To Raphael she seemed like a person whose head was so muffled with wrappings that she could not hear or see the symphony that thundered forth its exquisite music all around her; and she refused to take those wrappings off, preferring to sit in self-imposed isolation from the glory of the universe.

In the beginning of this decline, he only sat by her bed and offered his presence as consolation, for he thought that he would only irritate her by speaking to her of what he knew; but one day when her fear seemed particularly intense, she brought the subject up.

All she said was, "I do believe I am dying"; but Raphael knew that however joyful that declaration would have been on his own lips, on hers it was the ultimate expression of terror.

"I know you believe it," he answered. In pity for her fear, he took her hand in both of his and held it. He thought that she would only suffer that touch, and not return his grip; but in fact she squeezed his hands powerfully for a moment, before her enervated muscles became exhausted.

"Yes," she said, in increasing terror now; "I do believe I shall die very soon."

"Perhaps you may," he said soberly. "And perhaps you may not. There is no way that we can know. The surgeon himself does not claim to know. God alone knows; and so we shall have to abide the outcome."

She seemed to be glad that he was not dismissing the reality of this much-dreaded possibility; everyone else in attendance on her had made little of it, in a false and mechanical fashion.

"I wish I were like you!" she said fervently.

"Because I know God loves us and cares for us, do you mean?"

"Yes," she murmured. Then she added, "And for other reasons, too."

Perhaps she thought he would ask what they were, but he did not; and so she went on.

"Because you are good," she said. "And because you are so innocent. Because you found a way to believe that it is all worthwhile.—Oh, Raphael, you brought Rafe into our lives. I never would have done that—I never would have *believed* enough to do that. And having Rafe has . . . made the pain of it all so much less."

He felt he must respond to this. "I may seem good to you, and innocent; but I am . . . I am a poor excuse for a good person, in my own view. I am full of an assurance that I am the chosen of God one minute, and then the next I am convinced of my worthlessness; and sometimes I do not know which is a greater blasphemy, for I know God does not want us to despise ourselves. To despise ourselves is to be unable to act. No, God wants us to be useful, I am sure of that."

"And of what use have I been?" she asked. "To you or anybody?"

"You are a good mother to Rafe," he said. "And a good grandmother to all his children."

"Yes," she said. He could see that she took great consolation for this for a moment; but then her despair seized on her again. "But what is the point of it all?" she asked.

He hesitated. He thought perhaps it would only anger her if he answered her question; but again he thought that it would be wrong to keep his peace.

"The point is that we may increase in goodness," he said. "Do you not see that? Such growth is the order of things; it is the way the universe is made. We are called upon to be a part of the universe by growing. The goodness in us is always growing, as we love more and more, and as we turn our lives toward love more and more. Some are blessed and love and are good from the beginning of their lives; others are born to bitterness and must struggle to love. But if we achieve love in some measure, any measure, then when we go on to the next world we continue to grow closer and closer to the One—to God, I mean—or call God the *Perfect Love*, or whatever you like."

"The next world!" she said bitterly.

"Yes," he replied firmly. "The next world. Only it is not so 'next' as we like to think. It is all around us; we are bathed in it; its influences penetrate through us as rays shine through crystal, no matter how clouded. It is always there, directly on the other side of . . . of what we think of as real."

"And what do we do when we go there?" she asked skeptically. "Sing hosannas all day long?"

"No. We live, love, marry, learn; we bear the children we could not have here. We grow more loving; we turn inward, always more inward, toward the center, where the One dwells; and slowly, over eternity, we make our slow progression inward, growing in goodness as we go."

"Oh, Raphael," she said again, shaking her head. "You are *such* an innocent! Such an angel! You deserve such a belief—it protects you from the despair I feel."

He smiled. "You shall see," he said quietly. "I am not worried about that. I am only concerned that you arrive there with as loving a soul as possible. There is some danger, I admit it—danger that those who arrive there may prefer despair. And then they must live in darkness—I do not know how long; perhaps forever."

"Then I shall be one of them," she said haggardly.

"No—no, it is not so. You have loved Rafe, my dear; you have loved Amanda, and Lucilla, and Frederick, and little Reuben."

"Yes," she said; "but you know I could not love you. And how true it is to your goodness that you do not even mention that, as something I ought to have done."

"It is of no consequence."

"Of no consequence that a wife never loved her husband? Even that she . . . hurt him as much as she could? Nay, I shall say it—that she betrayed him, was unfaithful to him?"

"No—I say that in our case, it does not matter."

"Why not? If I were to arrive in this next world you believe in, would that unfaithfulness not count against me?"

"Not if you are sorry for it."

She began to weep; she grimaced bitterly.

"Sorry for it!" she repeated. "It was the stupidest thing I ever did. Ah, it was hateful—the whole thing. I took no pleasure from it—but you know that. It was hideous, a torment—I would rather have been beaten half-senseless. Thank God it was so brief!"

"Do not think of it," he said.

"But I suppose it must count in my favor that I did not enjoy it," she insisted.

"Of course," he said.

"But then again, I never could enjoy anything of the kind."

"I know," he said. "And I guessed why; I guessed why long ago."

She looked at him then; and he wondered if for a moment she was going to tell him what had happened to her so long ago, before he had ever known her, the awful event that had made her hate the pleasure between man and woman. But then her old stubbornness reasserted itself again, and she looked away and was silent.

And the moment passed, and the opportunity fled away, the chance to make some little healing of that wrong she had done him because of the wrong that had been done her. But in truth he did not mind; he only pitied her the more for this failure to speak, even as she approached death.

If she had spoken to him, he might have spoken to her, too, and told her the truth about Awen, and of how he and she had been married, before he and Veronica had ever met. But instead he kept that secret; and in truth he did not believe she deserved to know it. And she might yet recover, and be tempted to speak of such a confession to others, and live to injure Awen's good name; which he could not have borne.

"So," she said, resuming the conversation, after a little time. "You believe in marriages in heaven?"

"I do."

"But the Bible says we do not marry there."

"I believe that is spoken in symbol. It is not literally so. It would be difficult to explain to you what I believe that saying means; but I know for a fact that we do marry there."

"For a fact!" she said.

"Yes, for a fact."

"You have a strange definition of fact."

For a long time thereafter she was silent. Then she asked: "And if we marry there, whom do we marry?"

"The one whom we love."

"And . . . you and I shall be married there?"

He was silent a moment before he answered. "As you have just told me, you do not love me; and though in a sense I love you, it is not as spouses love one another. No, we shall have other spouses there."

She looked at him with something like panic. "But we . . . *must* marry there," she said. "We said our vows—and surely they must count for something *there* if anywhere."

"We vowed to be together until death parted us. When we die, our vows are fulfilled."

"And you . . . you do not *want* to be married to me anymore," she said accusingly—seizing irrationally, as she had always done, on the painful part of what he said.

He could not find anything unhurtful to say in response, so he said nothing.

"I understand," she said; but she began to weep again, and she went on, in an urgent voice, "Oh, Raphael, if I had another chance—I should be good to you! I should be a good wife to you! If only there were a God who loved me enough to unmake me and make me up again, but as a good person—how I wish it were so! How I wish I *could* have loved you as you ought to have been loved."

"You had another chance every day of your life with me," he said, "and you never took it. But I do not reproach you. No, there is a reason that all turned out as it did."

"A reason? Oh, you are mad, Raphael, if you think there is any good in all of this!"

"No, there was indeed a reason why I was given to you to be your husband."

"Because only *you* could bear with what I had to inflict on a husband, is that what you mean?" she asked bitterly.

"No. I mean there was a reason for *me*. I could not have a true wife here."

"Here?"

"I mean in this world."

"Why not?"

"Because I was and always have been truly intended for another, whom I have married in the next world."

"*Have married?* What, already?" she asked scornfully. "Are you in that much of a hurry?"

"For your sake I ought to have said, 'shall marry.' But it is the same thing. All time is one; and in eternity, in the mind of the One, I have married her already—or at least, so I do most humbly hope and pray."

This was all beyond her ken. "Oh, Raphael," she said, "you are a strange one indeed! I never could understand you."

"No, you never could, and you never shall. But you shall, sometime, know that I am right in what I say about love and marriage and the brighter world within which we live already, even as we think we live only in this dark and dim world."

She said nothing more; she had been wearied by her emotion and by their conversation, and she lapsed into silence now; and by degrees she fell into sleep. He stayed with her until he was sure she was no longer awake, and thus no longer fearful; and then he went away to walk in the Paradise for a time.

It seemed to him that here, in this little garden he had dedicated to his marriage with Awen, he could feel the presence of his true wife more intensely than anywhere else. On that particular day she was very close to him; she seemed to be walking beside him on the very gravel, pausing with him before the bench where they had sat together, and before the grave of the little cat whom they had both loved, and by the door through the wall that had separated their lives, their earthly marriages. At one point in his visit on that day, the symbolism of the wall struck him.

Always a wall between us, he thought to himself. *In those days the world had put the wall of convention and false marriage between us, and she was on her side, in Rush Hill, and I on mine, in Fulkothing. Now she is in the Bright World, and I still in the Dim. But the wall cannot hold forever—our love must breach it, make a door in it. The One is the Great Wall Breaker, or indeed say instead the Great Maker of Doors. And someday the One shall make me a door, and I shall walk through it into that brighter world and join her forever.*

How odd, he thought, *that Veronica seems to be dying first, and yet is loath to go. Well, not odd in Divine Providence, for it is only right that I should be here to offer what comfort I can, since I have it to offer. But I would be so glad to go onward myself. All here is in place, so far as in my mere human prudence I can make it so: Rafe is to have Fulkothing and all the properties, and he shall do well with them. He will look after Titus; and I do not believe Titus will linger here much longer in any case. The hospitals are to continue under their own funds. Lucy and Reuben are well-off, well-loved, happy; they have no need of me.*

Then he thought of how difficult Veronica might be for others, and he realized that it was right that she go first.

Yes, he thought. *I shall be here to care for her to the end. And then my task here may well be done, I do not know. And it may be well done—that I do not know either.*

Despite his uncertainties, he felt, as he often did now, a kind of approbation flowing into him from the other world, as if Awen knew his thought and approved it. Or rather, as if Awen felt the goodness of his intentions and seconded them, for he knew she could not know the specifics of the situation in which he then stood, since she was as blind to this world where he was as he was to hers. She did not even think of herself as lacking him now, for in that timeless place he was already with her. Only he himself was trapped in time; and yet he was finding that time was not as much of a prison as he had thought. By degrees he was becoming part of the timeless world. Indeed, it is another common experience of aging that, even as time accelerates, one increasingly perceives all time to be simultaneous. Raphael was in addition blessed with an uncommon understanding of the meaning of that simultaneity.

A short while later he went back up to the house to see whether Veronica had woken; and with him he carried the warmth of Awen's approval.

☙ ☙ ☙

Over the next two months Veronica continued to lose strength. Though there were days when she seemed to improve, those remissions were false halts on the way, and they seemed to leave her only more weary than before. Gradually she slept more and more. Rafe came to see her often now, and the grandchildren had been brought for what was known implicitly by all to be their final visit. Her periods of wakefulness were so unpredictable that Raphael had a runner in constant attendance outside the door of her room, so that he might be informed when she was conscious, and come back from his study or his errands on the estate to be with her then. More and more he returned only to find she had drifted off again, and he began to confine himself to the immediate vicinity of the house.

She became quite gaunt. But even as her skin stretched taut over the bones of her skull, and her muscles and breasts wasted away, and her arms and legs became mere frail twigs of bone, she continued to be strangely beautiful. He often puzzled about that, and decided that the One had set the mark of beauty on this woman as in the old story God set the mark upon Cain. Veronica's beauty was a promise that despite the pain she should suffer and the anguish she should cause, there was a goodness in her that should someday have a life in the mind of the One. Raphael had not been entirely wrong in loving her for it.

Then the time that must come to all, all who are in this time-bound world, came to her.

She was asleep; but some monition had brought him to her bedside; and by some impulse of his affection for her as a child of the One, he had taken her hand and was holding it.

And on a sudden he realized someone else had entered the room. He looked about slowly and saw three strangers, two men and a woman. He knew at once that they were not in this world with him, but in the Bright World, and he knew at once that they were good. Their clothing was not like that of the Image Makers, and instinctively he knew them to be of the society known as the Watchers and Welcomers.

He knew all about this, and yet still he felt as if he were dreaming as he watched the scene unfold. The woman, approaching on the other side of the bed, came to Veronica and, with extraordinary gentleness, placed her hand on her face and drew open her eyes; and Veronica—it was the strangest thing to witness—both sat up and remained lying down. That is, she seemed to sit up out of her body. Clearly it was her soul rising out of the flesh; and he realized that her body had now given up its last faint struggle and most peacefully died.

But the form that rose up was not the wasted form that had lain on this bed for weeks. It was the form of the woman with whom he had first lain on that night when they were married. She was naked, in all the fullness of youthful firmness and smoothness and beauty; her long hair, golden and gleaming and unbound, was glorious to see. She looked around in bewilderment.

"Greetings, dear one," said the woman.

Veronica gazed at her wide-eyed. "Who are you?" she asked.

The woman smiled. "I shall tell you all about that," she said. "As much as you want to know. But you are to come with us now."

"With you?" repeated Veronica uncertainly. "But I do not want to go with you. I want to stay here with my husband.—Look, here is my husband, Kerrsy, my own sweet Kerrsy."

The three visitors looked at Raphael, at first in a kindly but cursory fashion, and then with something like surprise and awe, for they realized that he could see them.

"He has been so good to me!" said Veronica.

And this was indeed sweet for Raphael to hear.

"It is long past time for me to begin being good to him," she went on. "Do not take me yet! I have so much to give him that I have not yet given."

"The time to give him those things has passed," said the woman. "But you may give them to him through someone else—and through the One."

"I do not understand," said Veronica.

"You will, I promise you. But you must come with us now, dear one."

"But he is my husband!" protested Veronica again. She turned to Raphael and appealed to him. "Tell them, Kerrsy—tell them who you are!"

"He is not supposed to speak with us," said the woman. "He is not supposed to even see us; though I see that he does—he is a wise one, your Kerrsy." And she smiled at Raphael with the air of one who shares a secret.

"But he is my husband!" repeated Veronica.

"No, he is not," said the woman gently but firmly. "Not anymore."

Veronica looked at Raphael. "Is that true?" she asked.

"It is," he said quietly.

"But when did you stop being my husband?" she asked.

Before he could respond, the woman gave him an earnest glance, as if to beseech him to keep silence, and so he kept his peace.

She answered for him. "He was never your *true* husband," she said. "And you were never his true wife."

Veronica was struck with wonderment by this. And with an insight of suddenness and force far beyond any she would have admitted to in her mortal life, she said: "Then he has loved me even more than I thought."

"Indeed, he has loved you more than you probably deserved," said the woman, with a hint of ironic amusement in her tone. "But that does not matter now. Now you are free to love, if you choose to; free to love equally. But it shall be another you love, not your Kerrsy."

There was no arguing with her. She made a motion to help Veronica rise from the bed, and Veronica obeyed; but still she looked back at Raphael regretfully. "But there is so much I must do for him," she objected. "I must repay him for all he has done for me. You do not know how patient he has been! You do not know how wicked I have been to him!"

"You will have the chance to repay him," repeated the woman, "by loving someone else—if you choose to."

Still Veronica was not satisfied; and she turned to Raphael one more time. "Is it all right, Kerrsy?" she asked. "Is it all right if I go?"

He was mindful of what the woman had indicated about his speaking, so he only nodded.

"If you say so, then," said Veronica. "But I want you to know that . . . that I did love you. I did love you, as much as I could." There was a hint of her old defensiveness in her voice; but he smiled at her, and the tears rose to his eyes. Even though he knew how little her love had been worth, it meant very much to him to hear her say this now.

When she saw his smile, she smiled back at him—such a smile! He had never in all his life seen such a smile of gladsome affection light her face.

And yet when she did now go, led by her guides, she did not give him a backward glance. And this was of a piece with the way she had always treated him—her affection, such as it was, had only been seen in flashes of faint light, and then had gone dark. And for the last time, the very last time, he was hurt by this; and then he gave her over to the care of the One.

And the words that he had read aloud to Awen, in their first little church service on Vigia so many years ago came back to him as a prophecy fulfilled: "This is thankworthy, if a man, for conscience toward God, endure grief, suffering wrongfully." And he thanked the One for having let him suffer in his care for this troubled woman.

He bowed his head and shut his eyes. In a few minutes, exhausted by his emotion, and by his vigils of late, which had occurred at all hours, he drifted into a refreshing sleep.

And it was in this state and attitude that the nurse found him, asleep but still holding the hand of the deceased Veronica Grancomb Kerr—the woman whom the world had for so long, and so very mistakenly, believed to be his wife.

Chapter 61

Duo illi, per mortem unius, usque non separentur; quoniam defuncti seu defunctae spiritus cohabitat jugi cum spiritu nondum defuncti seu defunctae, et id usque ad mortem alterius, quando iterum conveniunt et reuniunt se, ac tenerius quam prius se amant, quia in Spirituali Mundo. Ex his datur hoc consequens irrefragabile, quod illi, qui in amore vere conjugiali vixerant, iteratum conjugium non velint.

> Husband and wife, even after the death of one, are
> still not separated, since the spirit of the deceased
> lives continuously with the spirit of the one who has
> not yet died, right to the time when the survivor dies
> and they meet again and are reunited. And then they
> love each other more tenderly than ever before, be-
> cause they are in the spiritual world. Thus the irrefra-
> gable fact: those who have lived their lives in a truly
> married love have no wish to wed here a second time.
>
> —Swedenborg

Raphael's forgiveness of Veronica did not go untested. After she died, he found a notebook among her possessions, much like that she had made up when they had lived at Riverbight Lodge, the one that was full of the changes she would make at Dareweather-house after his uncle passed on and she and Raphael took possession. This later book contained her plans for what she would do at Fulkothing when Raphael died. How she expected to live on there when he was dead, he did not know; the book seemed to stem from the years before Rafe had entered their lives, a period during which Raphael had been without a proper heir and his death would have meant the loss of Fulkothing to a collateral line. It seemed all a part of the delusions Manwaring's spite had whipped into existence in Veronica's mind.

This notebook listed the servants she would have dismissed, the furniture she would have discarded, the wall coverings and carpets she would have altered, and the moveable property from the house she would have disposed of, including his entire library and many of the family heirlooms that were not even properly hers to sell. Still worse, it proposed in detail much major reconstruction, including the razing of entire buildings and the drastic recasting of the very lay of the land. First to go would have been the Paradise, which would have become the terminus of a new roadway and allee through the park, the trees of which she would have cut freely.

In short, it was the unmaking of Fulkothing at the whim of a tyrant. It was an odd final insult to add to the injury her life had been. He shook his head and puzzled over it, but he was past being hurt; he merely threw it in the fire. Like her dark spirit, it became vapor and departed.

He was not alone in feeling a lightening of heart at her going. All who had known Veronica from old times were glad for Raphael when she passed on. Lucy in particular had difficulty maintaining any kind of decorum when he brought her the news, as he did personally, riding over to Madgelet Lodge himself. She clung to him and wept copiously, in great relief at his release, and also in grief that he had been so long attached to such a person; and yet at the same time she genuinely mourned the woman who had been a second mother to her own child and who had loved her grandchildren well. Indeed, the keenest cut of loss often is the combination of relief and grief, and our sorrows would be shorter and less wounding if they were not compounded of contradictory emotions.

Lady Lanthan came at once when she heard the news, somewhat to Raphael's surprise. Lord Lanthan had died several years before, and Lady Lanthan was alone at Hawkover—as alone as a mistress of eighty servants, farmers, and sheepherders may be. She made Raphael promise to come visit her. He thought this to be a curious grasping at old times, and he did not give much thought to her insistence that he should wait to visit until three months of mourning was over—an odd stipulation that might perhaps have told him something of her motives.

He was now seventy-one years of age. He was, however, uncannily hale. He was still a great walker and rider; and in fact his riding and shooting and angling skills had only increased over the years, so that he was in those respects much admired by the men of the local gentry. The new Lord Kintillian in particular almost worshiped him; the heir of the old lord had lived at Rush Hill for many years before he came into his own, and had visited Raphael often during that time—not being put off by Veronica, who was in her good decades then, in her happy time with adopted child and then grandchildren. He had been present as a young man at the fishing contest when Awen had handily outcast all the men of the neighborhood but Raphael, and he had discovered that Raphael—when his wife was not among the company—had an endless willingness to listen to his account of that golden dawn.

Having detected this fondness of Raphael's for the slain Mrs. Quinn, the young Lord Kintillian had once made a point of relating further news about Quinn himself. He had met Quinn again by chance in London, in about 1835; the man seemed quite happy and prosperous. He was in the company of several grown children and their families—and it did not escape Lord Kintillian that these offspring were much more grown up than they ought to have been if they had been born subsequent to Quinn's removal from the neighborhood in 1816. The male children were well established in the church and the army, and the females had been married off to quite wealthy men of the upper class and had children of their own. But if Lord Kintillian had thought to provoke some show of disapproval or any strong emotion from Raphael in recounting this shocking surmise, he was disappointed; for Raphael only smiled in a kindly way and said something mysterious about divine providence.

Kindliness had become Raphael's foremost characteristic in later life. Yet the word *kindliness* did not do full justice to the sort of love he radiated to the world. It was such that children and even animals sensed it and came to him immediately, the children hanging on his knee or standing about gazing at him as if at some wonderful apparition, and the animals fawning on him quite shamelessly and vying to be petted. Dogs known to be vicious became happy puppies in his presence, and the most haughty and retiring of cats woke from their naps in the window seat and came to lie in his lap. If he walked by a paddock of twenty horses, there was not a beast among them that would not turn and look at him, and crowd to the fence as close to him as possible. When he walked through any assembly of humankind, whether at the assizes or at market, at a hunting meet, or even in the City, men and women stopped and gazed upon him, momentarily distracted from their cares; and where he was not known, he was inquired after, and the whisper would go up that this was Mr. Kerr of Fulkothing, in Norfolk, and even if people were not familiar with the name, they said, "Ah, yes," as if they knew him.

Young women in particular sought him out with a kind of fascination. They sensed his connection with Awen, or so he believed; it was the sort of connection they themselves craved. They thought of him partly as a fatherly figure and partly as a hero; and though they sat demurely around him, vying to serve him his tea and cake, they found themselves blushing under his gaze, much to their own surprise, and feeling physical sensations awaken in them that they had never felt before. They instinctively understood the rich sexuality of his marriage with Awen, and the buried thought of it, though formed only in their unconscious minds, was confusing and provoking to them. The result was that they doted on him past all common sense, and spent more time in his company at gatherings than they ought to have done—when they should have been dancing with partners their own age, they were instead drawn to the side of this ineligible older man by some power they would not admit to themselves. For his part, he seemed immune to their charms; and under his quiet gaze they felt themselves *lesser*—though lesser than whom, they did not know, for they did not think it could be Veronica; and they felt vaguely jealous of whoever it might be, and sulked a little inwardly, thinking that their youth and beauty ought to count for something more with him than it seemed to. And people do love to throw themselves at the unassailable, to see if they can make any mark on it.

Some of these women felt even stronger feelings for him. When Veronica died, there was a little flurry of interest among his single female acquaintance. Several very young and some not-so-young women went to their mirrors after they heard the news, and looked themselves directly in their wide eyes, and asked themselves if they would not like to try to be the new mistress of

Fulkothing, and perhaps give Mr. Kerr a genuine heir of his own blood. But it was only a momentary fantasy; for they found, on reflection, that there was something forbidding about Mr. Kerr after all, not so much his greater age but some purity that kept them at bay, as if he were still married. So Raphael was not troubled with them; or rather, was troubled by, or at least approached by—only one of them.

☉   ☉   ☉

He made the journey to Hawkover at the appointed time. That journey was very different from the old days, for in 1841 the railways were in their first big building boom. Though the many existing lines still had not been consolidated and well connected, the trip was much more rapid than it had been by horse, with no delay due to bad roads or ill weather; and Raphael had a fairly comfortable ride, swaying along the rails northward, with only brief lifts by carriage to and from the stations. Jackman, who had become quite rheumatic of late, was grateful for the relatively smooth and brief passage, and never stopped expressing his wonder at modern convenience throughout the journey. Raphael thought, at some point in his travel, how the railroad was proof of humanity's longing to annihilate space and time. It seemed to him a sign that we all unconsciously yearn for the state in which we are to live when we pierce the barrier and enter the Bright World.

Hawkover had changed very little since the visit on which he had unexpectedly encountered Awen. The downland through which the long drive wound was still pasture to great flocks of sheep; the trees of the final avenue were still all living, and even, in the way of their kind, had grown more stout and heavy in branch and limb than decades before; and the long, low front, with its taller wings beside, had needed no more for perfect preservation than the regular application of paint to the window trim. However, he found that no few of the servants who met the carriage and ushered him into the house were unfamiliar to him. *The human face of earth changes fastest of all things,* he thought.

He went straight to the room appointed for him, not that in which he had spent his hours with Awen, but the Green Room, the grander suite into which he had been carried on his return from Scotland. He was disappointed when he saw where he was to be—he had been imagining revisiting that other room again, because he was sure that he would be able to feel Awen's presence most strongly there—but on inquiry he found the housekeeper quite insistent that her mistress wanted her guest here in this place, and he yielded the point.

When he had refreshed himself and dressed for dinner, he went downstairs. He was brought into the gallery; and there, before one of the fireplaces, and veritably bathing in its heat and light, Lady Lanthan sat alone, but for a little dog on her lap.

She, too, was in a good state of preservation. Like the trees, her trunk and limbs had grown stouter, but it was a stoutness of strength. She was the mother of several children, grandmother of many more, even a great-grandmother to a few—a matron of a thriving and wealthy family. Yet there was still about her that air of youthful romanticism she had had forty-eight years before; and if he was not mistaken, she had taken extra pains with her appearance in the thought of meeting him again. Women do sometimes telegraph their intentions in that way; but a man is never sure whether a woman makes such assiduous preparations with him in mind or out of a desire to please only herself.

She rose from her chair, displacing the little dog, and greeted him almost like a man, shaking his hand, or rather say, *taking* his hand, for she did not give it a squeeze or a pump, as a man would have. And thus holding him captive, she said, "Here we are at last."

"Yes," he said, hiding his puzzlement over her precise meaning with an easy confidence. "We outlive our friends, it would seem."

"It is surprising how many of them are gone," she agreed. "We are not *that* old. You are one-and-seventy, and I am six-and-sixty.

And yet Harry has left us, and Veronica. Do you remember the Mileses? They have both passed on. And you knew that Mr. Peacock died last year—I hear that Mrs. Peacock has remarried." And on she went, through an accounting of various of her friends, some of whom he knew and some of whom were strangers to him.

"But we," she concluded, pressing his hand now in both of hers, "shall not lack for company, as long as we have the two of us." And she smiled at him happily, disarmingly, and he smiled back his agreement.

Then she relinquished his hand and they sat down for a few minutes before dinner was announced. He asked her about her sons, and heard all the news of them, and their wives and families, and families' families; which news she continued over dinner, interspersing her gossip with questions about his Rafe and about Rafe's children, whom she remembered in particular detail from her visit at the time of Veronica's death.

She was in every respect in earnest in all the interest she took in these matters; but all the same, Raphael began to suspect somehow that she had another intention that she was not disclosing to him; and it did not take him long to decide that she had summoned him here to ask him to tell her the story of Awen at last. He had once admitted his love for Awen to the lady before him, and once he had confessed something to Lucy; but for nearly fifty years he had denied the full knowledge of his time on Vigia to anyone. Now he began to feel tempted to tell at least one person; and that one person would be Lady Lanthan, if it were anyone. Lucy, he felt, did not want to hear; it would only have been painful to her, for any number of reasons, but mostly because it was past, all past, and she preferred to ride on the happy wave of the present, not looking back.

In small talk, then, the evening went by, not unpleasantly; and Raphael went off to the Green Room somewhat early, on the excuse of his journey.

The next morning began in a mist that lay over all the moors of Yorkshire. After breakfast Lady Lanthan suggested that they walk out together, on the path that had long been her constitutional. Raphael agreed gladly enough, thinking that it was only appropriate to renew the story of his connection with Awen at the place where he had last touched upon it, in conversation with Lady Lanthan years ago, on the bench at the top of the hill.

For a matron of sixty-six years, Lady Lanthan was remarkably light of breath, but her legs were short, and the walk to the high vista was long, even though she had Raphael's arm to lean on; or perhaps *because* she had his arm in hers, and she drew out her progress to enjoy that. She had dressed again with exquisite care, wearing a walking dress that borrowed something of the style of their youth at the turn of the century: the waist was high and thus flattering to her plump figure. Indeed, she really looked quite handsome in it, in a fashion peculiar to English noble ladies of a certain age, and she seemed to know she did. She looked the very Lady Lanthan, baroness, the former Honorable Miss Margarite Hobarris Redstone Carkwell Duplessy, daughter of a viscount. She made one concession to the current *mode:* today she wore the heavy, curled locks that hung from her temples along her cheeks, peeping out from her bonnet and framing her face pleasantly— the so-called spaniel curls, that characteristic fashion of the Victorian era. Her hair was colored, it was true, but skillfully, so that one almost believed the tint was real; and it did have the desired effect of making her appear younger than she was.

They made no pretense of any other wish: They went to the bench directly upon arriving at the summit, and there they sat for several minutes in silence, looking out over the moor to the south. The heavy morning mist and cloud were dispersing away, and the land was now waking to summer; even as Raphael and Lady Lanthan watched, all became either blushing green moor or pale blue heaven. Under the influence of this beauty, Raphael was ready to tell his story, or as much of it as Lady Lanthan was capable of believing.

"My dearest Raffy," she said finally, "is it not time for us to speak openly?"

"I do not see any reason why we should not," he said.

"Then must I be the one to state the facts of the case?"

He looked at her curiously. "You, my lady?" Even at his age, he was still an innocent.

She took his arm and leaned against him, but still looked into his eyes.

"Do you not see?" she said. "We are old romantics, we two. Ought we not to live out our last days together?"

This was utterly unexpected. And yet, in retrospect now, he saw that it should have been obvious and predictable, at least from the moment after Veronica's funeral when she asked him to visit her, if not from their very first meeting decades ago.

"Ah," he said. "Forgive me for not understanding sooner."

"But you do understand now?"

He smiled at her, feeling great kindness, and hoping he would not disappoint her too gravely. For the first time in his life he abandoned his reservations and addressed her by her first name, as she had long wished him to; and he went further than that in his compassion for her: he put his arm around her, even as he shook his head to say no.

"It cannot be, Margarite," he said.

She looked at him in amazement. "What do you mean?" she asked.

"It is forbidden; and indeed, it is forbidden by my own heart."

"Forbidden? Whatever do you mean? Why, widows and widowers marry all the time. You are a free Englishman, and I do not compromise my title or the title or estate of my sons—what can forbid it?"

"I am married already," he said.

She was now completely and almost violently taken aback.

"To whom?" she cried.

"You know to whom," he said. "Only you and perhaps my sister ever guessed. I am married to Awen—to Awen Kerr."

"Awen! But—God bless you, Raffy!—she has been dead for over twenty years! Why, it is *twenty-five* years now." She paused suddenly as a thought struck her. "What?" she asked peremptorily. "Were you *ever* married to her?"

"We were married in Scotland in 1792."

She now went beyond simple astonishment: she stared at him, her understanding reeling.

"We were robbed of our marriage by violence," he said.

"Violence? Of what sort?"

"Her father attempted to kill me, and very nearly did. He did succeed in killing our child."

"No!" she cried.

"Yes. And the circumstances of the affair were so terrible, they were such that . . . in fact, I thought he had killed Awen, and she thought he had killed me."

"Ah," she said now, nodding her head almost eagerly. "I knew it must have been something like that! I knew you could never have been willingly separated. And when you came to us here at Hawkover, you were shattered—in mind and still in body. I always knew you would not have been so spiritless if you had known she still lived somewhere in the world. And you would never have married Veronica Grancomb—or married anyone—if you had not thought Awen lost forever. Nor would she ever have married if she had not thought you lost to the world."

"Yes; our doom was a strange one. You know how miserable our marriages to others were. When we met again—through your help, Margarite—I wanted us to give up the false marriages we had made to others, to go back to Scotland and resume our life together—and in truth that life and marriage we had together was an idyll, an age of gold."

"And she *would not?*" exclaimed Margarite. The question was wild rhetoric; she knew the answer.

"She would not," affirmed Raphael.

"But *why?* At the time I thought you had every reason; but—a *prior marriage* to one another! How could she refuse that claim? And why did you not enforce it in law?"

"Do you want to know?" he asked.

"Want to know? Of course I want to know!"

"You think you do; but what if the answer I give you proves the strangest of all strange answers? What if it puts on trial the very way you think about this world—or instead possibly makes you think me mad? Are you willing to risk that? For I promise you, the story is indeed stranger than any you could imagine."

She looked a little frightened now: she could see he was in earnest. And perhaps guessing something of his intention, she said, "And you are going to prove to me that it is impossible for you and me to marry, Raphael?"

"Whether you will consider it proof, I do not know."

"If you believe it—then it will be proof, or as good as proof; for if you believe it, then there is no possibility."

"That is so. And perhaps we ought to let it rest there—you ought to rest content, knowing that it is impossible; and I shall be silent, except to express my sense of honor and obligation to you for considering a union with me desirable."

"Oh, Raffy! Do not be *too* gallant! What kind of a fool would a woman have to be, especially a woman of my age, not to want to marry you? Why, I dare say you could marry a younger easily enough, and have a child such as you never had of your own. No— we are past that foolish gallantry, you and I. You know I would marry you in an instant. I sometimes think you were the only man who ever understood me; and as for my feelings for you—you know that I have worshiped you for your mind for many years now. I loved my Harry dearly enough, God knows; but in his later years, he was all wine and card play; and whenever you came into the house, it was like a fresh and invigorating breeze, sweeping away all the fume and heat and dullness."

"Then I shall not force your patience to labor under any of my expressions of gratitude; for the truth is that I can hardly thank you for an offer I do not need."

"No, do not; but by the same token, you must tell me the story—I must hear the story, be it ever so strange, so . . . disturbing."

"Very well," he said.

Instead of speaking, however, he sat for a time in silence, as the morning waxed warmer and fairer; and Margarite, for all her romantic eagerness to hear what he had to say, respected his silence for that time.

And as he sat there, looking out on the rolling moor and the dark blue sky, he thought how very much like the Bright World this Dim World was becoming. It was an effect of his age, he thought. The process by which the Dim World seemed to be shedding its shadow and mist was continuing at a faster pace the older he grew; the Dim World was becoming more clear and bright, and he had no doubt it was because the Bright World was shining through more and more, infusing the dim symbols of this world with its own spiritual intensity.

At length he spoke.

"Sometime in the years when we were parted," he said, "Awen began to dream. These were not ordinary dreams—nay, let me unsay the word 'dream' entirely, because these had nothing to do with dreams. Let me say instead that Awen began to go into another world—the world you think of as *the* other world, the world beyond death. At night, lying on her bed, when to all appearances she must have seemed asleep, she yet rose up, in her mind, and went through the gate in the grim wall and climbed the slope of flints, to the very feet of the terrible angel who guards the way there; but instead of falling, failing, perishing, forgetting, she was permitted to go onwards.

"There she found a city. It is the city of our future; and there, having in her dreams bided many months, she was waiting when I joined her.

"I joined her, though at the time, in this world, I knew nothing of that other world; I did not even know that Awen was alive in this or any place. I was in the dimmest and darkest part of this world, and she in the Bright World. And yet, because time there is all one, I came to her there, in a kind of future present or present future. And we loved each other as always—more than always, more than ever—and we married again, and we had the child who had been lost to us in this dim place.

"And later, after she had died to this world, I too dreamt the dreams. I went to that Bright World too; and I found her there. Then again I knew the joy of marrying her, loving her, though for me the full knowledge of our history was cut short, because I . . . was still with Veronica in my waking life, and I had to live out that old history before I could truly know the new. But I did have a blessed interlude there; by night I went there in my dreams.

"Imagine that world as a great circle. It is not in fact so—it would be more accurate to think of it as a sphere—but it is simpler to think of it and to speak of it as a circle. On the outside of the circle, farthest from the Great Light that is at its center, are the Dark Lands. Life there is miserable, though that is exactly the life that the people in that place choose. To them, in their benighted state, there is nothing finer than violence, crime, rage, hatred. They have never known or thought anything better, so they find in promiscuity and immorality the highest pleasures.

"In the next innermost ring are the Lands of Light. They are beautiful, sweet, infinitely varied, containing cities, villages, wide plains and deserts, high mountains, sheltered valleys, inland seas. In those lands I wandered for some time, seeing inexpressibly good people. Sometimes I veered toward the Dark Lands, meeting people troubled by a dark morality, but a good power always led me back toward the light.

"Within that fair ring of the Lands of Light, at its center, are other realms. Some say there are three, but I think that three is only a symbol, or the number of their larger divisions; because if a person is willing to grow closer to the One—the One is what we here know as God—that process proceeds by infinite stages. How beautiful those inner realms are, you may guess from this: that Awen was once taken to the first of them and was overcome by it—fell in a swoon, overwhelmed in every sense by the beauty of the place, by the love and goodness that she felt there. And if Awen could be overcome by them, you know they are indeed great. But I think that as one goes inward, the appearance of the other world as made up of natural landscapes must fall away or dissolve. It is probably given that appearance initially only to help us on the early stages of our journey, and it gains a beauty we cannot yet conceive, that we could never conceive or even perceive without undergoing greater growth of our imaginations.

"In the center of all is the One, the great Uniter of all multiplicities and dualities. From that Center flows everything in a constant stream, the pure love and goodness that support the universe. It is true that we pervert that pure stream when it reaches us—we muddy it with our imperfections. But we are permitted to do so, because unless we are free to grow inward by our own choice, our growth could not be pleasing to the Loving One—would not be part of the Order of the One. This is the mystery of the universe: that the One sustains us, in love, and that we are all undergoing the long process of growing and evolving *back,* or returning closer to the Source.

"And this world in which we struggle and strive—it is a symbol, it is infinite symbol; it is countless symbols projected like rays from that more inner world. The inhabitants there throng around us, on their side of the barrier that keeps us apart, and our thoughts intermingle with theirs, though neither we nor they know it. If we think evil, the evil cluster to us; if we think good, the good stand around us, helping us onward in our thoughts.

"For me, Awen is always present. She is just on the other side of that veil of worlds, loving me, as she always did; loving me, as I shall always love her. I have never lost her; I have never forgotten her, not for a moment.

"And so you see why I cannot marry you. She is, she was, and she always will be my wife. My connection with Veronica—it was only an accident of this world. Through the grace of the One I was able to grow within it and become better, but now it is over—now it is forever over. Veronica has been released to whatever life she chooses for herself over there. I can pray that it is a good one, but to tell you the truth, I have had some doubt that it shall be. If she finds her old companions again, the ones with whom she consorted so long, she may be drawn back into her old ways. But I hope not, I pray not."

He had spoken almost as if to himself, not looking at Margarite to see how she was receiving this account; and now, thinking that she must believe him a madman, he turned to her.

She was gazing at him with an expression of wide-eyed and exalted wonder. Tears had streaked her face unheeded, even unfelt; and as he looked at her, a soft sob escaped her, and she clung to him suddenly and fiercely.

"Raphael!" she said.

He put his arms around her and held her in silence for several minutes.

"It is all true, is it not?" she said then, turning her face up to his.

"It is, my dear Margarite," he said gently.

"How wonderful, then! How wonderful, and how . . . romantic, that you . . . went to her there and . . . like Orpheus following Eurydice . . . it is as if you brought her back to this earth for a time, but she could not stay."

The comparison with that myth had struck him often; he nodded his head in token of agreement with it.

"But you will go to her," said Margarite. "You will go to her . . . perhaps not so very soon; perhaps not for another ten years, or fifteen, or twenty, or more. We shall be friends, you and I; and you will teach me everything you know, everything you are allowed to teach me, about . . . that other place. I have always thought there *was* such another place, but . . . no one knows anything about it."

Now, Raphael was in the habit of carrying a copy of *Heaven and Hell* in his pocket. He had had a small run of it specially printed in very small type on onionskin paper, and it was quite compact; and he took this out now and put it into Margarite's hands.

"What is this?" she asked.

"It is the account of one who went there. I would not say that it is all true, but it is as true as the man who wrote it could make it at the time. I am sure that if I wrote such an account of what I have seen, he would find fault with that in his turn; for I do not doubt that the other world is as individual and unique to our eyes as this one is. The One wills it so. It is in the perilous gap between what we see and know as individuals and what the One knows to be the universal and absolute Truth that we live and have our being. Or perhaps even the One's Truth is so infinite and rich and varied that it is wrong to call it a single thing at all. As wild and improbable as that book may seem to you, I can only say with the author of it that it is true, because I too have seen it, heard it, felt it, as did he."

She opened it to the title page and read it.

"Swedenborg?" she asked. "Was he not a crackpate, a mad-man?"

"Maybe," said Raphael, smiling. "And maybe I am one my-self."

She clutched the book eagerly. "May I keep this?" she asked. "May I read it?"

"Of course."

Now she thought of something else and looked troubled. "Will I . . . find Harry there, do you think?" she asked.

"Do you want to find him?"

She hesitated. "I . . . I would not mind *seeing* him, and talking over the old times with him; but I . . . God forgive me for saying this—you do not think it is wrong of me, do you?—but I do not want to be married to him there."

"Then you shall not be."

"I always thought I should like someone more like you."

He smiled. "That is flattering, I am sure," he said. "But there will be someone better than me, who will love you as you wish to be loved."

"Do you really think so?"

"I know it."

"Then this life is not the only chance I have?"

"It is the only chance you have to set your course straight for the next life. If you learn to do ill here, you will doubtless go awry there. But if you learn to do good here, you will doubtless do good there."

"Then I shall want your counsel," she said.

"I shall be glad to give you what counsel I can, but I think you will do quite well. You are a good person, Margarite."

"Ah, but I am so silly and romantic and self-indulgent—I know I am, there is no point in either of us denying it or pretending otherwise." And now, very winningly, she pleaded: "Do let us be friends, Raffy."

"We always have been," he said with a smile.

"Yes, we always have been. And always will be, I hope. And perhaps, *over there,* I shall come to visit you and Awen."

"Perhaps," he said, still smiling.

"Awen, you know," she said teasingly, "was a special protégée of mine; so I ought to be allowed some privileges when I see her again."

"Perhaps you will be a protégée of hers, when you come to the Bright World."

"Yes!" she said happily. "I know that in truth I always was her inferior in every way.—But you cannot imagine what intense pleasure I took in discovering her secret, and in throwing you two together again after all those years. And I have often thought of that as one of the best and cleverest things I ever did in life."

"And I shall always be grateful to you for it; though I think rather that you are not to get full credit, as it was the One who arranged it, and you only acted as the One led you to act."

"I am sure that is so," she admitted with another smile.

For some time longer they sat on the bench, speaking of Awen; and no conversation in this world could have been more pleasing for either of them. Then they walked again, much at random, over the hill and moor around Hawkover House. Sometimes she leaned on his arm, and sometimes they went along with their arms about one another, as lovers do, but in the innocent affection that old friends have for one another, having no thought or feeling of which to be ashamed.

◌ ◌ ◌

His visit to Margarite had an unlooked-for consequence in the following year. She wrote to him to say that one of her visitors at Hawkover during the winter was a Scottish jurist of great erudition and high repute, one James Malcolm McIlvaine. In conversation with him, she had put Raphael's case before him as that of a friend. He had responded with a great deal of legalese she did not understand, and she had asked him to write it down so that she could pass it along to the interested party. He had at first demurred to commit himself in writing, but she was so charming and begged him so wittily and prettily that eventually he was persuaded; and thinking that Margarite's friend would be as ignorant of Latin as she was, he even supplied helpful glosses of the Latin legal terms, or at least where he did not blush to do so. This précis she sent to Raphael; it read as follows:

> The case supposed is that of a man and woman of valid age marrying in Scotland without priest or witnesses, subsequently uniting by the consent of each *in copula,* but separated innocently before solemnization could proceed. Many authorities would hold that theirs was a *sponsalia de praesenti:* a written or verbal promise and consent to marriage by both parties effecting immediate marriage (as opposed to promising a marriage in future). Such marriage has been recognized as *verum matrimonium* (very marriage, or true marriage) since the time of Peter Lombard, though some call it a novelty because it is not based in Roman law. The judgment of Lord Stowell to that effect in *Dalyrymple,* though disliked by many, has been definitive in our time. Furthermore, theirs was a *sponsalia subsequente copula,* a consent to marriage followed by commixtion; which under Scottish law is irregular but still valid. In such a case it matters nothing that this couple failed to obtain proclamation of the banns, sacerdotal benediction, or legal witness. Their claim of marriage would be less liable to contestation if they both freely wished to maintain it, though obviously more difficult of proof in the absence of witnesses.

In the case supposed, the innocent separation of the parties, and their presumption each of the death of the other, would not effect any change in the condition of *verum matrimonium;* and thus any second marriage by either party, even though contracted *in bona fide* (in good faith), would be a nullity. The difficulty again would lie in the proof of the first marriage, especially if it be contested.

Raphael might, at an earlier time in his life, have received this dry confirmation of his own theory of the legality of his first marriage and the nullity of his second with some frustration if not bitterness. He might have said to himself that it only demonstrated that he and Awen ought to have left their second spouses, maintained the validity of their original marriage, and lived out their lives as husband and wife on this earth. But when he looked back at the ebb and flow of his life, at the slow working of Providence within its innermost forms and structures, he felt no frustration at the lawyer's pronouncement. Instead it gave him a secondary sort of satisfaction: it was pleasing to know that even the law of the mortal world recognized the truth and validity of his marriage to Awen.

He wrote as much to Margarite, thinking that she would never understand how he had been able to receive the opinion of her acquaintance in such good temper. But she showed how much she herself had come to accept the notion that our lives here continue into the next; for she replied that she understood perfectly.

Chapter 62

La vie est un songe . . . nous veillons dormants et veillants dormons.

Life is a dream . . . we go about sleeping when we are awake and waken when we sleep.

—Montaigne

Mistress mine, where are you roaming?
O, stay and hear! your true love's coming . . .

—Shakespeare, *Twelfth Night*

. . . Sleep on, my Love, in thy cold bed
Never to be disquieted!
My last good-night! Thou wilt not wake
Till I thy fate shall overtake:
Till age, or grief, or sickness must
Marry my body to that dust
It so much loves; and fill the room
My heart keeps empty in that tomb.
Stay for me there; I will not fail
To meet thee in that hollow vale.
And think not much of my delay:
I am already on the way,
And follow thee with all the speed
Desire can make, or sorrows breed.
Each minute is a short degree
And every hour a step towards thee. . . .

—Henry King

The One remains, the many change and pass;
Heaven's light forever shines, Earth's shadows fly;
Life, like a dome of many-coloured glass,
Stains the white radiance of eternity,
Until Death tramples it to fragments.—Die,
If thou wouldst be with that which thou dost seek!
Follow where all is fled!

—Shelley

                                        What if earth
Be but the shadow of heav'n; and things therein
Each to other like, more than on earth is thought?

—Milton

> He will watch from dawn till gloom
> The lake-reflected sun illume
> The yellow bees in the ivy-bloom,
> Nor heed nor see what things they be;
> But from these create he can
> Forms more real than living man,
> Nurselings of immortality.

—Shelley

Et amor aperit illam, et ducit ad conscios.

Our love opens the right path and leads us to our kin-dred spirits.

—Swedenborg

As it was, Margarite went on to the Bright World before him. She died in 1853, slipping away with relative ease in a bout of pneu-monia. Her sons were with her, but Raphael was not summoned until it was too late. She left him a packet that contained sundry notes and letters she had received from Awen in the short time they had corresponded, forty years before; and each was a pre-cious thing to Raphael.

By that time, Rafe and his family had moved into Fulkothing Hall. There was plenty of room for them all, and Raphael found it very pleasant to have a family around him: Rafe with his scholarly interests and his role in the community (he had become the mag-istrate, and was on the board of trustees for Raphael's two hospi-tals); Rafe's wife, Alice, a very intelligent and kind woman; their three daughters; and the sons who came home at holiday from school. His study and his Paradise remained sanctums, which the family respected implicitly; and on those rare occasions when he invited the girls into the garden, they walked about its graveled paths with a hushed sobriety that was charmingly at variance with their usual madcap behavior. Raphael seemed a holy man to them; and sometimes they teased him to tell them secrets, though they had no idea what secrets he might have to tell; but he only smiled, and promised they should know everything someday, even while he cautioned them that they must be patient.

In 1855, when he was about eighty-five years of age, he happened to be walking through a field on his way home from viewing the hay harvest in early June. It was a beautiful, warm afternoon, such as England offers in early summer. It had seemed to him for years now that in that beauty he could feel the closeness of the Bright World, but this morning it was especially close.

He was climbing a stile between field and pasture and he heard a sound—a sound of voices nearby; but strangely, it was coming from *above him.* He descended carefully to the ground before he looked at the source—he was hale, but arthritis had made him a little stiff, and it behooved him to be cautious.

There, about fifteen feet in the air above the pasture, several people were striding along, talking to other another. He had no doubt that they were in the Bright World. It was not in itself anything new to him to see inhabitants of that world while he stood in this; but this particular instance was different in many respects. Previously he had seen only the beings, good or evil, who were drawn to good- or ill-thinking inhabitants of this world; he had never seen people in the Bright World about their ordinary business. And previously the people whom he had seen were veiled somehow by the barrier between the worlds, so that he knew that they were *there* and he was *here.* But the people he saw now were not dim to him. They appeared in absolutely crystal clarity, or with a clarity even clearer than under the very best conditions in this world, as if he saw them with the eyes of his soul, not his body; that is, with eyes not subject to the infirmity of the body.

They were all women, as it happened. They seemed to be crossing some open ground in the Bright World, though he could see nothing of the land they traversed, only the figures themselves. They were all beautiful, but they did not possess that very high beauty that had struck him with awe in his first dream of the Bright World, when he visited the white city. Instead they had a very familiar and warm sort of beauty, and he felt in looking on them as he sometimes had felt when he saw his sister looking particularly attractive at some holiday gathering or social occasion. That is, he felt both pleased and a little proud of them. And yet he did not know any of them; he had never seen them before, and they were not wearing the clothing of the Image Makers.

They were speaking, and he heard the words clearly; they came to his mind without any interference from the breeze or from the distant sounds of the mowers or the occasional bleating of the sheep in the pasture. The purport of their conversation was of no consequence; they spoke only of something that concerned them at that moment:

And when is it to begin? said one.

When the ship comes in from the City of Resolve, answered another, who seemed to be the leader.

Oh, it will be great fun! enthused the first.

And there will be room for all of us? asked the third, who was following behind the other two, a position that seemed to be symbolic of her status as a newcomer to the Bright World.

Of course, my dear, said the leader. *We will use the largest of the amphitheaters. But you have not yet seen that one, have you?*

The third was so excited that she made no answer to the question. *What shall we sing?* she asked instead.

A pleasant laugh. *We must have a new song for the occasion, that is certain!*

Then we must begin to compose it this afternoon.

Indeed, we must.

And the subject?

This beautiful day . . .

Or this beautiful world! exclaimed the newcomer.

And with the affectionate laughter that met those words, the women faded from Raphael's vision and hearing.

Rafe, coming along a few minutes later, found Raphael standing in the very spot where he had halted, inside the fence of the pasture. He looked blissfully happy, and yet at the same time he wore an almost impish grin, such as boy might wear when he overhears his sisters telling of some crush they have and imagines how he can tease them about it.

"What is it?" asked Rafe, startled.

Raphael only grinned the more.

"Nothing, dear Rafe," he said.

"Ah, no, my dear Uncle," said Rafe with a laugh, "it is not *nothing*. You cannot put me off with that."

"You are right," said Raphael. "It is not nothing; but it is nothing I can tell you about. But it is good—call it a thought I have had, or a vision, if you will; but it is all good, so do not alarm yourself."

"At times you are so mysterious, Uncle!" said Rafe. "The girls are sure you are in possession of the ultimate secret of the universe."

"Perhaps I am," said Raphael. "Or at least, perhaps I have seen the outermost surface of the chest in which it is kept, though inside that chest there are an infinite number of other chests, each containing the next and smaller—or is each one the next larger?"

"Well, I shall trust you that whatever you have thought or seen has made you happy," said Rafe.

"Yes," said Raphael. "Take my word for that."

They continued on to the house together, Rafe surreptitiously observing his uncle for any signs of oddness or ill-health, but seeing none; and Raphael graciously and with good-humor suffering this observation, and grinning the more.

That proved to be only the first of these odd visions of the Bright World. Raphael had no doubt about what was happening: the barrier was breaking down more and more. He was beginning to live in the Bright World, even while he lived in this, somewhat as the Wonderful had done in his time on earth, only with less predictability and regularity.

Once, for example, he was looking out the window on a cool autumn day and he saw a little troupe of Image Makers—again, he guessed they might be singers, though he knew not how he knew that—walking up the hill before Fulkothing. Or so it seemed at first; on closer observation it became apparent that they were not walking on the ground that was visible to him, but were about a foot above it. This group was, again, composed exclusively of women, and in very high spirits, even more merry than the three he had seen over the pasture. Several were barefoot, carrying their shoes, and all were dressed in their finest, as for a great event. Their clothing was strangely radiant when seen in this world, and even their skin seemed to gleam as if with an inner light, especially the skin of their faces and the area of their breasts that was exposed above the low neckline of their gowns. They were tripping along at a great pace, leaning into their ascent of the hill eagerly, and at the same time prattling (and though he was delighted by what he heard, he could not have called their conversation anything else) about an event that was to take place in the city square. Although they were at some distance, and the glass of the window was closed between him and them, he could hear their words distinctly, because they were in the mental speech. Their conversation fell into his memory as a kind of sweet babble of images and female emotions, such as a man loves to hear at a distance in the house, as he sits in an easy chair or lies comfortably in his bed, and sweet feminine peace descends on him, and for a moment he slackens his grip on the weaponry that every man carries within him constantly, concealed in his heart.

The little troupe walked by several of Raphael's retainers, including his manager, Mr. Tralant (Mr. Kettie had long since died), and three or four young gardeners. The men could not see the visitors sweeping by them in the Bright World, but they all seemed to feel their passage. They stopped their work and stood straight, and to the last man of them they looked upward at the sky; and one of them took off his coat, as if he had received a vicarious breath of spring air and had grown warm. For the next five or ten minutes they were quite useless, and fell into what seemed from Raphael's distance to be an amiable and animated conversation, as if they suddenly were on holiday.

Another time he was traveling to Norwich in a carriage and looked down from the crest of a hill; and spread out before him there, in the gray dead of winter, was a beautiful fair taking place in the springtime of the Bright World. People from several cities were flocking to it from various directions, streaming into the sunlit meadow, where there were all the usual features of a country fair, but all reinterpreted in the style and for the purposes of the Bright World. There were booths filled with goods: books, sheaves of musical scores, clothing, food, furniture; there was sculpture and the work of artisans and jewelry rich in symbolism; and he knew not what other excellent things. There were musical competitions and sports and contests of oratory and elocution; there were meetings of old friends over cakes and hot drinks at long tables; and there was a kind of open-air chapel in which fairgoers paused from time to time to refresh themselves with gratitude. Raphael gazed on this vision with longing and wonder, craning his neck to look back at it as the carriage slowly left it behind; and though his companions questioned him closely about what had interested him in that barren landscape, he only smiled and would tell them nothing.

Now, too, he heard conversations from the Bright World. Most often he heard women speaking, and speaking no prattle but conversing on weighty topics—of the One, of love, of life, of the symbolic meaning of the passage from one world to the next, of how they hoped to penetrate deeper into the realms of light, approaching the One. Sometimes their talk was all of mathematics, of the most abstruse variety, and they discussed axioms and theorems and proofs; and other times they spoke of art, visual or literary, or of moral law, very weighty topics.

He also caught very fleeting glimpses of the other world at random. He saw towers in the distance, sometimes whole cities; or mountains, rivers, beautiful plains. On a couple of occasions he recognized those places: he saw the plain before the city of the Silver Folk, he saw the Temple of Marriage, and once he saw the white city. But he never saw the City of the Image Makers, and never saw Awen; nor expected to, nor, truth be told, dared to wish it; for he felt that his heart would burst then with joy and longing, and he would pass to that world before the allotted hour.

From time to time, when there was no wind, he heard the breeze passing; not in this world, but the other. When there was no rain, he heard rain falling there; sometimes in the dead of night, he felt sunlight on his face. Walking through a frozen field here, he smelt the grass and the blossoms there. Strains of music came to him, more and more frequently; he heard them especially when storm raged in the Dim World and the wind wuthered around the gable ends; for the peace and beauty of the One is hidden, imperturbable, even in the fiercest violence of this earth.

And all these whispers of the other world, all these glimpses, called to him, called him away; and he was ready, more than ready, and he longed to go to it, but he bided patiently, waiting the proper time.

◎ ◎ ◎

The spring came back to the Dim World. Early one day Raphael put a flask of water in one pocket of his coat and some bread and cheese in the other, and he went out of the house, going north, taking the long way around the wall that lay between Fulkothing and Rush Hill. He had told the housekeeper where he was going; and though she had looked dubious, the family was away that day, and no one could interfere.

He had not been back to the spot where Awen had died for many years now. The new owner of Rush Hill, who knew only vaguely of the former history of the estate, had harvested much of that particular copse many years before and turned the ground around the stone into an open height; he had once told Raphael that he and his family liked to picnic there.

Was her beloved blood still there? He thought he could see it; or was that an effect of the light, or a hue of the lichen? At any rate, when he sat on the stone and put his hand upon the spot where the blood had been, he felt her love and life flowing into him again; and he sat there for a long time, basking in the sunlight of the Dim World, symbolic of the radiant love of the One; and thus, vicariously, in the sunlight of Awen's love.

After he had sat in this manner for some hours, the barrier between worlds yielded to his sight like a dissolving mist. From bright Dim World he looked into bright Bright World.

There he saw, instead of the vignettes of daily life that had appeared to him at intervals in the past year, a vision much like that evoked by the music of the Image Makers on his wedding day. He saw the One; though he could not have articulated what the One *looked* like, yet he *saw* the Human One through the eyes of his heart; for there was the One, the mystery at the heart of all, the Center at the center. From the One there poured forth, ceaselessly, without defect in any radius, an infinity of love, piercing through the entire universe so perfectly and powerfully that nothing stood in shadow.

And yet the universe was so much less than the One that it could not absorb that love and become it, except with an almost immobile slowness. In his vision, Raphael saw the vast emptiness of space, its inhospitableness; saw worlds of seething gas and molten stone, or of gas frozen harder than water ice; saw airless expanses between terrestrial oases; saw death, violence, uselessness everywhere. In the same vision, in some kind of instant magnification, he saw the universe of human life as well, filled with similar death, violence, uselessness. Still the streaming love of the One filled it, creating it, from moment to moment, even in its imperfect state; and still, he knew, despite all its violence, it evolved by infinitely slow degrees into a state more loving and more nearly perfect. This change was symboled by the changing planet Earth itself, absorbing the light of the sun for untold years, and gradually building that heat into a rich and complex system of water and air and living life. Gradually Love won; and not through violent persuasion, but by persistence; and all violence, misery, death was ultimately subsumed into the love of the One, transmogrified and transubstantiated, until it became perfectly Love, though still distinct from the One, in the outward-streaming love of the One.

This was the order he saw; that was his glimpse of the order of the universe. It was an order in which love ruled, and anything done in opposition to love was against true order. Every truth uttered, if not uttered in love, was a violation of the order of the One; for love preceded all, even truth; and even truth and its wisdom were only the description of the means through which love found a way to act.

The vision dimmed as the barrier reasserted itself. For a long time thereafter, Raphael sat considering its meaning. And in its light, he looked on the woes and pains of his life and laughed softly. His bitter grief in losing Awen, again and again and again—all vain and blind; for what was that loss for, but to gain her again forever? His long contest with Veronica—he had thought her a curse and a millstone, but she had been, if not a teacher, yet a lesson set by the Teacher. And he to her, too, had been a teacher and a lesson. All his loves and his quarrels over the years—his quiet assistance to Lucy, his patient help to Titus; and then his contrasting dislike of others, such as Prosper and Quinn and Manwaring— these were all the slow workings of the One. He saw himself in all his past worldly interactions, in humble metaphoric retrospect now, as if he had been a gangly and awkward boy on the athletic field, wanting to perform, but unpracticed and unsure, yet loved all the more by his watching parents for that very uncertainty. So the One had loved him as he ran hither and thither on the field of life, stumbling at times, missing his opportunities, inadvertently failing his teammates, or distracted by some byplay that had nothing to do with the goals he had been set.

While he sat in this manner, gazing deep into the catoptic glass of the past, the sun of the Dim World (symbol of the Sun of the Bright) climbed to the nooning. At that hour the barrier suddenly opened before him again.

His view was from within the gate of horn. He was looking up the slope into the mist of the borderlands.

He rose from the stone where he had been sitting and walked forward into the Bright World. He was a little frightened; he was not sure he ought to be doing this; but he continued to walk, and slowly, with unsteady step, he climbed the slope. At the top of the hill the mist parted, and all of an instant he was confronting the angel who had been set to guard the way.

He expected to be stabbed, burned, annihilated by the fiery sword; but the angel, seeing him and recognizing him, lowered the sword from before him. Then, without a word, that guardian turned and walked away into the mists.

Raphael was confused by this unexpected retreat. He, too, turned away, and he stumbled back down the slope hastily. At the edge of the hill he came out into the Dim World again; he *saw himself* seated on the rock, and he went and, sitting there again, somehow became one with his body again. The barrier closed.

He knew not what to think of what had happened. Was he being invited, was he being summoned? He was not sure.

The day grew on past the nooning. And the barrier opened up again; and this time he was smitten deep in the heart by what he saw; for there was the City of the Image Makers before him, on its tree-clad hill by the lake. On the commons at the foot of the hill, a festival of song was in progress, and the sweet singing of the musicians came to him like the calling of sea-sirens.

He rose abruptly to his feet and walked forward into the meadow; and, pausing just within the threshold of that world, for a long time he listened, reveling in the joy of the music, yearning to join his friends there, and most of all, to find Awen once more.

The music ceased in intermission. He backed carefully away, backed into the Dim World again, and sat down on the stone. The barrier closed.

He prayed: *Ought I to have stayed? Tell me, oh One, do you now invite me to leave this world and join her there?*

The Dim World whirled on, and the sun sank toward mid-afternoon.

Then the barrier opened yet another time. He was looking on the shore between land and lake near the very spot where he had last seen Awen in the Bright World.

He could not help himself. The scent of her surged powerfully over him; it drew him to his feet like a mighty cable and pulled him—quite unresisting, it is true—into the Bright World.

His feet were on the sand; he looked around, again confused; and as he stood here, hesitating, the Wonderful came to him again.

He smiled at Raphael and said, *You have come back.*

Yes, said Raphael. *Tell me—am I here to stay? Is it permitted now?*

The Wonderful laughed. *I see you have learned a little humility. The last time we spoke on this spot, you insisted you must be allowed to stay.*

I hope I have indeed learned humility, said Raphael. *But if my lessons in that must first be perfect, I fear I shall never be allowed to return.*

No, said the Wonderful. *Here you shall make them complete; but I think they are well begun, and that is all that the One asks of you.*

Then I may stay? asked Raphael. *Then I may truly be married to Awen at last?*

The Wonderful smiled and responded only with a quotation: *And Jacob fulfilled her week,* he said: *And Laban gave him Rachel his daughter to wife also.*

Then, like the angel on the misty hill, he turned away and vanished.

Raphael looked down the strand before him. It wound around a point of land; he could not see what was there, but Awen's aura came to him powerfully from that direction; and now he saw that in the sand were two sets of footprints, a woman's and a man's; and he knew that he could run after her and *rejoin himself* in that world.

He did not look back. He began to run—to run forward into his future life.

⦿　⦿　⦿

When Raphael ran away down the strand in the Bright World, he did not notice that he had left his elderly, rheumatic, earthly body behind and that he was youthful and powerful again; he instantly accepted that new form as his true body in the Bright World. When his son, Rafe, came looking for him later that day in the Dim World, he found Raphael's body lying sideways on the stone where Awen had been slain years ago. Though Rafe did not know it, Raphael's heart was pressed against the very place where Awen's blood, symbol of her life, had spilled forth from her heart on the stone, symbol of truth.

But no more did Raphael need to press his heart against the mere mark of her memory; for in another world, a place without time, he stood holding her, pressing his body to hers, heart to heart with her again, within a single, shared, bright aura.

L'Envoi

οἳ δὲ δὴ ἂν δόξωσι διαφερόντως πρὸς τὸ ὁσίως βιῶναι, οὗτοί εἰσιν οἱ τῶνδε μὲν τῶν τόπων τῶν ἐν τῇ γῇ ἐλευθερούμενοί τε καὶ ἀπαλλαττόμενοι ὥσπερ δεσμωτηρίων, ἄνω δὲ εἰς τὴν καθαρὰν οἴκησιν ἀφικνούμενοι καὶ ἐπὶ γῆς οἰκιζόμενοι. τούτων δὲ αὐτῶν οἱ φιλοσοφίᾳ ἱκανῶς καθηράμενοι . . . εἰς οἰκήσεις ἔτι τούτων καλλίους ἀφικνοῦνται, ἃς οὔτε ῥᾴδιον δηλῶσαι οὔτε ὁ χρόνος ἱκανὸς ἐν τῷ παρόντι. ἀλλὰ τούτων δὴ ἕνεκα χρὴ ὧν διεληλύθαμεν, ὦ Σιμμία, πᾶν ποιεῖν ὥστε ἀρετῆς καὶ φρονήσεως ἐν τῷ βίῳ μετασχεῖν: καλὸν γὰρ τὸ ἄθλον καὶ ἡ ἐλπὶς μεγάλη.

But those who are found to have excelled in living a righteous life are set free from the regions within the earth, like people released from prison, and they attain to a pure and high dwelling upon it. And of these, the few who have duly purified themselves with love of wisdom . . . come to homes still more beautiful. To describe their dwellings would not be an easy matter, nor even possible in the time we have. So, given the facts I have set out, Simmias, ought we not to do everything within our power to acquire virtue and wisdom in this life? After all, the reward is a splendid one, and our hope of it is great.

—Plato

www.ingramcontent.com/pod-product-compliance
Lightning Source LLC
Chambersburg PA
CBHW071150180726
48291CB00007B/2399